S.J GATHERCOLE

The People We Trust

First edition

ISBN: 9781836907725

This book was professionally typeset on Reedsy.
Find out more at reedsy.com

Chapter One

"So, how much does he know?" Gareth muttered as he followed a heavily pregnant Faith up the stairs.

Parmer Investigations was based in an old building in the city centre. Gareth guessed it probably dated back to the 18th century. The floorboards creaked under their combined weight. At least no one would be able to sneak in and catch him by surprise, he thought. Assuming Faith's boss agreed to take him on as her maternity cover.

"Don't worry. I haven't spilled all your dark secrets." The familiar Welsh lilt in Faith's voice had been the little slice of home he'd needed since he arrived in Leeds. But right then, it wasn't doing anything to settle his nerves. Sensing this, Faith continued, "I just told him we'd grown up together and that if anyone was going to keep him in line while I'm away, it would be you. That seemed enough to get him interested. Besides, I think he has a thing for the Welsh accent."

"Do I need to tell Robin to worry?" Gareth finally felt himself relax enough to crack a quip at her expense. He knew Faith was utterly devoted to her partner Robin, but her flirtatious nature was always a good source of banter between them. It had been since they were kids.

"Robin's got nothing to worry about as far as Scott's concerned. I don't think I'm quite his type." Faith winked.

They reached the brightly lit landing, and Gareth quickly stopped, catching Faith's arm before she opened the office door. "Hold on, this isn't some elaborate set-up, is it?"

"Would I do that to you?" Her round face was flushed, and he wasn't sure if it was from being caught out or from the effort of climbing the stairs in her condition.

Gareth rolled his eyes. "That's exactly the kind of thing you'd do." He sighed heavily. "Look, Fay, you've been great these last few months, and I really appreciate the help, I do. But I'm just not..."

"Not ready for anything like that. I know. I'm teasing." She rested a soothing hand on his. "For what it's worth, I genuinely think you'll be brilliant at the job. Maybe even better than me."

"I don't know about that." Gareth chuckled lightly. "I don't know the first thing about investigating, other than what I've read in books and seen in films."

"Neither do I! The job is just managing his diary and making sure he doesn't forget to file his reports or eat lunch. Sometimes I help him file his paperwork or do a quick background check. But you never know. You love all those mystery novels and such. You might find you catch the bug for it in real life. Besides, I think being able to help some of these people will be cathartic for you. It's mostly hurt spouses trying to confirm their suspicions and leave bad relationships." She gave him a sympathetic look. "If anyone knows how relieving getting out of a messy relationship can be, it's you. You'll be helping them and probably find it helps you work a few things out yourself."

Gareth took a deep breath and nodded. He straightened his tie and ran a hand through his dark hair, relieved he'd had it cut the day before so the morning's rain hadn't turned it into a dark curly mop.

This was it. His new start was just beyond that door. The opportunity he'd been looking for when he'd fled Cardiff six months ago. After the last few years he'd had, he really needed to shed his old self and start again. In his more poetic moments, he'd thought of himself as a phoenix being reborn from the ashes of the life he'd left behind.

Faith swung open the door and led Gareth into the office waiting area. The room probably wasn't much bigger than Gareth's living room in his new flat. There was a small, black leather sofa against the left wall, coupled with a matching armchair. On the opposite wall stood a small wooden desk with Faith's computer on top. A worn, blue carpet covered the floors, and a slightly lighter blue-grey paint covered the walls. Gareth thought the room could do with some updating, maybe some artwork. But then, he supposed interior design probably wasn't high on Scott's list of priorities.

"The kitchenette is just through there." Faith pointed to the door on the right of the back wall. "It's not much, but it's got a microwave, kettle, and coffee machine. Scott's a bit of a coffee nut and always wrinkles his nose up at my having instant. Another reason I think you'll get along. On a strictly professional basis, of course." She shot Gareth a wink, and he had to resist rolling his eyes at her.

She'd insist she was joking, but he knew her well enough to know that even her jokes always had a hint of truth to them. She was unfalteringly honest and open, which often meant that she lacked tact and discretion. It was one of those things that either endeared her to people or scared them off completely. A straight talker himself, Gareth had always felt far more relaxed around her. He didn't have to second-guess what she was thinking or plotting because it was usually written all over her face.

"Loo's just down the corridor to the left, you probably spotted the signs on the way in." Faith looked around her as if trying to think of anything else she could use as her introductory pitch. Coming up blank, she decided to bring Scott through. "I'll just knock on the office door and let him know we're ready for him. He's probably got caught up on the phone with a client."

Gareth stood awkwardly as Faith peeked her head around Scott's inner office door. The deep baritone of Scott's American accent floated through the open door as he chatted away with someone on the other end of the phone.

Faith mouthed to her boss that Gareth was here, and he gave her a signal that he'd be another couple of minutes. She smiled at him warmly and nodded.

She closed the door and turned back to her childhood friend. "Come on, you can make him a cup of coffee while I get a herbal tea. That's probably the thing that'll clinch the deal for you."

With Faith's rounded belly, there wasn't much room in the kitchenette for them to move around. There was a lot of shuffling around one another as Gareth quickly whipped up a fresh pot of coffee. The machine was almost the same as the one he had at home. Closer to a professional machine than one you'd find in most people's homes, but one that any real coffee buff knew would do the job.

"If you'd told me beforehand, I could have brought one of my blends," Gareth said over the hiss of the kettle.

Faith looked at him open-mouthed. "Of course! God, why didn't I think of that? Bloody baby-brain. That would have been perfect."

Gareth chuckled and laid out sugar and milk on a small tray he'd found in the bottom cupboard.

"I really don't think you need to worry, Gareth. Something tells me you'll be just fine. You've only been here five minutes and you already know your way around this kitchen better than I do after five years."

"Well, that's you all over, isn't it? The only bit of a kitchen you're familiar with usually is the wine fridge."

Faith let out a booming laugh. "I know, I've not needed to go in our kitchen at all for months."

Still giggling, the two friends headed back towards the waiting area. Gareth set his coffee tray on the small, black glass table and took Faith's mug of tea from her so she could lower herself onto the sofa, using both hands to keep her balance. Once Faith was comfortable, Gareth gave her back her mug and sat by her side.

"I know I've already said it, but thanks for setting this up, Faith. It could be just what I need to get back on my feet."

"Don't mention it," she smiled. "I meant it when I said you'd be perfect for this place. I think the two of you will be a perfect fit."

"You mean me and the job, right?" he asked with one eyebrow raised.

"Of course." She smirked at him over the rim of her mug, and he shook his head fondly. He just hoped that she'd be too distracted to try and meddle in his love life once she went on maternity leave. She was like a dog with a bone once she got an idea in her head.

As Gareth poured his coffee, the inner office door opened, and Scott stepped out into the room.

The first thing that struck Gareth was just how large he

was. He was probably a height similar to Gareth at around six feet, but he was much broader in the chest and shoulders. His dark blue shirt fit his toned chest well without looking too much like he was deliberately trying to show off. His tapered trousers hung loosely around his long legs, and Gareth had to shake off the wave of disappointment that washed over him at only being able to see the front of what he was sure was a spectacular 360-degree view. He shot Faith a quick glare as she grinned maniacally. Damn, she was good. Not once in all their discussions about him covering her maternity leave had she mentioned that her boss looked more like a movie star than a private detective. Trying to keep his face neutral, Gareth mentally reminded himself that he was here for a job, not to drool over this green-eyed, dark-haired God. He wasn't in the right headspace to be getting involved with anyone, let alone his new boss.

"Gareth, right? Faith's told me a lot about you." Scott held out his hand, and Gareth shook it firmly.

Scott's American drawl was incredibly charismatic. Gareth could see it would likely come in handy when trying to charm witnesses to give up information.

"All good, I hope," he replied, immediately chastising himself for letting a hint of flirtatiousness slip into his voice.

Scott smiled broadly, perfect teeth framed by soft lips. "Of course."

Gareth felt Scott's gaze burning into him as the two men sat back down. He couldn't quite decide whether that was a good or bad thing, as he felt his heart rate increase. It had been a while since he'd been comfortable with anyone's attention on him for fear of the repercussions it might bring. He still had to wrestle with his inner panic to remind himself that his situation had changed.

He cleared his throat and spoke up. "I just wanted to say thank you for agreeing to meet me. I was fascinated from the moment Faith told me about P.I. Investigations, so to think you might have a place for me is extremely exciting."

Gareth noted a small wince pass over Scott's face as the words tumbled from his mouth. Trying to control his nerves and panic, he glanced at Faith.

"You said P.I. Investigations. That's Scott's biggest bugbear," she giggled.

"It's just P.I. – Parmer Investigations. Otherwise, it'd be Parmer Investigations Investigations," Scott grumbled.

Faith's giggle bubbled into a full belly laugh, forcing Scott and Gareth to chuckle along with her.

"I'm so sorry," Gareth laughed. "I'd never thought about that."

Scott waved his apology away. "I get it all the time. It's my fault for trying to be too clever. I just liked the idea of a private investigation company with the initials P.I. – I never realised how much it would annoy me when people got it wrong."

"No, I think it's totally understandable. It's your business, of course you want people to get the name right."

Scott smiled at Gareth's understanding. It was a soft, warm smile, a million miles from the huge grin he'd sported at their first introduction. Somehow this seemed more personal.

"Gareth knows all about the frustration of having your name said incorrectly." Faith smiled.

"I've had Gaz, Garry, Gar, G. Winds me up no end. Just Gareth is fine for me."

"I'll remember that." Scott smiled again as he raised his coffee cup to his mouth. As the warm liquid touched his tongue, his eyebrows shot up his forehead. "Wow. Faith wasn't kidding, you do make good coffee. Great in fact. She's been here years and never mastered it."

Gareth laughed as Faith stuck her tongue out at her boss, who chuckled warmly.

"I worked as a barista through university. The owner of the shop was Italian and very, very particular about his coffee," Gareth explained.

"Well, their loss is certainly my gain," Scott replied, taking another sip. He drained his cup before placing it back on the small tray Gareth had brought through.

"Look, I know this hasn't exactly been the most usual of interviews. But I'll be honest, from what Faith's told me I'd already made up my mind. The most important thing to me is being able to trust who I'm working with; the skills and know-how can come further down the line. Faith trusts you; I trust Faith. Have faith in Faith, that's what I say." Scott shot a warm smile at his long-time employee and friend.

"Besides," he continued. "Now that I've tasted what you can do with a coffee machine, I've no choice but to take you on. Can't have you going elsewhere and supplying someone else with your skills."

"I'll have to bring in one of my blends next time," Gareth said. "Then you'll be really wary of letting me go."

"Oh, I don't doubt that." Scott smiled. His green eyes held Gareth's gaze for long enough that Gareth felt his cheeks start to heat. He blinked and cursed his pale skin which had always been too quick to blush.

"I'm sure Faith has already explained, but the role will predominantly be office-based. I need someone to manage calls, sort my calendar, and greet clients when they arrive,"

Scott continued. "She'll be able to train you up on the system we use but it's nothing overly complicated."

Faith nodded in agreement. "I thought Gareth could come in on Thursday. That way I'll have a couple of days to talk him through how everything works before I finish. I don't think he'll need much more than that. I'll come back and he'll have more of an understanding of things than I ever did."

"Sounds like a plan to me." Scott smiled. "Does that suit you?"

"Absolutely," Gareth replied. "An immediate start suits me just fine."

"Excellent. Always helps when someone's nice and eager to get going," Scott winked and chuckled deep in his throat.

Gareth felt his face flush again and was thankful when Scott excused himself to answer his ringing mobile. As soon as Scott was safely closed off in his office, Gareth turned to Faith and glared.

"What?" she protested innocently.

"You know what, Faith. What did I say? I don't need setting up."

Faith raised her hands in protest. "Who said anything about setting you up? You're the only one who keeps mentioning it. I didn't know you'd find him so attractive that that would be your first thought."

"Oh, come off it, Fay. You've got eyes." Gareth folded his arms and slumped back against the sofa. His mind was spinning. "I don't want to make the same mistakes again, Faith. I can't do it again."

The mischievous glint in Faith's eyes faded fast, and she reached out to pat her old friend on the knee. "Gareth, no one's going to force you to date him. Like I keep saying, I really think this job will be good for you. I think you'll be good for each other, and if something beyond a working relationship develops, what's the harm? He's kind, and loyal. He has a wicked sense of humour, just like you. He's not Liam, Gareth."

Gareth let out a shaky sigh and nodded his head. It was stupid to compare everything to his past experiences. He knew that. But he also knew he couldn't take being burnt again. Starting again in a new city was hard enough. And God knows where he'd go if he had to move away again. He certainly couldn't go back home. He gently patted Faith's hand where it still sat on his knee and gave her a small smile.

She smiled back before looking at him with concern again. "If it's going to be too much for you, I can always tell him you had a change of heart. Or that something else came up. The last thing I want is to make you unhappy."

Gareth squeezed her hand. "Thank you. I'll be fine; it's not like I've got employers lining up to take me on with no references, is it? Might as well see how it goes first. I have to stop running sometime. Besides, despite myself, I trust you."

Faith grinned and winked at him. "Have faith in Faith."

"Something like that, yeah." Gareth snorted a laugh. He stood up and brushed himself off. "I best get going and leave you two to it. Do you need anything else from me?"

"Nope, I think we're all good. And I can pass him your number in case he thinks of anything I've forgotten." Faith smiled. "You still coming over for dinner? I think Robin's planning on doing a lasagna."

"Absolutely." He smiled.

Robin's lasagna went down a treat, as usual. Gareth had lost count of the times he'd eaten lasagna at Faith and Robin's, but he hadn't tired of it yet. They'd spent most of the evening discussing the couple's impending parenthood and kept most of the focus away from Gareth and his new chapter.

By half-past eight, dinner was done, and Faith had dozed off on the sofa, one hand resting protectively on her stomach. Even in sleep, she couldn't help but show her doting, caring side. Gareth and Robin stood in the hall as Gareth slipped quietly into his coat and wound his scarf around his neck.

"Thanks for dinner, Robin. It was delicious as always." Gareth smiled.

"No problem, mate. I'm just sorry the company wasn't as lively as normal." The broad Welshman chuckled, nodding his head towards Faith, who snuffled in her sleep and brought a second hand over her bump.

"Ahhh she's growing a baby, I'll let her off." Gareth smirked. "Thanks again, and give her my love when she wakes up."

The two men embraced and said their final goodbyes, Robin seeing that Gareth safely made it into his taxi.

Once Gareth had given his address and was on his way back to his small and, he hoped, temporary flat, he finally started to reflect on how far he'd come in the last few months, culminating in taking the jump back into work. When his life in Wales had fallen apart, his confidence had taken a huge knock, so he was grateful that Faith had the awareness to welcome him into a role where he'd have her familiarity and support when he needed it. On the other hand, in doing so, she'd removed one of his primary concerns and replaced it with another by introducing him to Scott.

He'd done the whole workplace romance scenario. It ultimately left him broken-hearted, with no home, and no job when it all fell apart. Of course, he knew that a large part of that downfall was due to Liam's behaviour and personality and had nothing to do with how they'd met. But convincing his now trepid heart of that fact was another matter entirely. As attractive as Scott was, he wasn't willing to risk his heart, home, or job again.

Gareth dragged himself out of his thoughts and noticed they were close to his flat. He let the driver know he was happy to get out anywhere along the road, paid his fare, and hopped out. Head ducked against the night's chill, he scurried towards the front of his building and let himself in. His flat wasn't exactly in one of the nicer areas of the city, but it would do until he'd got enough of a footing to find somewhere better. Yes, the lift was broken, leaving him to climb four flights of stairs to his flat. Yes, the paint was peeling in most of his rooms, and there was a suspicious damp patch by the battered French doors that led to his Juliette balcony. But beggars couldn't be choosers.

As he climbed the stairs, he did his best to avoid the occasional puddle he found sitting on the vinyl and tried not to listen to the loud arguments from some of his downstairs neighbours. If they'd started early, they might be finished before midnight tonight.

On autopilot, Gareth prepared his favourite coffee blend and took his cup through to the living area on the other side of the narrow hall, settling on the worn sofa. The bare bulb overhead was exceptionally bright and filled the room with a harsh white light that made every white surface look slightly radioactive. He needed to sort out a shade for that.

As he took a deep calming breath, the aroma of freshly brewed coffee wafted into his nose, and a serene smile grew on his face. He was a man of few luxuries, but instant coffee was a low he refused to stoop to. He'd invested a considerable chunk of his furniture budget in his coffee machine.

By nine-thirty, his coffee was gone, and he was busy flicking through his phone to find a decent playlist to listen to in the shower to drown out the ominous clanging of his water pipes. His phone started to vibrate as he browsed, and he jumped, almost dropping the device on his peeling lino floor. His body froze at the sight of an unknown number flashing on the screen. It couldn't be. Fear swept through him as he racked his brains, trying to think of someone, anyone else, who might be calling him at such a time. He answered with shaking hands, swiping the green symbol to the right of the screen.

"Hello?" he asked, cursing the way his voice broke.

"Gareth?"

He immediately felt his body relax at the sound of the American drawl on the other end of the line. "Scott?"

"Yeah! Listen, I know it's late and feel free to say no, but I could use a hand. How'd you fancy getting started in your new role a little early?"

Chapter Two

"Sir, it's nine-thirty."

"I know, I know, I wouldn't ask if I didn't have to. And please, none of the 'sir' business. It makes me feel like some kind of general. Just Scott is fine."

"Okay. Scott. It's nine-thirty. I don't see what..."

"Okay, so I'm at The Viaduct bar in town, do you know it?"

"Yes..." Gareth did know The Viaduct very well. He'd been dragged there a few times by Faith in her attempts to get him 'back out there' as she put it. Every time he'd protested profusely on two counts. Firstly, she'd already been at least five months pregnant when he'd moved nearby, and he was afraid of her getting hurt in such cramped and rowdy conditions. Secondly, as he'd told her multiple times, he hadn't been comfortable even making eyes at someone at that point. Back then, even thinking about how good-looking someone was triggered a fight-or-flight response that had him freezing up and preparing for a bollocking. He supposed the very fact that he could acknowledge his attraction to Scott without being completely overwhelmed by panic was a step up from there.

"Okay, great," Scott continued. "So, I tracked a guy here whose wife is paying us to prove he's cheating so she can divorce him without leaving herself completely high and dry.

The only problem is it's tricky to go unnoticed in a place like this when you're on your own. I kind of stand out, and everyone keeps approaching me, so I can't get a clear view of this guy or get any of the shots I need."

"That makes you sound a bit cocky," Gareth mumbled.

"Maybe," Scott chuckled. "But it's what's happened. So, I need someone to come, keep me company, keep prying strangers away, and let me do my job."

"And you were hoping that someone would be me?"

"Only if that's okay with you." Scott tried to sound neutral, but he needed to get this job done, and as much as he knew he could call on someone else, he had a strong gut feeling Gareth had been the right call.

Gareth checked his watch and counted in his head. "I can be there in ten minutes."

Scott let out a small whoop, and Gareth could picture him punching the air. "Gareth, I could kiss you! You're a lifesaver. See you in ten."

Gareth felt a hot blush creep up his cheeks towards his ears and was more than thankful no one could see his reaction.

They hung up and Gareth caught himself quickly tidying his hair, despite knowing full well it would have rustled back up again by the time he'd walked to the bar. He tutted at himself, rolled his eyes, grabbed a pair of shoes and a jacket, and headed back out into the night.

Gareth had never really been an impulsive kind of guy. He'd never thought of himself as boring, but he liked to be sure of his decisions before acting, which meant he constantly battled his internal doubts over every move he made. It was a bad habit that had only worsened over the years he'd been with Liam.

As a result, he'd found himself considering turning around and heading back to his flat at several points along the walk, but every excuse he came up with sounded like exactly what it was – an excuse. Every time he tried to think of something new, he remembered what Scott had said at their meeting earlier. Scott trusted him. That was something Gareth hadn't heard in a long time, and he was reluctant to lose that trust before they'd even properly gotten to know one another.

By the time he got to the bar, his hands were frozen, despite being wedged deep inside his jacket pocket. He was thankful that there was no queue like there typically was on a Friday or Saturday night. The sudden wall of stale heat hit him as he walked through the doors. Considering it was a Tuesday night, The Viaduct was still heaving.

The low lighting around the bar and outdoor area was a strong contrast to the bright lighting on the stage, where the night's drag act belted out the typical camp showstopper he'd come to expect from the bar. He smiled to himself. He knew precisely why Faith had brought him here so many times. It was exactly the kind of place they went on nights out in their late teens. Somewhere they could dance together, sing along to the acts – possibly even end up on stage at some point – and laugh until their stomachs hurt. Of course, then he'd met Liam, and before he'd even realised it, those fun nights out with his best friend had become a thing of the past.

"Gareth!" A booming American voice pulled him from his thoughts as a strong pair of arms wrapped around his waist. He blinked in surprise at Scott as the American man pulled him closer.

"Just follow my lead but let me know if you're uncomfort-able," Scott murmured in his ear, his lips ghosting close to his cheek.

Gareth nodded and smiled, surprised by how comfortable he felt and how much of his pre-Liam persona rose to the surface in Scott's presence.

He hadn't felt so 'himself' in years, to the point where he'd been sure he'd forgotten who Gareth Hughes had been before Liam Clarke had entered his life.

The realisation of his relaxed body language in the arms of another man almost threatened to overwhelm him with guilt and panic, and he could feel his body prepare itself to bolt out the door. He steeled himself and grabbed Scott's hand, pulling him towards the bar, where it was a little less crowded, so he could catch up on exactly what they needed to do.

He leaned his arms against the bar and ordered a whisky and Coke before turning his body towards Scott, who was looking at him with a massive smile.

"Thank you for coming," he said.

Gareth returned the smile, reminding himself that he was doing Scott a work favour. "No problem."

They leaned closer together. To outsiders, they looked like any other couple in the bar, murmuring and enjoying each other's company.

"The guy in the green shirt, buttons undone," Scott said into his ear. "You see him?"

"The bald guy currently grinding on the younger bloke in the Hawaiian shirt?" Gareth replied as he glanced over Scott's shoulder onto the dance floor.

"That's the one. He's been working on that guy since I called you and judging by their body language, I'd say they're not far from heading off for somewhere more private."

Gareth took his drink with a smile and paid the bartender.

"Well, we best not waste time then. You got a plan?"

Applause rang through the bar as the act on stage finished their set and handed over to the bar's DJ for the rest of the night. Both Scott and Gareth kept a close eye on the couple on the dancefloor, ensuring neither moved away during the downtime. Thankfully, the DJ didn't waste any time, keeping the night's momentum going with an upbeat 80s track that Gareth vaguely remembered his mum playing in the car from time to time.

Scott grinned at him and grabbed his free hand. "Come with me."

Gareth followed Scott into the centre of the dancefloor. They were close enough to have a reasonably clear view of the man they were after but far enough away that they shouldn't catch his attention. Not that he looked capable of being distracted from the slender young man in his arms.

Scott turned them so they faced each other, Gareth looking towards the bar and Scott facing their target. Gareth flinched slightly as Scott placed his hands on his hips before getting a grip on himself. *It's okay*, he reminded himself. *You're okay. You're safe.* Repeating his mantra inside his head, Gareth quickly relaxed.

Scott nodded to him, checking in. Gareth returned the nod and smiled before taking a swig of his drink. As the whisky burned down his throat, he was glad of its distraction, dragging his attention away from Scott's body swaying in time with his, their thighs rustling against each other.

He watched Scott's face as his dance partner shot occasional subtle glances at the couple behind them. Occasionally, they caught each other's eyes, Gareth checking in wordlessly to see if anything was happening behind them and Scott shaking his head almost imperceptibly. Now and then Scott would mouth, "You okay?" and Gareth would surprise himself by smiling and nodding.

One song rolled into the next, and the two men continued to dance. Both were secretly glad that they were each keeping half their attention on another couple. Gareth knew he was blushing brightly but took comfort in the fact that he could pass it off as a flush from the heat of the stuffy bar.

Suddenly, Scott pulled back slightly, pulling his phone from his back pocket. He lifted the device and gestured at Gareth to move somewhat to the left. He immediately did so, smiling and posing awkwardly with his drink, knowing full well that he wouldn't be the focus of Scott's photography skills. He watched the concentrated look on Scott's face as he snapped several pictures. He almost spilled his drink when Scott dragged him closer seconds later, hooking an arm around his shoulder and leaning into his side. Scott brought the camera up in front of them, but instead of seeing himself on the screen, Gareth could see the bald man they'd been watching leaning in to suck the neck of the young man he was still dancing with.

Scott took a few more shots, and Gareth instinctively switched his position slightly each time to look like he was posing. Scott smiled at his new employee's intuition and snapped more pictures than he'd expected.

Once Scott was done, he spun himself around so that he was once again facing Gareth. He slipped the phone back into his pocket and leaned his forearms on Gareth's shoulders as he started to dance again.

Gareth felt his heart stop as Scott leaned in closer again, their cheeks pressed together as Scott moved his lips closer to his ear.

"Let me know if they move," he murmured.

Gareth swallowed heavily and nodded, his cheek rubbing against Scott's as he did so.

With plenty of pictures secured, Scott seemed to relax a little more, as if he trusted Gareth to keep an eye on their target. Gareth continued to move in time to the music, unsure if the thumping in his chest was from his pounding heart, the heavy bass, or Scott's heart echoing through their joined chests. Just for a second, he could convince himself that someone like Scott could see him as anything other than someone to use to fulfil his needs, that they were just like any other couple on that dancefloor, caught up in the heat of the night and the rhythm of the music. It had been so long since he'd been in that position that even pretending for a while made him feel better than he had in years. He dropped his hands to Scott's hips, the left gripping him tightly, the right resting against his hip bone as he balanced his now half-empty glass.

As the song came to an end, the man in the green shirt leaned into his companion and spoke into his ear. His companion nodded and allowed himself to be led away from the dance floor. Gareth tapped his fingers against Scott's hip bone and flicked his gaze in the couple's direction. They watched as the man in the green shirt led his dance companion toward the exit, his fingers wrapped around the other man's wrist.

Gareth moved to the bar to place his glass down, waiting a few seconds for Scott to come and stand by his side.

"You ready to go?" he asked his boss.

Scott glanced at the front door, waiting for the couple to clear it and watching through the glass as they turned right. He nodded, took Gareth's hand, and led him out of the bar.

Once they hit the pavement, they pulled their jackets tighter, and Gareth fiddled with his zip as he glanced around the street, looking for the other couple. He quickly caught sight of the young man in the bright Hawaiian shirt pressed against the alley wall alongside the bar.

"Right," he told Scott. "I'm back up this way." He nodded his head up the street, knowing it would draw Scott's attention to the couple who were now completely wrapped up in one another, so drunk on booze and lust that they hadn't twigged that they could still be seen, even if only slightly.

Scott smiled at him. Not the huge, megawatt grin he often gave, but that softer one Gareth had noticed in his informal interview. One that was more intimate, more familiar.

"I'll walk you back," Scott told him, gesturing for Gareth to lead the way. They moved past the alleyway, checking that the couple were still engrossed in one another. Once they were far enough past not to be seen, Scott paused to snap a final photo, the red shirt visible and the hand of the young man in the Hawaiian shirt tucked inside the back of his trousers.

Mission accomplished, Gareth and Scott exchanged triumphant smiles and continued up the street and away from the club.

"Where did you park?" Gareth asked.

"What? Oh, I didn't. Got a taxi into town. If it's okay with you, I thought I'd walk you back to your place and order a taxi from there? Maybe try out that special blend you mentioned?"

Gareth smiled softly, keeping his eyes on the ground, suddenly concentrating on putting one foot in front of the other. "Probably a bit late for a coffee, don't you think?"

"Nah, just the one won't hurt. Unless you'd rather I didn't," Scott rambled.

"No, no I don't mind. I don't need to be up in the morning so no problem for me. Just don't go using it as an excuse to sack me if you end up late yourself tomorrow," Gareth deadpanned.

Chapter Three

It was ironic how full of life a potential murder scene could be. Alex slid out of her car and joined the swarm of officers buzzing around the familiar council house of Beth O'Neil, the star witness in the biggest case of Alex's career.

The modern, clinical uPVC door hung open to allow easy access for the CSI team, but it didn't appear to be damaged. The windows of the front room were still intact too. An uneasy shiver ran down Alex's back. No signs of a fight or disturbance. Nothing to point towards an attacker.

As she approached the crime scene tape barrier, she caught the eye of a young, slightly overweight officer. His gaze shifted over his shoulder briefly and he shuffled his feet. When she got closer, she could see fat beads of sweat on his forehead despite the chill in the air. He looked as uncomfortable as she felt. No matter how Beth had died, it didn't look good for their case.

Her phone buzzed in her back pocket and she quickly pulled it out to check the screen. Marcus. She rolled her eyes and declined the call. She'd ring him back once she was finished. There'd be hell to pay for ignoring him, but she'd deal with it.

When she looked back up, the officer had been joined by the familiar, large frame of DCI Pickering. She quickly rolled her shoulders back and held her head high as she strode across the paved driveway.

"Scullon not with you?" Pickering asked brusquely as Alex ducked under the tape.

"Nah. I called him but he said he had a stomach bug. Sounded rotten. I figured it was better he didn't come and spew up all over a crime scene."

Pickering hummed in agreement. "Elevate's defence lawyers are going to have a field day when this gets back to them," he grumbled.

"We're definitely thinking suicide then?" Alex asked.

"Certainly looks that way. No sign of forced entry. No obvious wounds. Overdose would be my guess, but we'll have a tox report done just to be sure. Had she mentioned anything to you? Any concerns she had?"

Alex shook her head. "Scullon handled most of the communication with her, to be honest, but he never raised any concerns with me. Last I heard she was nervous about the trial date but no more so than you'd expect."

"Let's not rule anything out," Pickering affirmed. "Her death would certainly make a lot of people's lives easier."

"Not ours, mind."

As they crossed the threshold into the house, Alex winced and stifled a sudden cough. "Bloody hell. It stinks of bleach in here." She looked around the hallway, taking in the pristine, cream-painted walls, and the freshly cleaned carpets. The style was a little sterile for her tastes but would have suited Marcus perfectly. Her husband believed in keeping everything as clean, tidy, and uncluttered as possible. These days she assumed that was because he had no personality to show off in his decor anymore.

"Yeah, looks like the whole place was deep-cleaned top to

bottom," Pickering grunted as he shifted up the stairs.

Alex frowned. "Why would anyone deep clean before killing themselves? It's certainly not how I'd want to spend my final hours."

"Maybe she was trying to help us out? Making it easier for us to shift the house after she was gone?"

Alex raised an eyebrow at his back. "Or she was trying to cover something up."

The further up the cream-clad stairs they went, the more the stench of bleach faded, replaced instead by the sour, rancid smells of vomit and death.

As they reached the top of the stairs, Alex's nostrils flared involuntarily at the offensive odour assaulting her senses. The pristine facade of the downstairs gave way to a scene of disarray and filth. Bed covers and a thick sweater lay twisted and strewn across the hallway. The cream walls were stained with splatters of what looked like dried vomit, and the pale carpets were now marked with dark splotches. The contrast was stark, almost as if the house was trying to hide its secrets beneath a thin veneer of cleanliness.

"Jesus," Alex muttered under her breath, suppressing the urge to gag as she surveyed the scene before her. Blood and gore she could handle. Somehow this seemed worse.

Pickering grunted in agreement, his jaw clenched tightly as he took in the sight. "Looks like we found where the cleaning skipped a beat," he remarked dryly.

Alex's gaze fell upon the bathroom door at the end of the hallway, slightly ajar and revealing a sliver of darkness within. She approached cautiously, her footsteps muffled by the thick carpet beneath her feet. As she pushed the door open, the full extent of the horror revealed itself.

The bathroom was a scene of chaos and despair. Beth O'Neil's lifeless body lay sprawled on the floor, dried vomit clinging to her lips and fingers where she'd tried and failed to clean herself up. The once-white tiles took on a sickly shade of yellow, and the air was heavy with the rancid smell of bile.

Alex's eyes scanned the room, taking in every detail with a sense of grim determination. By the sink she spotted a discarded bottle of bleach, its contents spilled haphazardly across the tiled floor. Beside it lay a dirty rag.

"It looks like she tried to clean up after herself," Alex murmured, her voice barely above a whisper.

Pickering nodded grimly, his expression unreadable. "Or someone tried to clean up for her."

As Alex's gaze lingered on the body before her, her phone buzzed once again in her pocket, interrupting the grim silence of the room. She glanced at the screen, her heart sinking at the sight of multiple missed calls from Marcus. Ignoring the pang of irritation that flared inside her, she silenced the device and turned her attention back to the task at hand.

There would be enough time to deal with Marcus later.

Chapter Four

Gareth and Scott continued through the centre, passing through the deserted high street in companionable silence. In the final hours of Tuesday night, there were very few people on the streets. A few stragglers from the few bars that were still open. A few homeless people searching for somewhere to lay their heads. Even the majority of fast-food restaurants were closed or in the process of closing.

"Do you really think I'm arrogant?" Scott asked suddenly.

"Sorry?"

"Earlier, on the phone, you said I sounded arrogant."

Gareth chuckled. "Well, you did say you couldn't get any work done because people kept hitting on you. And I think I said cocky, not arrogant."

"Semantics." Scott waved his hand in the air. "Besides, I think what I said was people kept coming over to me. You assumed I meant they were hitting on me."

"Semantics." Gareth smiled a lopsided smile. "You implied they were hitting on you."

"I think that's just what you inferred."

"Whatever." Gareth smiled, kicking a stray pebble across the pavement.

"So, do you think I'm arrogant?" Scott prodded again.

"I think you're persistent," Gareth laughed. "We need to turn left up here."

They turned into the square where Gareth's building was. Most of the streetlights were out, so the only lights were those that illuminated the main entry door of each building. Gareth grimaced slightly and prayed his new boss wouldn't judge him too harshly for his current residence before chastising himself again. *It's safe*, he reminded himself. *That's all that matters.*

"The joys of starting over, huh." Scott smiled knowingly.

"It's only temporary," Gareth bit back, wincing at his harshness.

Scott held his hands up. "Hey, I'm not criticising. The decision to start over in a new city takes some serious guts. Besides, it's not where you start; it's where you finish, right? You gotta do what you gotta do in the meantime."

"Sorry." Gareth bit his bottom lip and fiddled with his keys. He smiled at Scott, who waved away his apology. He sensed that he might have a kindred spirit in Scott, someone who understood what it meant to give up everything to start again. The American accent alone showed he'd come a long way from wherever he'd started. Gareth wondered if he was happy with where he'd ended up.

"Watch yourself on the stairs, they're usually wet and I'm never sure why," he warned, leading the way inside.

For once, the stairwell up to his flat was quiet. His neighbours had clearly worn themselves out shouting for the night. With any luck, he might get to sleep before dawn broke.

He unlocked his door, waiting for his furry squatter to scurry away before he flicked the light on. He heard Scott close the door behind them and immediately forced down the ice-cold fear that threatened to climb his spine.

The fear was irrational. He knew that. He replayed Faith's words in his mind – *he's not Liam.* He repeated his mantra, willing his body to calm down. He reminded himself he'd moved on. He was perfectly within his rights to have someone in his flat. There was no one to belittle or accuse him anymore. Desperate to give himself some space to calm down properly, Gareth put his keys on the hall table and gestured to his sofa.

"Make yourself comfortable, I'll brew the coffee," he forced out, avoiding Scott's eye contact as he dove into the kitchen. Once he was alone, Gareth set the coffee machine brewing and placed his hands on the counter, hanging his head between his arms. He sniffed loudly and shook his head, refusing to let the tears of panic drop. A shaky breath escaped his lips as he forced himself to calm down. *Stop being pathetic.*

"Everything okay?" Scott's American drawl floated through the doorway. It was the grounding force needed to pull Gareth out of his head and back into the present.

He stood up straight and managed to shoot a quick but wobbly smile in Scott's direction. "I'm good. Sorry."

Scott held up his hands and leaned against the doorframe. "Nothing to be sorry about. You need me to do anything?"

"No, all good. Milk and sugar?"

"Neither for me, thanks."

Gareth nodded silently in approval. He'd always preferred the purist approach to coffee as he felt it was the best way to taste the flavour of the beans.

They settled in the living room, Scott keeping a comfortable distance and checking in with Gareth with the simplest of looks when he could. The gentleness of his green eyes was so far from the intense scrutiny Gareth had grown so used to that it took him a second to register. But once he had, he nestled comfortably against the back of his sofa and pulled his feet up underneath him. He'd yet to find a coffee table at a reasonable price, so their only options were to hold the mugs or rest them on the floor. Both men decided to hold the mugs, wrapping their hands around them protectively to avoid constantly bending down.

Scott leaned over the rim of his mug, closing his eyes and inhaling the rich aroma with a soft moan. "I don't think I'll ever be able to go back to standard coffee after this. How do you do it?"

"That would be telling." Gareth smirked. "If I let you in on the secret you might decide you don't need to keep me around anymore."

"Oh, I don't know, I get the impression you're a man of many talents." Scott smiled. "You were a great help tonight, you made things so much easier, so thank you."

"No problem." Gareth blushed.

Scott's smile grew wider as Gareth felt his blush creep up his cheeks. Faith had told him multiple times that she found his blush endearing, but it was still a constant source of embarrassment for him, preventing him from hiding his emotions when he needed to.

Scott looked away suddenly, breaking the moment, and Gareth shifted in his seat, careful not to slop coffee everywhere.

"How're you settling into life 'up North'?" Scott asked in a terrible imitation of a Yorkshire accent. He grinned cheekily but kept his eyes hovering around his coffee cup as if he was trying to avoid looking at Gareth too much.

"Fine." Gareth shrugged. "I mean, I think it'll be a lot easier now that I'm working. Don't get me wrong, the time to myself was great and it gave me a lot of time to, you know..." he paused for a moment. Took a breath. "It gave me a chance to sort myself out. But I'll be glad to have something to do again. What about you? Have you been here since you moved from the States?"

Scott had been nodding knowingly as Gareth talked and took a large swig of coffee before responding. "Yep. Came over four years ago now. Seems like it flew by. Having the business to focus on certainly helped, I think you're right in that. It's good to have a purpose when you're starting somewhere new."

"The income will be nice too," Gareth teased. "Might finally be able to start filling this place. Make it feel a bit more like home."

"You didn't bring stuff with you when you moved?" Scott enquired.

Gareth shrugged and hid behind his mug. "I didn't have much that meant anything to me. And I couldn't exactly fit my coffee machine in my suitcase so..."

Scott laughed. "Well at least you managed to buy a new one. Great model too. Excellent choice."

"Oh yeah." Gareth smiled. "I know my priorities."

They chuckled, their gazes catching for just a moment. Gareth held his breath, drinking in that soft, glinting look in Scott's eyes for as long as he dared. He could feel the heat simmering on his high cheekbones, but couldn't bring himself to stop looking.

Once again, it was Scott who looked away first. He cleared his throat and pulled out his phone. "I should probably book a ride home. Don't want you complaining to the boss about late working hours." He winked.

Gareth huffed a laugh, grateful that Scott hadn't teased him about the blushing. Or the staring. He watched as Scott tapped on his phone, his brows suddenly shooting up his forehead.

"Oh wow. That was quick. They'll be here in two minutes," Scott said. Gareth thought he'd maybe detected a hint of disappointment mixed with his surprise. "I guess I should make a move. Don't want to have to race down those stairs in case I slip in one of those mysterious puddles."

"Good thinking," Gareth replied, offering up a small smile. Something tugged in the pit of his stomach as Scott stood to leave. He held out his hand and took Scott's mug. Both men fumbled slightly as their fingers brushed together during the exchange. Avoiding eye contact, they stepped away from each other, both desperate to keep the look in their eyes hidden from the other.

"I'll see you Thursday," Gareth called, his feet rooted to the spot for fear that if he followed Scott to the door, he might do something inadvisable. He received that soft smile and a nod in return. Their gazes lingered on each other, just for a second. Gareth held his breath, wondering. Scott cleared his throat, breaking the moment and waved, before the front door closed, and Gareth was left alone in his flat again.

As he carried their empty mugs to the kitchen, he began to think about the night's events in more detail and how they might impact his new role. He was in no doubt that he was incredibly attracted to Scott, and he got the impression that Scott was perhaps slightly attracted to him too. But at the same time, he knew that a mutual attraction didn't always mean it should be acted on, especially not in a work environment. *Been there, done that*, he thought.

He thought of Scott's words in the club. He'd wanted to ensure Gareth was comfortable at every stage, even when heading back to the flat. The delicate concern he'd shown at every stage of their night had been a refreshing change to the treatment Gareth had grown so used to with Liam. Of course, even that relationship had started well. It had turned sour slowly. He'd lost himself, piece by piece, until he'd suddenly realised, years down the line, that the damage was too far gone, and he'd no escape route left. He'd become so used to having to run his plans for the day, right down to what he intended to wear, past Liam and not being allowed to speak to anyone without facing a backlash.

He'd hoped that getting so far away from Wales, setting up in a brand-new city, would mean he could shake free of those enforced habits and heal his scars far quicker. At times he felt he had, but nagging fear and doubt still crept up on him from nowhere once in a while.

He locked the front door and shuffled his way to the bedroom – he'd wait for the morning to shower now to avoid his neighbours complaining about the clanging pipes. Gareth shook off his clothes and folded them neatly into his wash basket, his mind racing and tripping over feelings of irrational guilt and fear and a small amount of hope. He pulled on a pair of pyjamas, moving quickly to avoid the chill that always seemed to settle in his bedroom, and bundled himself into bed.

Chapter Five

The following morning, Gareth cleaned his flat from top to bottom, cleared out every cupboard in every room, and made a mental inventory of everything as he went.

Then he called his landlord about the scurrying and suspected furry residents. While he hadn't found any signs of life during his cleaning frenzy, he had seen multiple droppings in the back of his boiler cupboard, so he knew he wasn't alone in the flat – which wasn't a comforting thought. Surprisingly, his landlord had apologised for the infestation. But, Gareth supposed, that didn't mean he'd sort it in anything like a timely manner.

Once he'd cleaned and organised everything, Gareth headed to the supermarket and stocked up on food and rodent traps. Then, laden with bags of food, he returned home and set about cooking his meals for the week. If his experience with Scott the previous night was anything to go by, Gareth was pretty sure he'd struggle for time to cook a well-balanced meal every night. But he was nothing if not prepared.

He batch-cooked several of his favourite meals, with at least four portions of each. Bolognese, meat stews, chicken bakes, homemade curries, pasta sauces. Once they'd cooked and cooled, he spread the dishes between his fridge and freezer, ready to dish out on an evening with minimal fuss.

Finally satisfied that he'd done everything he needed to do, Gareth set his prized coffee machine brewing and decided to settle down for a peaceful evening with a few of his favourite films. As the machine brewed, he carefully set up several coffee bags with his own blends ready to take into the office in the morning. From Scott's reactions to his coffee so far, he had a keen idea of the man's tastes and which blends he'd like best.

Coffee brewed, Gareth dropped onto his battered sofa and fished his mobile out of his pocket to finally respond to Faith's text from earlier.

All set, thanks. Just put together some coffee bags to stock up the kitchen with.

Within seconds of hitting send, Gareth saw another message from Faith on his screen.

Not that you want to impress him too much, eh.

Gareth rolled his eyes at the screen and tapped out his response.

He's my new boss, of course I want to impress him. Need to make sure he'll keep me on or give me a good reference when you come back.

When Faith's reply came through, Gareth felt torn between a chuckle and another eye roll.

I get the impression he doesn't need much of an excuse to keep you around. You still need to give me the details from Tuesday night.

He put his phone on the arm of the sofa and pulled his legs up, sitting with his feet tucked under him. As he inhaled the strong scent of his coffee, he tried desperately to block out the memory of Scott's pleasured moans when he'd smelt and tasted Gareth's coffee before. He didn't need the images those memories conjured in his brain. Especially not the night before he started working for the guy.

He hit a button on his remote control, and the DVD he'd set up earlier began to play. He'd gone for Guy Ritchie's *Sherlock Holmes* movie. It was a personal favourite. He'd always enjoyed Robert Downey Jr.'s take on the elusive Holmes and felt he had the proper rapport with Jude Law's Watson. He was slightly loath to admit it, given his love of the quieter plots of the original novels, but Gareth also loved the action sequences Ritchie had included in the films. He'd always felt it brought the fantastic characters and other elements of the classic mystery novels up to speed for a more modern audience, which he had hoped would encourage more filmmakers to tackle his favourite stories. But now he wondered if it had been a poor choice given his simmering nerves. He should have picked something utterly unrelated to his new job.

With his hands wrapped around his coffee mug, Gareth hunkered down into the sofa cushions and focused on the film in front of him. As ever, he found himself frequently imagining himself in Watson's shoes. However, this time, he also envisioned a particular American instead of Holmes. Eventually, afraid that if he shook his head any more it might fall off, Gareth turned off the TV. He took his empty mug to the kitchen, rinsed it, and headed for the shower. There, he planned to drown out his thoughts with a soundtrack of running water, clanging pipes, and some of his favourite rock bands.

He cranked up the volume on his phone to try and drown out the heavy clanging before he dove under the warm water. He usually liked his showers scalding hot, but he'd learned that wasn't possible in his current flat – not without risking the pipes sounding like they might burst.

Once he'd cleaned most of his body, he took the small brush from his shower caddy and used the rough bristles to clean beneath his fingernails. He knew his obsessive cleaning came from thoughts of washing away the shame and guilt he held over Liam from his body but had long ago decided he could have far worse habits from that time of his life. In fact, he did.

Once he was done, he rubbed his skin with a rough, old towel, watching as his usually pale Welsh skin turned steadily redder from the friction. Dressed in clean pyjamas, Gareth padded back to his bedroom and settled deep under his covers. He set his alarm for seven-thirty a.m. and put his phone to one side, determined as ever to limit his screen time before bed. By the time he was settled, it was nine-thirty p.m. *Just enough time to read a little*, he thought as he grabbed his book from the floor. Just a few chapters to unwind. He wriggled around until he found a comfortable position that didn't expose him to the chill of his bedroom and still allowed enough movement to turn the page when he needed to. He stifled a yawn and hoped that he might manage a decent night's sleep ahead of his big day.

Gareth was awake again by six-thirty a.m. Between the nerves and vivid dreams racing through his mind, he knew he wasn't going to get back to sleep. After what felt like an age of staring at his ceiling, he pushed himself out of bed and shuffled to the bathroom to freshen up. He splashed cold water on his face, forcing his body to wake up and catch up with his mind. As he brushed his teeth, he wandered through the flat, making double sure he had everything he needed for the day. His best shoes were already lined up by the door, and his bags of coffee were sat neatly on the kitchen counter, ready for him to grab on his way out. He'd also remembered to hang a suit on his wardrobe door the night before, so he wouldn't have to stress about picking one out in the morning. Not that he had many to choose from anymore, but he'd picked what felt right for a first day – although now he was looking at it in the early morning light, he wondered if it was too late to change his mind.

This time he'd paired it with a deep red shirt and a grey-striped tie, but now he was worried the red was too much for a first day. He surveyed his wardrobe again. His clothing selection was far more limited than it had been, as he'd not been able to pack everything into his cases when he'd left his old life behind. He made a mental note to try and build his wardrobe back up once his wages started coming in. Finally settling on a slightly more muted shirt, Gareth dressed and fixed his hair. Despite its recent cut, he could already feel it starting to curl on the nape of his neck, so he ran to the bathroom and wet it down, hoping that would hold the curl at bay for the day.

Once he was ready, Gareth returned to the kitchen, set a pot of coffee brewing, and threw some porridge oats in the microwave. With his palms resting on the counter behind him, Gareth started tapping his feet as he listened to his coffee machine and microwave whirring. The ping of the microwave made him jump slightly, pulling him from the world inside his head.

Too nervous to sit down, Gareth placed his mug on the counter behind him and cupped his bowl of porridge in one hand while eating with the other. The sticky substance was usually his favourite, especially when he got the pack with an extra drizzle of honey. But that morning, he had to force it down his throat and it settled heavily in the pit of his stomach. With half a bowl left, Gareth gave up on breakfast, downed the rest of his coffee, and grabbed his things.

He was still far too early to meet Faith outside the office, but he usually found that a short walk through the city centre's deserted streets helped calm his mind. The soft buzz in the air as the city began to wake was soothing and invigorating at the same time. It let him know that another day was beginning with endless possibilities and opportunities. Plus, he could take in the local area with fewer people crowding the streets. These quiet walks often helped him spot new coffee shops or green spaces perfect for reading or people-watching. It was a chance to see the city in a way that wasn't possible when you were caught up in the throngs of city workers, commuters, and shoppers. As he wandered in the direction of his new office, this time with fewer people in his path, he made a mental note of a handful of artisan bakeries and delis en route. He took a little extra time to memorise the phone numbers in the windows of those advertising delivery services. He'd always been good at remembering and recalling details. He only needed to look at something for a short time before he could bring the image back to the forefront of his mind.

At his leisurely pace, it took him until eight a.m. to reach the area around the office. Faith had said she didn't usually get to the office until around eight forty-five, so he headed across the road to the green square opposite the P.I. building. The weather had been fine for a few days, so the benches in the courtyard were dry enough for Gareth to sit on. He settled with the office on his right and whipped out his current read and his coffee thermos.

Time passed by as he lost himself in his latest mystery novel, the morning grew brighter, and the streets became busier, but all went unnoticed as Gareth immersed himself in the words on the page before him.

"Brushing up on your investigative techniques, are we?" A familiar drawl surprised Gareth out of his book.

He jumped slightly and flicked his eyes up to meet the bright green eyes of his new boss. He shoved his bookmark into the pages of his book before putting the book itself back in his bag and grabbing his thermos.

He shot to his feet nervously. "Sorry. I'm not late, am I? I got here early and thought I'd get a spot of reading in while I waited for Faith. I sort of lost track of time."

"No, you're fine, it's only half-past. Faith just called to say her bus was stuck in traffic and that you'd probably be waiting in the courtyard having got here obscenely early." Scott smiled lopsidedly.

"She knows me far too well," Gareth chuckled.

"Let's get inside. We can have a cup of that coffee of yours, if it's on offer, and I can give you an initial induction before Faith gets here to talk you through the details of what you'll be doing."

Scott took a step back and gestured for Gareth to lead the way out of the courtyard. Once they reached the front door of the old building, Scott stepped back in front and let them inside. As they headed up the stairs, Gareth couldn't help admiring the way Scott's dark jeans clung to his pert arse. He'd been right at his interview. He hadn't had much of a chance to admire it when they'd been running surveillance at The Viaduct, but the 360 view was spectacular. He swallowed loudly as he watched Scott unlock the door on the second landing that led to their private offices.

Once inside, Gareth dropped his bag by the desk and bent down to retrieve the coffee blend he'd brought. He forced down the blush that burned his cheeks as he felt Scott's gaze on his rear as he bent. He stood up and cleared his throat, brandishing the coffee bag in front of him.

"I have been dreaming about this moment since the other night." Scott winked, which elicited another deep scarlet blush in Gareth's cheeks.

"Let's hope it lives up to the memory, then," Gareth said. His throat felt dry and tight, his nerves and heart racing.

In the kitchenette, Gareth placed his palms on the countertop and took a deep breath to settle himself. A small smile grew as he thought about how Scott's eyes had followed him. Unlike when Liam had watched him, it didn't leave an unsettled feeling in his stomach. He didn't feel judged or suffocated under Scott's gaze. Instead, it warmed him to know that, maybe, Scott was as intrigued by him as he was by Scott. Chuckling to himself, Gareth poured two cups of coffee and took both to Scott's office on a tray. He knocked lightly on the open door and offered a shy smile when Scott looked his way.

"You take it black, right?" Gareth asked.

"You remembered." Scott smiled back at him as he took one mug from the tray and leaned against the edge of his desk.

Gareth shrugged. "Always easy to remember when someone takes it the same way as you do."

Scott snickered softly, causing Gareth to roll his eyes. The two men stared at each other over their mugs, sporting small smiles. The noise of the door opening broke the moment.

"Sorry boys, traffic was mad this morning," Faith called from the main room. She waddled across the waiting room and leaned with her shoulder against the door frame of Scott's office. "Looks like you've managed fine without me so far." She grinned.

"We haven't gotten any further than coffee." Scott grinned back. "You got here quicker than you thought."

"Yeah. Once we got out of the villages it seemed to ease up. Must have been something on at one of the schools or something. Kids everywhere." She rolled her eyes and rubbed her stomach absentmindedly.

"I'll make you a tea," Gareth said softly. "Then you can get started on showing me the ropes."

"Thanks, pet," Faith said, patting his arm as he passed her.

Chapter Six

It wasn't quite midday when Faith sank back in her chair and whistled. "I know we used to joke about your photographic memory in school but seeing it in action is another thing entirely. You know his diary better than I do already."

Gareth blushed bright red and shrugged his shoulders, not knowing how to respond. Positive feedback still seemed alien to him.

Scott came out of his office and smiled at the pair. "Everything going well, by the sounds of things."

"He knows more than me already," Faith laughed.

Scott grinned again. The soft, soppy grin he'd had on his face when they'd had coffee in Gareth's flat. It almost made him look a bit dorky.

As if suddenly struck by an idea, Scott clapped his hands and said, "If you're both comfortable with this, why don't you take off, Faith? I know you still have lots to get done before the baby comes. If Gareth's sure he can manage, of course."

Gareth smiled at his old school friend. "Go, I can manage. And if I get stuck with anything I'll give you a call."

"You sure?" Faith asked, one hand already lifting her jacket from the back of her chair.

"Absolutely. Go," Gareth told her.

Breathing a sigh of relief, Faith smiled again. "Thanks guys." She wrapped her two friends and colleagues in firm hugs and kissed their cheeks before heading towards the door. "Don't have too much fun without me."

"Not possible." Scott smiled.

With one final grin at the two men, she was gone.

Silence crept into the office as Gareth raced to think of something to say.

"Do you want a coffee?" Gareth eventually settled on – assuming a coffee offer was a safe first step in their working life as a pair.

"That would be great." Scott beamed at him.

"No problem, I'll brew a pot and bring it to you so you can enjoy it before your meeting with Mrs. Howard at twelve-thirty."

"Shit." The colour drained from Scott's face so quickly that Gareth became a little concerned.

"Sir?"

"I'd completely forgotten about Mrs. Howard. We were supposed to meet yesterday and she rearranged so I put off writing up my report and processing the photos we took the other night and then totally forgot to get back to them. Fuck." He ran a hand through his hair, ruffling it in such a way that Gareth thought would probably resemble the way he looked first thing in the morning. "Forget the coffee. I need to get everything sorted and I don't want to be too distracted and waste your efforts."

"I could always sort the photos for you. That way all you'd have to do is type up your notes – assuming you made notes."

Scott let out a long breath, a weight visibly lifted from his shoulders. "Are you sure? They only need copying across from the memory card and printing. My computer is just so old it can't manage to do both things at once. I should have updated it years ago and just never seem to get around to it."

Gareth smiled, pleased that he was already cementing his usefulness to Scott. "You go crack on. I'll brew us a pot of coffee and collect the memory card from you when I bring you a cup through."

Scott bowed his head in thanks and quickly disappeared into his inner office.

Gareth made his way into the kitchenette, pulled his coffee bags from one of the upper cupboards, and set the machine running. As it whirred into life, he gathered two mugs from the draining board, dried them off, and put them to one side. Over the hissing of the coffee machine, Gareth heard and felt his stomach growl. It had been several hours since he'd abandoned his half-eaten bowl of porridge, and with midday fast approaching, he was starting to get peckish. He recalled the deli he'd walked past that morning and decided he'd call them while he waited for the photographs to copy across to his computer.

Before he turned back to the coffee machine, he remembered Faith's passing comment that Scott often forgot to sort his lunch. He checked the fridge and found it bare. If Scott hadn't brought something with him that morning and had his meeting with Mrs. Howard at twelve-thirty, he'd have little chance to collect lunch at a reasonable time. He'd order two lunches in that case. The calendar on his computer had highlighted forty-five minutes for Scott's meeting, so if Gareth arranged delivery for between quarter-past and half-past one, he'd be bang on time.

Conscious of Scott's time crunch and wanting to ensure he

had the photos ready in plenty of time to relieve Scott of any extra panic, Gareth quickly poured the coffee and took a mug to his boss.

Scott looked up the second he stepped through the door and smiled broadly. Gareth returned his smile and placed his mug on the desk in front of him.

"I'm going to order some lunch from this little deli I saw on my walk in this morning. I could order something for you too seeing as there's nothing in the fridge."

"Gareth Hughes, I could kiss you. I already don't know what I'd do without you." Scott grinned lopsidedly.

Gareth blushed again and reminded himself for the millionth time that he needed to find a way to control that particular reaction. He cleared his throat and willed the flush to go down. "Do you want me to bring up a menu for you?"

"No, I'm not fussy." Scott smirked. "Whatever looks good to you is fine by me."

Gareth nodded, plucked the memory card from Scott's outstretched hand and scurried back to his desk, hoping it would hide the fact that his cheeks were starting to turn red again.

Once he was sure he was out of sight, he took the opportunity to take a few calming breaths. His mind was at war with itself. One side of him was jumping for joy at Scott's mention of kissing, already daydreaming about how those full lips would feel against his. The other half chastised him, reminding him that it was probably just a phrase Scott used. It hadn't necessarily meant anything.

But Scott had been grinning again. That grin that Gareth was starting to recognise as Scott's more natural, relaxed smile.

God, he needed to get himself under control.

He turned his attention back to his task. Once the photos

were printed and in his hand, he knocked softly on the door to Scott's office. Scott raised his head and smiled. Gareth tried to keep his face neutral as his fingertips brushed against Scott's hand as he passed the pictures across the desk.

"Thank you. For the printing and for keeping me calm," Scott said, their fingers still dangerously close as they both held the photos.

Gareth swallowed and pulled his hand away, hyper-aware of just how close they'd been. "Just doing my job." He smiled and shrugged. "I'll let you know when she arrives."

"Thank you," Scott repeated.

Gareth nodded and turned to leave, feeling the soft warmth of Scott's gaze on his back as he went.

Chapter Seven

Alex sighed and curled her lips into a frown as her phone buzzed for the umpteenth time, indicating yet another call from Marcus. She glanced at the screen, frustration bubbling up inside her. With a flick of her thumb, she declined the call once more and fought embarrassment as DCI Pickering stared at her from across the desk. His eyes narrowed in knowing and mirrored the irritation she felt.

Shoving off her emotions, she stared at the report that had just come in and chewed on her thumbnail. The three days it had taken for the lab results to come back had been so tense that a permanent knot had formed in her stomach. And now they had answers. They'd found high levels of cardenolides in her blood, indicating she'd been poisoned. Potentially deliberately.

"That's not quite everything," Pickering warned.

Alex sighed and straightened her back. That knot pulled tighter on her insides again. "Okay. Hit me with it."

"We found Jake Scullon's fingerprints on the inside handle of the front door."

Alex's heart dropped into her stomach. Her throat felt dry and tight, but she tried to keep her face stoic as Pickering continued to talk.

"The lawyers for Elevate are already kicking off, seizing that as evidence of mishandling the case." Pickering stopped and gave her a sympathetic look. Alex's skin prickled. "We're going to have to ask you to step down from the case, Alex. If Jake Scullon is involved, neither of you can be seen to be involved in the investigation from here on out. You're too close to this."

Alex rolled back her shoulders and lifted her chin. "With all due respect, sir. It's not that unusual that Jake's fingerprints would be in that house. He did handle the correspondence with her, and with the court date coming up, he was bound to have been there recently."

"No, but it is strange that his fingerprint is the only thing to have survived that mass cleaning."

Alex's shoulders ached. She could already feel the weight of their accusations bearing down on her. She and Jake Scullon had worked on the Elevate case together for months before Beth had finally come forward with her witness statement confirming that the pension giant was selling its customers' data on the dark web. They'd then guided her through the prosecution process and set up the necessary protection when it became apparent that Elevate were determined to do anything to keep her from testifying. The idea that they would have done something to her wasn't just absurd, it was insulting.

Pickering's voice broke through her thoughts, his expression grave. "We can't afford any missteps, not with the stakes this high."

Alex nodded, her mind racing with possibilities. Was someone setting them up? Had someone within Elevate gotten to a member of the CSI team? Or had she and Jake truly just let Beth down and left her vulnerable to the very people trying to silence her? Her heart pounded and she could feel sweat pooling under her arms. She shoved her hands in her pockets, hoping Pickering hadn't noticed their shaking.

Her phone vibrated and she closed her fist around it.

"I need to take this," she lied.

Pickering nodded. "Of course. And maybe get yourself home. I know this will have come as a shock to you. We can handle everything from here. Just make sure you leave all the info on your desk for us."

Alex tried to give him a smile in thanks and somehow managed to walk out of his office even though her legs felt like jelly. She could feel her blood thrumming through her veins. This wasn't right. Her instinct itched underneath her skin. She quickly gathered her investigation notes, grabbed her coat from the back of her chair, and left the station – Beth's file still gripped tightly in her hand.

She needed help. And with the rest of the force being told to give her a wide berth there was only one person she could think to go to. Declining Marcus's latest call she scrolled through her contacts and dialled the number for Scott Parmer.

Chapter Eight

As the end of the day rolled closer, Gareth was feeling more and more confident in his new job. He'd spent most of the afternoon looking through a series of process documents that Faith had left for him. It all seemed straightforward enough and he was fairly sure he'd memorised it within a few hours. He'd also managed to book a few consultations with prospective clients who phoned throughout the day and made some headway in getting back to a few query emails that had been stacked up in Faith's to-do pile. He was so engrossed in working through everything that he didn't hear Scott come into the room until he spoke.

"You can head off if you're all done."

Gareth jumped slightly at the sudden disturbance but settled fairly quickly when he set eyes on Scott leaning against the doorframe. It was strange how quickly Scott's presence was able to soothe his nerves. He felt comfortable around Scott, like he could be himself. Although he was still relearning who that was after the damage Liam had done. Suddenly realising he'd been staring and hadn't yet responded, Gareth cleared his throat and started shutting down his computer.

"Great, yeah, thanks," he mumbled. "I'll close this down and tidy up, and then I'll be off."

"No problem." Scott smiled. His phone rang in his pocket. He fished it out to quickly decline the call, turning his attention back to Gareth. "Did you notice how much was left in the petty cash after you paid for lunch by the way? Do I need to top it up?"

Gareth paused and frowned.

Scott must have read his confusion because he chuckled. "Faith forgot to tell you about the petty cash, didn't she?"

"She did, yeah. It's fine though. It wasn't much," Gareth insisted as he gathered his empty coffee mug and made his way to the kitchen.

"Don't be silly," Scott called from the other room. "I can't have you paying for my lunch. Especially not on the first day."

As Gareth came back into the room, Scott fumbled with his wallet. "Oh, no, no. You don't need to do that. It didn't cost much, and I honestly didn't mind sorting it. I needed to get something for myself too anyway. If anything, buying for both of us made it more worth the delivery fee."

Scott looked up from his wallet and frowned. "You're sure?"

"Absolutely." What little pride Gareth had managed to rebuild for himself and the desperate need to please Scott overruled his money worries. He could sacrifice a tenner to keep his pride intact.

Scott smiled back. The room was silent for a moment as both men looked at each other, trying to assess what to do next. With a small nod to signal he was done, Gareth pushed in his chair and slipped on his coat. He was just about to say goodnight when Scott interrupted.

"Do you fancy going for a drink?"

Gareth froze, one arm inside his coat, the other hanging awkwardly by his side. His heart pounded in his chest, and he could feel his throat drying with every second that passed.

"Just to say thank you for lunch and to welcome you to the team properly," Scott clarified.

Gareth swallowed, willing his throat to loosen up a little so he could talk rather than gawp helplessly. He slowly slipped his other arm into his coat sleeve and started buttoning it up, giving himself some time to think. A thank you and welcome drink was completely normal, wasn't it?

"It's the least I can do after you paid for lunch and helped me out with Mrs. Howard's case earlier."

Gareth took a breath and forced himself to relax. "If you're sure. You don't have any other plans? I wouldn't want to take up your time." He was sure his voice sounded strange. It was more strained than it should have been. But he managed to offer up a shy smile that he hoped made his hesitation look more like typical first-day nerves than anything more.

"Nope. Free as a bird." Scott smiled.

There was something in that smile that made Gareth relax. He felt his spine soften and his shoulders drop to their normal height. Before he knew it, his smile began feeling more natural too.

"Great. Well, thank you." He nodded.

"I'll just grab my coat and we'll head off," Scott said before disappearing back into his office.

Once he was gone, Gareth's mind began to whirr once again. He closed his eyes and took a breath. It was just a drink. There was a small part of him that almost dared to hope that it had been more of a personal request than a professional one, but he soon squashed that thought. Scott was his boss. It was nothing more than just a polite, professional courtesy.

Gareth shook himself, forcing his body into what he hoped

looked like a more relaxed stance just as Scott came back and gestured for him to lead the way.

Chapter Nine

Gareth settled his back against the hard wooden chair as he watched Scott weave across the pub with two half pints and a warm smile. He returned the smile on impulse, despite the nagging voice in his mind reminding him to keep things professional. Scott's phone vibrated against the knotted wood of the table, drawing Gareth's attention. Alex calling. He flicked his eyes back up to Scott again, hoping it wasn't obvious he'd looked.

As Scott sat down, he glanced at his phone and quickly slipped it into his jacket pocket.

"Do you need to get that?" Gareth asked, unable to contain his curiosity.

"I'll call her back. Just an old friend I haven't caught up with in a while. She'll be fine." Picking up his half pint, Scott glanced over at him. "You didn't need to have just a half because I was. It's not like you're driving home."

"It's fine, I didn't do it to stop you from feeling lonely. I don't tend to drink much these days anyway."

Scott nodded in understanding. "I'm much the same. I need to have my wits about me in this job."

"I think that's fair advice for life in general."

Scott chuckled but quickly sobered up when he looked at

Gareth. "You're far too cynical for your age."

Gareth snorted. "You going to go all detective on me? Try and investigate my past to work out why?"

Scott smiled softly. "No. No. I was hoping to be a friend you opened up to about it. But if you're not ready, I completely understand."

Gareth put down his drink and stared at the man in front of him. Green eyes bore into blue. There was something about Scott that tied Gareth's stomach in knots. But Faith trusted him. She wouldn't have introduced them after everything he'd been through if she didn't truly think it was the right thing to do. Faith was many things. Impulsive. Stubborn. Feisty. But she was always good-hearted and had the best intentions for those she cared about – and the knowledge that he was one of those people warmed Gareth.

He refocused on Scott. Warmth spread through him again as Scott continued to look at him reassuringly. Something inside Gareth crumbled. Like a dam bursting. It was a feeling he'd only felt once before. But this time, Scott's steady presence made it far easier to do so without shattering completely.

He took a deep breath. "Liam. My ex. We met at work when I was straight out of uni. He was in HR. I was a PA. When we first started dating, he was great. Attentive. He was always checking in on me. Made sure I got home safe after dates. He'd come to check on me at work if I'd been too busy to reply to his messages. I thought he was being sweet. Protective. He asked me to move in with him after a few months. Quick, I know. But he was so excited and made it all sound so romantic. He couldn't be without me, hated being apart or not hearing from me, going days without seeing me. It was about then that he started to change." Gareth lifted his eyes to look at Scott. He hadn't even been aware he'd dropped his gaze, but Scott was still looking at him with concern and support in his eyes.

Taking a calming breath, Gareth continued, "He hated me going out without him, so I only ever went anywhere if he was invited. My friends said he was overbearing, but...He told me his ex had been attacked, and he was terrified of it happening again. I thought he was just protective and insecure. Before I knew it, most of my friends had stopped asking after me. Faith had moved up here by then so we weren't in touch as much as we had been. If I got upset about that he'd tell me not to be so needy. He said it was no wonder everyone left me if I suffocated them so much – even my family didn't want anything to do with me, so I was lucky he stuck by me, and he always would. He took control without me even realising. Eventually, he had a say in everything I did – how I dressed and who I spoke to. Anything he didn't like earned me some kind of punishment. He'd humiliate me and make me feel so worthless that I began to believe him. I loved him so much that I would always find a way to blame myself or excuse what he'd done. I didn't see it happening until I was so deep, I couldn't get out."

He felt two warm, soft hands cover his own. He hadn't even realised he'd balled them into fists.

"But you did." Scott reassured him with a gentle squeeze. "You got away. And you're safe now."

Gareth smiled. "Faith came to visit. She surprised me for my twenty-third birthday and took me to one of my favourite bars. We had such a good night. But then I went home. Liam wasn't happy we'd been out. He accused me of deliberately worrying him or preferring being with Faith to being with him, that I was pining after her. He'd often used my bisexuality against me that way. That was nothing new. But that night was the first time he hit me. Faith must have known something wasn't right because she came round the next morning after he'd left for work. I told her everything. It just came spilling out.

"She got me to report him. But he'd already set rumours going at work that I was a drunk. He'd told people that was why we never went out anymore and why my behaviour had been off. He made me sound completely unreliable. Destroyed my reputation. I was isolated the second I accused him. The flat was his too, so within the space of twenty-four hours I lost everything."

"So Faith set you up here." Scott smiled.

"She's the best friend anyone could ask for." Gareth nodded.

"I don't know. I think you give her a run for her money." Scott patted Gareth's hands again. "Thanks for telling me."

"Doesn't feel as hard to say to you as I expected." Gareth shrugged. They were silent for a moment as they processed everything Gareth had shared. But, afraid that the silence would become awkward, or give Scott too much time to start seeing him as nothing more than a weak victim, Gareth asked, "So what about you? Anyone special in your life at the minute? Girlfriend? Boyfriend?"

Gareth pulled a hand away to take another gulp of his drink. He could feel Scott watching him as he did so as if assessing his body language for any signs of lingering trauma. It was a look he'd often seen from Faith and one he'd learned to accept as concern, rather than judgement. He swallowed his drink and tilted his head from side to side as he made a conscious effort to relax. He loosened his shoulders and unclenched his fists, hoping Scott would get the message that he was okay. Eventually, Scott nodded and started recalling his own story.

"No girlfriend. Women aren't my thing. And David, my ex,

left about four years ago; there hasn't really been anyone since. We met when he was in the States for a research project, and I was so besotted I came back to the UK with him, set my business up, and thought we were happy. About a year in, I woke up one morning to find he'd gone. Didn't think too much of it – he often got up early to head home before going to work. But then, a week went by, and I didn't hear from him. Turns out he'd decided to go travelling again and just failed to tell me. I had to find out through mutual friends."

Gareth nodded knowingly. "Well, here's to having a terrible romantic past."

"And hopefully a more promising romantic future." Scott grinned as he raised his glass and the two men toasted.

They settled into an easy conversation as they finished their drinks. They talked about Scott's mother, who still lived in the States. She came over for the holidays most years, and they tended to take a holiday abroad together. Despite the distance, they had a close relationship.

Gareth felt a fit of lingering jealousy over their relationship. He had a large family: mum, dad, an older sister, and a niece and nephew. But they didn't speak anymore. He still got a Christmas card from his sister every year, but that was it. It was just another thing Liam had managed to damage.

Eventually, Scott convinced him to stay for something to eat, as a thank-you for lunch. Gareth had worried about veering away from his pre-planned meals for the week but was eventually convinced that he could put something in his freezer to keep and readjust his planning accordingly.

Scott was just returning from putting in their order at the bar when Gareth's phone started ringing. Seeing it was Faith, he quickly silenced it and tapped out a text to say he'd call her back.

"Everything okay?" Scott asked as he placed two pints of Coke on the table.

"Faith. Probably wants the gossip from my first day."

"Ah." Scott grinned. "How long do you reckon until she tries to get hold of me?"

"If she lasts any more than five minutes you can have some of my chips."

The sentence was barely out of Gareth's mouth before Scott's phone started ringing. He laughed as he waved the device at Gareth to show him the caller ID – Faith.

"No chips for you then," Gareth mumbled as he gulped his drink.

Scott answered with a grin, "You just cost me chips...No, nothing. Yeah, fine. More than fine. He was, is, great. In fact, I think introducing Gareth to your role was probably the best thing you've ever done..." He gave Gareth a quick wink as he listened to Faith on the other end of the line. "Yeah...Okay. Well, I'm sure he'll get back to you soon...Yeah. Okay. Rest up." He hung up and burst out laughing as he caught Gareth's eye. They tamed their laughter as their dinners arrived – steak and ale pie with chips for Gareth and a chicken tikka masala for Scott.

They thanked the waitress, and Scott watched as Gareth laid out a paper napkin in his lap and gave his cutlery a once over.

"I was only half joking, you know. I think this might be the best thing Faith's done for me."

"Don't judge too quickly. It's only been one day." Gareth smiled as he cut open his pie.

"I don't know about that. You've constantly impressed me since we met, and I get the impression you'll only continue to.

You're very impressive, Mr. Hughes."

Gareth blushed furiously but smiled nonetheless. "You're not so bad yourself."

Scott grinned back as he shovelled food into his mouth, and they continued to eat in companionable silence.

As he swallowed his last mouthful, Scott asked, "You want me to walk you home?"

"Bloody hell, I've only just finished. You want to get rid of me that quickly?" Gareth raised an eyebrow.

Scott laughed. "I didn't mean immediately. I was just trying to bump myself up from 'not so bad'."

"Isn't your car over this side of town? You'd have to walk all the way back here afterwards. Seems a bit silly."

"Alright, let me drive you then."

Gareth smiled softly. "It's fine, after this and the big lunch I need a good walk. That okay?"

Scott dropped his gaze to the table and pushed the dregs of his meal around his plate. Gareth almost felt sorry for what he was now sure was disappointment on Scott's face. Something inside him blossomed into life and he almost backtracked. But his therapist's words echoed in his mind. He needed to learn to do what he wanted, not what he thought other people wanted from him. And as much as Gareth wanted to make Scott happy, and spend more time with him, he also wanted to get some fresh air and walk off the two less-than-healthy meals he'd had that day.

Before Gareth could linger in his thoughts for too long, Scott raised his head and smiled. "Of course. Got to make sure those delicious suits still fit."

Gareth pouted and grinned slyly. "Just the one suit for now. I had to sell my best ones to pay for a new start. Maybe you'll have to help when I come to buy a few new ones since you seem to have such a good eye."

As he unlocked the door to his flat (and noted the familiar scurry on the other side), Gareth fished his mobile from his pocket and immediately started dialling Faith's number. Clearly eager to hear his gossip from the afternoon, she answered almost immediately.

"What took you so long, I called you ages ago!" she panted.

"Sorry, I stopped out for celebratory first-day-at-work dinner and then walked home. I literally just got in."

"Oh, sweetheart you should have said if you wanted to go out to celebrate. You didn't sit on your own, did you?"

"Of course not! How sad do you think I am? Scott took me to the pub and got dinner as a thank-you for my getting lunch earlier."

Faith gasped. "The little...Were you there when I spoke to him?"

"Yep." Gareth laughed, popping the "p" at the end of the word.

"He never took me out to thank me for buying lunch before. He already likes you more than me," she joked.

"Well, in fairness, you usually pay for lunches out of the petty cash, which I didn't find out about until after," Gareth told her as switched on his coffee machine.

"Oh shit. I knew I'd forgotten to show you something. At least you managed to get a date out of it."

"It wasn't a date, Fay," he sighed. "Just a good boss taking his new employee out to say thanks."

Faith snorted down the line. "Yeah right."

There was a long pause as Gareth finished preparing his

coffee and made his way through to his living room and lumpy sofa, a sappy smile on his face as he inhaled the coffee aroma.

"Is this a good silence or a bad silence?" Faith asked warily.

"It's good, Faith. I'm good. Thank you."

Faith let out a loud sigh. "Well thank God for that. So, you're gonna be okay working together, it's not going to make you too uncomfortable, is it?"

"No." Gareth smiled. "No, I think you were right. This might just be exactly what I needed."

"I told you. Have–"

"Have faith in Faith, I know," Gareth laughed loudly before sobering up. "I might really like him, Fay."

"You say that like it's a bad thing."

"I don't exactly have the best track record when it comes to picking people to date. And he is one hell of a flirt."

"As if you're one to talk on flirting. I remember you at eighteen, don't forget." Faith giggled. "Listen, Gareth. I've known both of you for years. Do you think I'd be encouraging you if I didn't think you stood a chance?"

Gareth didn't respond. He couldn't. Because he knew she was right. He'd already told himself as much. But old wounds were hard to heal, and he questioned his judgement regardless.

"Besides, the flirting is harmless. He'll flirt with anything, but he's one of the most loyal people I know. He was really beaten up for a long time after everything went wrong with his ex. Scott was still pining when I met him, and the guy had already been gone a year by that point. I get the impression that when he falls, he falls hard. Just like you."

Gareth laughed softly but didn't answer her. In the background, he could hear Robin's muffled voice before Faith laughed.

"Alright, I'm gonna let you go; Rob reckons I've pestered you enough."

"Tell him thanks," Gareth laughed.

"Yeah, I don't think so," Faith snarked. "You know where I am if you need me, okay?"

"Absolutely. Don't worry about me."

They said their goodbyes, and Gareth dropped his phone beside him on the sofa. He took a large swig of his coffee, letting the flavours dance on his tongue for a moment, his eyes sliding closed. Few things in life gave him the same pleasurable thrill as a perfect cup of coffee. As if he'd opened the floodgates, several images of other things that might give him such a thrill began flooding his mind. He let them hover there for a moment before his eyes sprang open, and he shook his head rapidly to clear it. After everything Liam had put him through, his sex drive had been on a hiatus for the last couple of years. Feeling like a worthless piece of trash didn't leave much room for feeling sexy. But now, his body felt more awake than it had in a long time as his brain painted some rather vivid images of his new boss doing incredibly wicked things to him. He gulped down the remains of his coffee and headed for his bathroom, hopeful that a cold shower would help wash the images away.

Chapter Ten

The following morning got off to a slow start. Scott was holed up in his office, working through reports for cases he'd closed, so he saw little of Gareth except for when he'd popped his head in to ask what Scott wanted for lunch. Scott wasn't entirely sure whether the space between them was calming or concerning. On the one hand, Gareth probably needed a little space after their meal at the pub the previous evening. But on the other, it made him feel slightly paranoid.

Had he pushed too hard and left Gareth uncomfortable? Was Gareth taking a step back to avoid any misunderstanding around their dinner last night?

Rolling his eyes, Scott mentally chastised himself and tried to focus back on the report that lay on his desk. He was being ridiculous. Gareth hadn't spoken to him because they were both busy. Besides, he'd seemed happy enough to take lunch together again when he'd asked what Scott wanted.

When Scott finally emerged from his office, Gareth was just putting the phone down. He watched as Gareth stretched in his chair, curling his back like an elegant feline. He swallowed and avoided looking too closely at the way Gareth's shirt clung to his shoulders and upper arms as he moved. Instead, he busied himself with his phone, realising with a jolt that he had several missed calls from Alex. That wasn't like her. Worry started to gnaw at his gut. He should have called her back last night but after his drinks with Gareth, it had totally slipped his mind.

Gareth cleared his throat, breaking through Scott's worry, and said, "Lunch should be about forty-five minutes."

"Thank God. I'm starving." Scott smiled. Perfect. That gave him enough time to call Alex back, but wasn't so long that his stomach would start grumbling embarrassingly.

"Didn't I see an empty packet of biscuits on your desk just now?" Gareth teased.

Scott pouted and folded his arms. "There were only a few left. And I had them early this morning."

Gareth rolled his eyes, but the soft smile on his face gave away his amusement at Scott's defensiveness. Gareth opened his mouth to respond but the loud creaking of a floorboard outside interrupted what would likely have been another jibing retort. Scott saw him jump slightly and snapped his head to look at the door as a petite Asian woman burst into the room. Her dark, almond-shaped eyes immediately locked on Scott as she gasped with relief.

"Thank God you're in. I've been trying to get hold of you for hours. You've not got an appointment, have you?"

Scott looked around at Gareth, who shook his head and responded, "No, the diary is clear now for the rest of the day." He didn't mention that lunch was likely on its way.

"Alex, this is Gareth. He's my new assistant while Faith is on maternity leave. Gareth, Alex. She's a cyber-crime expert with the police. We go back years," Scott told him with a mischievous glint in his eyes.

"Nice to meet you," Gareth said politely.

"You too," Alex replied hastily, before turning her attention back to Scott. "I need your help with something."

"Of course! Sorry! I meant to call you back last night but I sort of lost track of time..." Scott frowned with worry. He stepped forward and placed his hand on the small of Alex's back with comfortable ease as he guided her towards the sofa. Scott could feel Gareth's eagle eye watching them curiously. As he looked back, he saw Gareth's previously relaxed expression shift, as if a cool, impassable, and unreadable mask slipped over his face. Suddenly self-conscious of his physical ease with Alex, Scott stepped away, removing his hand from her back as she sat down.

Alex's phone vibrated loudly in her pocket, and she quickly silenced it, but not before they caught sight of the caller ID. Marcus. Scott rolled his eyes. Of course. Who else would it be?

"Do you want a coffee while we chat?" Scott offered, instinctively stroking a comforting hand down Alex's arm.

"No, thank you. I'm jittery enough as it is."

Scott frowned. He'd known Alex for years, and if there was one word he'd never thought to describe her as, it was jittery. They'd met about a year after he'd moved to the UK. He'd been nursing a broken heart at the time, and despite not knowing each other well, she'd been a strong force in helping him pull himself back together. Plus, she'd been able to introduce him to a few other like-minded people to get him through his breakup.

Scott beckoned for Gareth to join them on the sofa and Gareth raised a questioning eyebrow but quickly moved from his desk.

"Remember the Elevate case?" Alex asked, her eyes pinned on Scott.

"Only by name, I never got the details," Scott replied, edging up on the sofa to let Gareth sit down. He tried not to register the hurt that swept through him as the young man shuffled as far away as the small sofa would allow.

Alex quickly ran him through the basics of the case. Pension company. Customer Data. Dark Web. Millions and millions in dirty money.

"Three days ago a woman named Beth O'Neil was found dead in her own home. Poisoned. She was our key witness in the case. We initially thought it was suicide, but blood tests suggested huge amounts of toxin in her blood. She could have ingested it accidentally, of course, but I think she was killed to keep her quiet and stop her from testifying in court. Without her testimony, we really can't pin the case on as many of the people responsible as we'd like. The defence is denying it, obviously, and trying to imply something's gone wrong on our end. So now the whole investigation is under scrutiny from every angle."

Scott winced. Alex was a consummate professional. He knew she lived for her job, much to the annoyance of her husband. She did everything by the book.

"Jake and I can't touch the case while it's being reviewed. His fingerprints were found in her otherwise spotless house and naturally, that's been snagged on and used against us."

Scott scoffed. "Ridiculous. Jake's no angel, but he's a good cop."

"Well, we know that. But until the whole thing is sorted we're being kept at arm's length. And I'm not saying I don't trust the review board to sort it, but if the defence team are involved in her death, who knows what else they've done." Alex rolled her eyes and grunted as her phone buzzed again. She silenced the call and shoved her mobile back into her handbag. "Sorry."

Scott nodded in understanding before she continued. "Just be careful who you talk to about the whole thing. I'm not sure who we can trust right now."

Gareth's eyebrows shot up his forehead. "You think someone on your side is stitching you up?"

Alex shifted her gaze to him for the first time in the conversation. "This case was huge. We made a lot of powerful enemies when we brought down Elevate. The company was run by some truly powerful people, and with the money at their disposal it would be easy for someone on the inside to take a payoff to make it look like we'd done something wrong and get the case thrown out."

Gareth nodded in earnest.

"Alex, I promise you. I'll get this sorted." Scott leaned forward and placed a hand on her knee.

Alex smiled softly at him and covered his hand with hers. "I know you will. Why do you think you were the first person I came to?"

Scott squeezed her hand and pulled away. She slipped her hand inside the leather portfolio she'd set by her side and pulled out a brown Manilla file. Scott took it from her, grabbed his phone from his pocket, and pulled up his notes app. "What can you tell me about who we can talk to if the force is out of reach?"

"There's her brother. I've put his details in the file. Jake says she'd started working at a hotel in the city centre after Elevate shut down, so there might be someone there you can talk to. Again, I've added all my information to the file."

"Okay, what about forensics?" Scott asked, starting a new section in his notes.

"Other than Jake's fingerprint, nothing. The place had been obsessively cleaned. I did note a few things that looked out of place. Empty spaces on the shoe rack and coat hooks. Like someone had stolen or moved her stuff."

"Or taken their stuff back to remove themselves from the scene," Gareth pondered.

Alex nodded, her eyes flicking down to look at the file now in Scott's hands. "Once they found Jake's fingerprint they shut me out, so I don't have anything else to go on I'm afraid."

"Why would they shut you out if it was deemed a suicide?" Gareth asked.

"Something felt off from the minute I got to the scene. Just odd little things. The missing items for one. The place stunk like cleaning products for another. Rumours started flying pretty quickly and whenever there's a rumour someone might be dirty, cops tend to close ranks, especially when it jeopardises such an important case. I tried calling in a few favours but got no response. I had to hand over all my notes to the review board, I took copies to give to you guys, which I shouldn't have. I'd be in even more trouble if anyone knew I had them." She dropped her head into her hands. Her straight, dark hair fell over her face like a curtain. Her shoulders sagged as her spirit seemed to crumble in front of them.

Scott's concern for his friend rose in his throat and he reached out for her once again, grasping her slight shoulder. He watched as Gareth bit his lip nervously.

Slowly, Gareth stood up and moved to crouch in front of Alex.

"Listen, I get it," he told her. His voice was low and soft. "You've worked hard to build a reputation, and then one accusation tarnishes everything."

Alex lifted her head to look up at him. Her dark almond-shaped eyes were wet and red-rimmed as if she were fighting back tears that threatened to ruin what little composure she had left.

"What is it, exactly, that the Elevate defence team are accusing you of?" Gareth pushed gently. "We can't prove them wrong if we don't know what we're trying to disprove."

Alex took a deep breath and pushed her hair behind her ears. "Their current theory is that we unjustly coerced Beth into giving us information and that she was going to pull out and expose us. They're saying..." Her voice cracked, and her face reddened. She gritted her teeth and spat her following words. "They're saying we had her killed to protect our careers. But they have no evidence. It's pure speculation. I mean, for God's sake, Beth was the one who approached us! We'd put out some feelers discreetly, tried to encourage some of the workers to talk, and she responded."

Scott leaned forward and grabbed his friend's hand. He'd never seen Alex so distraught in all the years he'd known her. She was always the cool, collected one. Jake was the emotional hothead. Usually, she was able to balance him out. Scott gave her shoulder a slight squeeze. "Listen, Alex. We've got this. I promise you. We'll find who killed Beth and get you back in the job you love."

A soft knock at the door alerted the group to the arrival of Gareth and Scott's lunch, which Gareth dealt with swiftly while Scott comforted Alex.

Once he'd collected the food, Alex had gathered herself enough to leave. She thanked Scott as she wrapped him in a tight hug. Her phone began to buzz again, and she pulled away from Scott with a loud tut, gave Gareth a quick nod and left, finally putting her phone to her ear. "Marcus, you need to stop. If I don't answer, I'll call you back as soon as I can..."

Her voice faded as she left the room and headed down the stairs.

Chapter Eleven

Gareth laid their lunches on the coffee table and settled himself in one armchair to face Scott on the sofa. His emotions and thoughts were racing, and he wasn't sure he could handle being near his boss at that moment. The attraction he felt towards Scott was strong, probably even stronger than the initial attraction he'd felt towards Liam. But so much of what he'd seen just now confused him. He could go from seemingly caring for Gareth's wellbeing, checking he was comfortable at every step, to being impossibly touchy with married women. Although he had said he wasn't interested in women, so perhaps it was all friendly and harmless. Gareth could barely keep up.

He watched Scott settle into the sofa and pick up a pork pie. For all his grace and charm, Scott was not a tidy eater. He chomped into his food, dusting his front and the area around him with pastry flakes and crumbs. As another smattering fell between the sofa cushions, Gareth winced before reminding himself he'd seen a small vacuum in one of the taller kitchen cupboards. He took a neat bite of his sandwich, carefully catching the crumbs with the paper plate the deli supplied. Scott's plate lay abandoned on his lap and seemed to repel crumbs rather than catch them.

"So, this Elevate case – is that the same one that was in the news a few months back?" Gareth asked, hoping to distract himself from his discomfort at the thought of the mess Scott was making.

"The very same," Scott answered, swallowing another mouthful of steak bake. "Do you remember much about it?"

"Only what I read in the papers. One of their employees shopped them into the police after overhearing two directors discussing the profits. They weren't named in the paper obviously, but I assume that employee was Beth."

"Yeah, I'd say so too. I'll see what else I can find in the files Alex left me. Could you do some research into Beth for me? Check her social media, see if anything she's posted raises any red flags."

Gareth raised eyebrows. "Did Faith ever help this much with investigations?"

Scott grinned at him. "How long have you known Faith?"

"Years – since we were at school."

"And have you ever known her to be discreet or tactful about anything?"

Gareth laughed and shook his head. "Yeah, okay. You have a point."

Scott's smile faded as a thoughtful look crossed his face. "Of course, you don't have to either if it makes you uncomfortable. It wasn't technically in the job description, I just thought... seeing as you helped so much with Mrs. Howard's case. And you were great with Alex when she came too."

"No, no. I'd love to." Gareth bumbled as a slight blush tainted his cheeks. "I always loved puzzles and mysteries. As a kid, I wanted to be either Sherlock Holmes or James Bond when I grew up."

"Well, you look far better in a suit than Bond ever did." Scott winked.

Gareth cleared his throat and stood to tidy away their finished lunches, hoping he'd moved fast enough to hide his rising blush. "I'll make us some more coffee before I crack on, shall I?"

"Putting all your skills to use in one afternoon. I could certainly get used to having you around Hughes, Gareth Hughes."

Gareth chuckled and shook his head as he dipped into the kitchenette. His mind whirred and his stomach churned as the coffee brewed. Doubts and questions bounced around noisily in his head. By the time the coffee was ready, his blush had mercifully faded, but the noise in his mind was still raging.

He placed Scott's coffee on the desk and held the other in his hands as he sat in the opposite chair.

Scott looked up to thank him and blew on his coffee, his eyes watching Gareth closely as if he could tell something was on Gareth's mind. But he didn't push. Didn't urge Gareth to say what he thought. Instead, he waited. That soft look in his eyes let Gareth know he was safe to speak his mind.

Reassured by Scott's patience Gareth spoke, "Are we completely sure this case is clean? Is there a chance the accusation is right, and something underhand went on?"

Scott's face turned to stone, and his back stiffened. "Alex is one of the most honest, by-the-book officers I've ever known. She lives for that job. I always joke that she loves the job more than her husband, Marcus. There's no way she'd risk sacrificing it in any way."

"Okay," Gareth receded, slightly afraid of the hard look on Scott's usually soft face. But, feeling braver and more comfortable in himself than he had for years, he decided to push forward. "What about the rest of the investigation team? It sounds like her partner has a bit of a reputation."

Scott sighed. "Jake's a little unorthodox and a bit ham-fisted but he's not corrupt." He raked a hand over his face and groaned. "If he'd been up to anything unsavoury, Alex would have spotted it."

"I wouldn't be too sure. When you trust someone, it can be hard to see them clearly. I'll get on with that research." Gareth made his way out of the office before Scott had a chance to probe further.

Chapter Twelve

By six p.m., Gareth had scrolled through more social media than he'd seen in the last two years. Liam had always been against social media. He claimed it was a toxic place where people pretended to be better than they were to make their friends and family jealous. The irony of that belief was not lost on Gareth now that he was out of the relationship.

Through his research, he'd found two critical things.

One: while Beth had Twitter, Instagram, and Facebook accounts, she wasn't particularly active on any of them. Her profiles were all public but there were very few photos and very little engagement on the posts she shared.

Two: her Facebook page had become far more active since her death, thanks to one friend in particular. Marie Arnold. It seemed Marie was very vocal about searching for information on her friend's murder and did not seem convinced that the police were doing all they could to catch the killer. She regularly posted to Beth's Facebook page, telling her friend how much she missed her and that she wouldn't rest until she saw her killer behind bars. She even claimed to have a hunch of who the killer was. That was particularly interesting.

Gareth quickly scanned Marie's social media and found she regularly took her young toddler to a local park just around the corner from Beth's home. He checked her previous posts and outlined the typical timings of her visits, hoping they could catch her there in the coming days.

Unlike Beth, Marie was an avid poster, regularly adding photos to her Instagram and Facebook profiles and frequently tweeting her opinions and musings about the goings-on in her life. She seemed the type of person to document every tiny detail, which would surely be helpful in any investigation. The odd thing was that none of her photos or posts involved Beth. Based on her recent activity, Gareth had assumed the two women were exceptionally close, but he found that Beth had vanished entirely from Marie's profile in the last six months. She no longer appeared in Marie's pub garden selfies or alongside the chubby toddler in the park. She wasn't tagged in her 'Ladies that Lunch' posts. Something about that didn't add up. Either the women had fallen out, or Marie felt guilty about their distance leading up to Beth's death. Or something had made Beth request Marie give her less social media attention. Both would make sense, especially based on Beth's role in the Elevate case, which would undoubtedly have caused her to become paranoid and skittish.

Gareth didn't have to try hard to imagine how the young woman must have felt once she'd given her statement to the police. That constant feeling of being watched, like the person you'd betrayed was going to find you at any moment. The desperation to hide and stay away so you would be safe. Of course, Beth hadn't left the home she'd lived in for years, but then, she had police protection on hand. Besides, running away too close to the trial would only look more suspicious.

Gareth quickly jotted down his notes and made his way back across to Scott's office. He gently knocked on the open door to Scott's office and offered a soft smile to let his boss know he held no awkwardness from their earlier encounter. Scott looked up and immediately returned the smile. His green eyes twinkled in the early evening sun streaming through the windows.

"Hey, you. Find anything useful?" Scott drawled.

"Maybe. Beth wasn't very active on social media, but I suppose she'd want to keep a low profile ahead of the trial. There is one woman who seems quite vocal about her death though."

"Okay, great. Give me her name and I'll try and find a phone number so we can give her a call." Scott nodded as he twirled a pen between his fingers.

"No need. From her social activity, it looks like she goes to a parenting group in Harehills every Saturday and Wednesday at ten a.m., then takes her son to a nearby playground. Should be easy enough to catch her there tomorrow," Gareth said as he handed over his notepad.

Scott raised his eyebrows and gave that familiar, just-for-Gareth, lopsided smirk. "Looks like all those mystery novels did you some good. I found something useful too. Sort of. We've got contact details for the hotel Beth was working in and a number for her brother, so we can get in touch with both of them. I tried both already and couldn't reach them. I've left a message, but we can try them again later. Also, it turns out the doctor that did the autopsy is an old friend of mine. Well, I say friend; he knew my ex well, and we've crossed paths professionally a few times too. Might be able to get more details from him in person than I can from his initial report. I reckon he'd talk to us."

"Us? You want me to come with you?" Gareth spluttered.

Desk research was one thing, but heading out to question witnesses was another.

"Of course. A second pair of eyes and ears never hurts. Especially ones as talented as yours seem to be." Scott grinned.

Gareth felt something warm stir inside of him. It'd been a long time since he'd felt particularly good at anything. The last few years had gradually worn away his self-confidence until he'd felt worth little more than a Freddo in the 90s. He chuckled internally. At least he was getting his sense of humour back, it seemed. In fact, he felt like he was getting more and more of his old self back the more time he spent around Scott. Amazing what being around the right people could do. Not that Faith and Robin hadn't been great, and he'd always felt welcome at theirs. But they were each other's priority, and with their baby on the way, he felt less and less able to impose on them. With Scott, Gareth finally felt like he might be important to someone again. Even if that never exceeded professional importance, it was more than he'd thought he'd deserved for a long time.

"Do you want me to give him a call and see if I can sort a meeting?" Gareth asked, keen to continue proving his usefulness.

"If you wouldn't mind." Scott smiled as he scribbled a name and phone number. "I'll clean up in here while you do and then I say we head off for the day. It's getting late and it looks like we have an early start tomorrow, as long as you're sure you don't mind working on a Saturday."

Gareth took back his notepad and smiled shyly. "No problem for me."

Once he was back at his desk, Gareth dialled the number Scott had given him for Doctor Oliver Hart. As he listened to the dial tone, Gareth chuckled over the irony of a man who worked predominantly with dead people named Doctor Hart. The chuckle died on his lips as a harsh Northern voice answered the phone.

"What do you want, Parmer?"

"Doctor Hart? My name's Gareth Hughes, I'm Mr. Parmer's new assistant," Gareth introduced himself, hoping he hadn't inflated his role.

"What happened to the woman? She shag him and have to leave?" The doctor snapped.

"Faith is enjoying some time with her fiancé and taking maternity leave, sir," Gareth replied through gritted teeth as he tried to keep his frustration out of his voice, both at the idea that Faith would betray Robin like that and that Scott clearly had a reputation. He wasn't sure he'd ever dealt with anyone as blunt or rude as Oliver Hart. Some friends Scott seemed to have. "Mr. Parmer did at least hire another Welsh employee to keep things familiar for everyone," he snarked.

The man on the other end of the phone barked a laugh, and Gareth felt himself relax slightly. Perhaps the doctor simply had a biting sense of humour.

"He was hoping you'd meet with him so he could ask you a few questions about a case he's working on. Tomorrow afternoon, maybe?" Gareth asked.

"Tomorrow is Saturday."

"Well observed, sir."

"Still doesn't know how to take a day off, I see. Tell him to stop by my office Monday eight a.m." With that, the Northerner hung up and left Gareth gaping.

He pulled himself together and added the meeting to Scott's calendar. He'd get the address from Scott later so he could meet him there on Monday morning.

As soon as he'd shut down his computer, Scott emerged from his office and closed the door behind him.

"Doctor Hart said he'd meet us at eight am on Monday at his office and then hung up before I could clarify where that was, so I'm hoping you know," Gareth told him.

Scott snickered and shook his head. "Yeah, polite conversation isn't his thing. Good thing his patients aren't the chatty type. I'll pick you up Monday morning, and we'll head straight to him."

"I can make my own way there if you give me the address," Gareth protested. The idea of relying too heavily on Scott sat uncomfortably in his gut.

"Don't be daft. We'll be heading the same way there and back here after, I can give you a lift. Saves you getting blown through the city first thing."

Gareth nodded reluctantly and slipped his coat over his shoulders. "Alright. I guess I'll see you tomorrow then. I'll meet you at the park."

"Yep. Bright and early." Scott smiled and spread his arms as he gestured for Gareth to lead the way out.

Chapter Thirteen

A light breeze ruffled the old pages of Gareth's book, and he tutted at the inconvenience. He smoothed out the pages, finished his paragraph, and checked his watch: eleven-forty. Scott had said they'd meet at quarter-to, so he had a few more minutes. He turned back to his book but didn't take in any of the words he read. What if Marie didn't show up? What if she didn't know anything, despite her social media activity? Or what if she did have information but wouldn't share it with them? The last thing he wanted was to waste Scott's time – especially on a weekend.

He looked up from his book again and felt a warm flutter as he spotted Scott striding across the square. His navy shirt and grey blazer framed his broad shoulders perfectly. Gareth swallowed hard and bundled his book back into his rucksack. He suddenly felt very self-conscious about his outfit. He'd picked a far more casual outfit that morning: black boots, jeans, a dark denim jacket, and a plain white T-shirt.

He fumbled around in his backpack before pulling out a thermos and two plastic cups, pouring one for himself and another for Scott. When Scott reached him, he already had the man's cup of coffee held out to him.

"Well, this is already the best witness questioning I've ever been involved in." Scott grinned, his eyes warm with a hint of a mischievous shine.

"I just hope she turns up and I haven't wasted your time."

"Believe me, it wouldn't be the first time a stakeout hasn't gone my way, and it certainly won't be the last. At least this one will have great coffee and company." Scott winked as he took a slurp of his drink.

Gareth grinned and offered up his cup in a 'cheers' motion, hoping his actions distracted from the blush he was sure was spreading across his cheeks.

As they settled on the bench beside one another, Gareth was hyper-aware of the space between them, hoping he'd kept the distance professional without being standoffish.

"Do you have a plan for this meeting then?" Gareth finally asked.

"Oh, I always have a plan. Doesn't mean things go that way though."

Gareth laughed softly. "Okay, so how are you wanting this to go?"

"Let her get here and settle, mostly so we can be sure she's on her own. Then we introduce ourselves and ask our questions. I'm guessing she'll be open to talking based on her social media activity, but you never know."

Gareth nodded in agreement. "Okay, any specific questions in mind?"

"Nah, I'm hoping we can just get her talking and see what she gives us."

Gareth took in the plan, or what little of one there was, and poured two more cups of coffee from his flask. They still had fifteen minutes before the parent and baby group ended, and it would take Marie at least five minutes to get to the park. The two men passed the time amicably and chatted comfortably. Gareth couldn't remember the last time he'd felt so relaxed and normal just talking to someone new. Scott asked about the book Gareth was reading and expressed a desire to get back into reading again. Gareth promised to pull together some recommendations that he thought Scott might like.

By the time Marie stepped through the rusty metal gate with a small red-headed boy, Gareth had almost forgotten they were there for work. He'd almost dared to hope he might be more than a colleague to Scott. They continued to chatter and drink their coffees, but both kept half an eye on the young woman with dark blonde hair as she pushed her son around on the rickety red roundabout. Her voice was high, and she was doing her best to stay bright and upbeat for the little boy, but even from a distance, Gareth could see the lack of light behind her eyes. When he'd seen Marie's social media rants, he had wondered how many of them were fuelled by a desire to get her name in the spotlight. Now faced with the woman herself, Gareth felt a wave of guilt wash over him at the assumption.

After a while, the young boy toddled away from the roundabout and headed for the slide, allowing his mum to sit on a nearby bench. Scott patted Gareth's knee and began to stride across the playground. Despite his size, Scott looked to be keeping himself as small as he could, as if, like Gareth, he'd picked up on the young mother's body language. The last thing they wanted to do was intimidate her into silence. Scott's shoulders had rounded and he seemed to sink into his hips to mask his height and width. Gareth followed closely behind and tried to emulate Scott's approach. Though he wasn't nearly as broad as Scott, he wasn't lanky either, and at just over six feet tall, he knew he could come across as intimidating to someone as vulnerable as Marie seemed.

As they got closer, Marie took her eyes off her son and gave them a questioning glance. Scott took the chance to introduce them without risking startling her.

"Marie, my name's Scott Parmer and this is my assistant, Gareth Hughes. Could we speak to you for a moment about Beth O'Neil?"

Marie's lip curled into an almost snarl. "I'm not talking to the press. Everyone's already tried to make me look like enough of an attention seeker as it is." She folded her arms tightly across her chest and turned her body away from them.

Gareth stepped forward and slowly lowered himself onto the opposite edge of her bench. "We're not reporters, Marie. We're investigators. And we agree with you that something doesn't add up about Beth's death."

"She was murdered," Marie snarled again, but this time her eyes brimmed with tears as she turned her face to Gareth. "She was murdered, and the police want to keep it all on the hush, so it doesn't look bad on them. They was supposed to be looking after her. They said they'd keep her safe." Her chin wobbled as she tried to keep herself together, and she again turned her face away.

"So, you think the police failed in keeping the people she was testifying against away from her?" Scott probed gently.

Marie snuffed loudly and raised her head. "I don't know what to think. Everything seemed to change all of a sudden for her. I couldn't tell if she was here or there recently."

"You think she was nervous about her involvement with the case?" Scott asked.

Marie rolled her eyes and tutted. "Well, duh. Of course she was. But there was more to it than that. Her life didn't revolve around that case. Not that the police cared about anything else, like."

"How do you mean?" Gareth pushed.

Marie stared at him for a moment as if sizing up whether she could trust him. Eventually she spoke, her voice barely registering over the gathering wind. "She'd been seeing someone. Kept it very hush, hush though. I think he must have been married. She wouldn't even give me his name; she'd just cancel our plans at the drop of a hat because he said he was free. Anyway, when I did see her, she seemed so obsessed with him that I couldn't question her about it. Then last week she comes to me in tears. They'd had a huge row because she wanted to go public with their relationship – and he wouldn't. She thought she was pregnant and didn't want to go through it alone. She'd seen how tough it's been for me, you know?"

The two men nodded in understanding. The higher winds had turned the air chilly, and the sun had hidden behind the clouds. Marie called her son to say they were going soon. He protested but soon relented after being promised three more goes on the slide. Marie turned back to the two investigators.

"Anyway, we set the world to rights over a few cups of tea. I teased her because she was on this herbal remedy for her nerves, and it looked like piss." Marie smiled sadly at the memory of her friend before her eyes filled with tears again. "I never saw her again. She cancelled our next catch-up because she felt poorly."

Gareth glanced over at Scott, who gave a slight nod. Beth's sickness may not have been entirely related to a suspected pregnancy. Alex had said she'd been poisoned, and sickness might have been connected. They needed to talk to this secret boyfriend.

Gareth gently patted Marie's knee and pulled a pack of tissues from his backpack, offering it to her. The young woman took it with a quiet thanks as she wiped her eyes and stood to scoop her incoming son into her arms.

"We appreciate your help, Marie. We know it can't be easy for you," Scott told her. "Is there anything else you can think of related to the man she was seeing? It would really help if we could find and speak to him."

Marie shook her head, and Gareth caught a flash of anger in her eyes as she spoke, "No. But, if you find him, give him hell. She deserved better."

Scott gave her a warm smile and shook her hand, passing her two small business cards as he did. One with his office number on, in case she thought of anything else, and the other for a free counselling service that specialised in helping victims of crime and those closest to them. She stuffed them in her jeans pocket alongside the tissue Gareth had given her before saying a quiet goodbye and leading her son away. They watched as she pulled herself together, chatting with her son and listening enthusiastically as he told her about the fun he'd had on the slide. Gareth felt his heart splinter as he heard the boy ask her if Aunty Beth was coming with them again next week.

As soon as she was out of earshot, Gareth turned to Scott and asked, "Do you want me to head into the office and type up a report for this?"

Scott's eyebrows shot up. "No. No way. I'll type something up at home, but if you wouldn't mind giving it a once over on Monday, I'd appreciate it."

"Of course," Gareth smiled as he hoisted his backpack onto his shoulder. "I best get going myself. I can catch a bus from just around the corner if I'm quick."

"I could give you a lift? Looks like it might rain soon?"

"You sure? Isn't it out of your way?" Gareth asked. As much as he wanted to squeeze as much time with Scott out of this afternoon, he didn't want to be a burden.

"Nah, it's fine. Can't have you getting all wet after you did such a good job setting all this up and then helping to keep her comfortable." Scott waved his hand and started in the direction of his car.

Gareth followed closely. "Well, we don't know if she gave us anything useful yet. The boyfriend might turn out not to be involved."

"She gave us something, and that's always useful." Scott winked. He fished out his car keys, stopped by a battered Ford Fiesta and unlocked it manually. "Central locking gave up about a year ago and I haven't gotten around to fixing it yet," he muttered.

Gareth frowned at the car. It was around ten years old, and the exterior desperately needed a wash and had more than its fair share of dents and scratches. When he looked closely, he noticed the rear bumper was held down with sticky tape.

Scott caught him glaring and groaned, "Oh Gods, you're a car person aren't you?"

"What?" Gareth started, shaking himself out of his thoughts. "No, no. Just, I expected you'd have something a little more... well...flash." His lips quirked into a smirk, and his eyes twinkled.

Scott laughed as he slid into the driver's seat. "I'll have you know, Fords are some of the sturdiest, most reliable vehicles on the road. You can't beat the built-in-America factor."

"Uh-huh. Sure," Gareth teased as he slipped around the front of the car and got into the passenger seat. He tried desperately to ignore the collection of clutter in the rear seat. It looked as though Scott had collected an entire spare wardrobe in the back of his car. The front wasn't much better. The footwell was clear, but the glove box was overflowing with old receipts and scrap bits of paper. Gareth just hoped that was all that was stuffed in there.

"So, what would you choose to drive?" Scott smirked.

Gareth stared at him, a wry smile on his face. "Oh, I wouldn't. I don't drive. I ride. Had a motorbike for years until Liam got me to sell it. Said he was scared I'd get hurt."

Looking back now Gareth could see Liam's request for what it was – a way to take away his freedom more than fear of him being hurt.

"Well, aren't you just full of surprises," Scott grinned – again that goofy, sloppy grin that Gareth was becoming so fond of.

Finally dragging his eyes back to the road, Scott wrestled the car into gear and pulled away from the kerb.

Chapter Fourteen

The drive back to Gareth's flat passed quickly with idle chit-chat. Gareth invited Scott in for a coffee but seemed surprised when Scott accepted.

"You sure you don't have anywhere else to be?" he asked as they got out of the car.

"Nope. Free as a bird. I was going to ring the hotel Beth worked at and check when her shifts were and who we could talk to, but I can do that from your place." Scott grinned before a wave of doubt crept over his mind. "Unless you didn't want me to come in?"

Gareth rolled his eyes and tutted as he opened the door to the building. "I wouldn't have offered if I didn't. I just assumed you'd have better things to do with a Saturday afternoon than hanging out with your employee in their dingy flat."

Scott followed him up the stairs, trying desperately to keep his eyes from settling on Gareth's arse. The image of tight biking leathers that Gareth's earlier revelation had aroused hadn't entirely shifted yet.

"I like to think we're more than just boss and employee. We're friends right? And the flat isn't that bad."

Gareth raised his eyebrows as he looked back and watched Scott step gingerly over a puddle on the landing.

"Okay, okay. Maybe that last part wasn't entirely true. But the company and coffee more than make up for it," Scott laughed.

Gareth rolled his eyes again and felt his cheeks burn. "You're such a charmer."

"You think so?" Scott wiggled his eyebrows and grinned.

Gareth shook his head and pushed open his front door. "Come on, get in. If you can fit your head through the door."

The fact that they both had huge smiles on their faces wasn't lost on Scott. It had been a long time since he'd been able to genuinely laugh and be himself with a guy. One-night stands weren't typically a chance to relax.

Once inside, Gareth slipped off his shoes and jacket, storing them neatly to one side. Scott followed suit and grinned as he caught an approving look from Gareth.

They headed to the kitchen, dancing around each other as Gareth moved to collect mugs and beans. When everything was laid out and the machine switched on, Gareth turned around, bringing them almost nose to nose. He heard Gareth's sharp intake of breath and took a steady step back towards the counter, giving them a little extra space.

With the space to relax, Gareth cleared his throat and asked, "Can I trust you to pour those when the pot's ready? I've got a book I can grab for you before I forget."

Scott smiled softly, the kind he reserved for the people he trusted, rather than the bold Hollywood smile he often hid behind. "I think I can manage that."

"Alright," Gareth smiled back as he slid along the counter and out of the room. "I'll leave it in your capable hands."

"I'll show you just how capable they are, don't you worry," Scott called after him.

Gareth took a deep breath, desperate to calm his heart rate and thankful that other areas of his body hadn't started to react to the tightness of his kitchen. That was the last thing he needed. A small voice in his mind suggested that at least Scott was flirting and taking an interest back. But a much louder voice reminded him of his last workplace romance and how well that had gone. He huffed out a breath and dove into his bedroom. He crouched down, pulled a box from under his bed, and unclipped the lid. He ran a hand through his hair and puffed out his cheeks before routing through the contents. Most of the personal items he'd managed to get out of Cardiff were in that box. A few photo albums, a couple of his favourite films and books. He quickly found the one he was looking for and put everything else back inside. His fingers lingered over photos of him and Faith in their late teens. He'd need to find frames for those. As he stood, he brushed the dust from his knees and made a mental note to clean the carpets again – they never seemed to be clean. If it were his flat, he'd have wood floors rather than carpets that clung to every scrap of dirt – someday.

Book in hand, he stepped into the hallway just as Scott emerged from the kitchen with Gareth's coffee tray, topped with two mugs and a pack of biscuits.

"I hope you don't mind," he said. "I spotted them on the side and thought we'd earned ourselves a little treat."

"Got a bit of a sweet tooth, have you?" Gareth asked.

"Yup. Never been able to resist sweet things." Scott winked as the two of them settled on the creaky leather sofa.

Butterflies swooped inside Gareth's stomach, and the voices in his head were screaming contradictory things. He took an impatient sip of his coffee, wincing as it singed his tongue. The need to know what Scott was thinking overruled the nerves he felt. He took a deep breath and asked, "Are you...flirting with me?" There was a pause. Just long enough for alarm bells and regret to start clanging in his head. "Sorry. That was...wildly inappropriate. I shouldn't have even...sorry." God. Gareth could feel his cheeks burning, the blush invading almost every inch of his skin as his embarrassment roared through him.

Scott was watching him closely, a biscuit halfway to his mouth. He lowered it slowly and looked Gareth in the eye. "And if I was? Would that...be okay?" He shifted in his seat. His gaze dropped momentarily before flicking back to Gareth's face.

A shy smile quirked the corners of Gareth's lips as he also struggled to hold eye contact. His inner critic was still ranting and raving, but a gentler, more hopeful voice that reminded him of the person he'd been before. He could feel that version of himself timidly raising its head. Desperate to enjoy the good in life again, but that lingering fear of pain still gripping its wrist, holding it from running into the open too soon. He swallowed. "Only if you promise me one thing," he mumbled.

Scott nodded and waited for Gareth to continue.

"I don't want to have to start over again." Gareth could barely manage more than a whisper now, but he was just relieved the words were coming out at all. "So, whatever happens, I want to keep it as separate from work as possible."

Scott caught his eye again and looked at him softly. "I can do that."

Gareth smiled and took a swig of his coffee. He watched Scott do the same before he shook himself out of staring and grabbed the book he'd placed on the floor.

"Here," he said, handing it across to Scott, grateful for the obvious change in subject and hoping it would give his blush time to recede. "This is the book I went to get. I'll make you a list of recommendations once I know what you think of that one."

Scott looked at the copy of *Ready Player One* in his hands. The front cover was pristine, though judging by the cracks in the spine and slightly crinkled pages, it was clear the book had been well-loved.

"A favourite of yours?"

Gareth nodded. "It combines a few of my favourite things: gaming, reading, and the 80s."

Scott laughed loudly. "You're not old enough to remember the 80s."

"My parents were, though, and they were obsessed. With the amount of 80s pop culture I was exposed to, I may as well have grown up then," Gareth chuckled.

"It's sci-fi?" Scott asked as he scanned the back cover.

"Yeah, it's set in the future so there's some pretty cool imagery in there," he paused. "This is when you tell me you're not into sci-fi, isn't it?"

Scott laughed again. "No, I like sci-fi. I think I actually saw the film of this advertised a few years ago and thought it looked good. Never got around to seeing it though."

"Same. I saw it advertised but Liam wasn't really interested so I never managed to see it at the cinema and then never got around to getting the DVD."

"Well, maybe after I finish the book, we could watch it together? That should help motivate me to actually get through it."

"Sounds good to me." Gareth smiled.

A couple of minutes passed in comfortable silence before Scott pulled out his mobile and notepad. He flicked through the pages of notes, frowning as he looked for the information he needed. Once he had the correct page, he pulled up his feet and got comfortable.

"Right, do you want to take her brother, or the hotel?"

Gareth blinked at him. "You want me to help?"

"Well, yeah. You helped organise today, didn't you? And you set up that meeting with Dr. Hart for Monday."

Gareth nodded and took another sip of his coffee. He shouldn't have been surprised. Scott was right. He'd helped plenty so far, so why should this be any different?

"Alright, I'll check in with the hotel."

Scott smiled and spun his notepad around to show Gareth the number he'd need. "Double-check when her shifts would have been and when it's best for us to talk to the people she would have worked with most regularly."

Gareth nodded and tapped the number into his phone. "No problem."

Scott grinned. He stood and moved into the hall as he hit dial.

Once he was out of earshot, Gareth hit dial on his mobile. As soon as the receptionist answered, he was ready.

"Hi, could I speak to the manager please?"

"Speaking. How can I help?" The woman on the other end asked.

"My name's Gareth Hughes. I'm currently investigating the death of one of your employees. Beth O'Neil. Could you tell me when her regular shifts were? We're just trying to get an idea of her timeline in the weeks before her death."

There was a pause, and Gareth wondered if she'd hung up on him. Maybe he should have tried a more subtle approach?

"We're not speaking to the press," she eventually said.

"I'm not with the press," Gareth reassured her. "I'm from

an independent investigation."

Another long pause.

"Look," the manager spoke in a much lower, quieter voice now, "what happened to Beth was a tragedy. But we're really trying to distance the hotel from the whole thing. The last thing I need is guests getting wind of what's happened. I don't want people making the wrong assumptions about the hotel."

Gareth gritted his teeth and tried not to swear. A woman was dead, and her boss was more concerned about how that looked for their business than finding answers. "We won't be a bother. Won't even come to the hotel," Gareth lied. "We just want an idea of her shift pattern."

The woman sighed, and he could hear her rustling through some papers. "We change the rota every few weeks to try and keep things fair," she explained. "Beth was working four days a week. Sunday, Monday, Wednesday, and Thursday for the last two weeks. She typically covered the afternoon shift, starting at twelve o'clock and finishing up at about six p.m. Is that any use?"

Gareth bit back the sarcasm he could feel bubbling under his veins. Instead, he kept his voice light and polite. "That's great. Any chance you could give me an idea of who best to speak to? Any colleagues she was close to who might know something?"

"I'm afraid we're not able to give out the personal information of our employees," the woman snapped. "We're quite busy. I have to go."

With that, she hung up. Gareth sat blinking rapidly as he tried to process what had just happened. He quickly grabbed a pen and noted the days and times the manager had given him. He then pulled up the browser on his phone, giving the hotel a quick search. It didn't take too long for him to find the webpage, and once he had that, it was only a few more taps of his fingers before he found the manager's name. Rachel Morris.

He gave her a quick search too, and soon found her social media profiles. For someone who had seemed so keen on privacy, she didn't apply the same logic to her personal accounts. A few clicks and he had enough quality photos to commit to memory – at least this way, they'd know who to avoid when they paid a visit to the hotel.

Scott's footsteps on the creaky floor pulled his attention back into the room. Scott settled himself back into the sofa, took a long swig of his cooling coffee and shovelled a biscuit into his mouth before asking, "How'd you get on?"

Gareth handed him the notepad. "I managed to speak to the manager, although she wasn't keen on us asking too many questions. She did give me Beth's shift information from the last two weeks, but I think we'll need to do some more digging to find out if anyone there knew anything."

Scott nodded as he read the notes Gareth had made. He absentmindedly popped another biscuit in his mouth, and Gareth couldn't help but wonder how he kept such a svelte physique when he ate like a horse.

"This could work for us," Scott nodded. "Paul – that's her brother – said he's going to be in town tomorrow to sort out a few things. We could meet him first thing and then stop by the hotel afterwards. If you don't mind giving up some of your Sunday. I know we've already worked a lot this weekend."

Gareth smiled over the top of his coffee cup. "Fine by me. It's not like I have much of a social life on weekends anyway."

Scott smiled softly and shook his head. "Okay, just don't let me work you too hard. I don't always know when to switch off."

"Dr. Hart said as much," Gareth laughed. "I'm sure you can find a way to make it up to me." He looked away as he felt the familiar, unwanted blush creep back up his cheeks.

"I'll think of something." Scott smiled, drinking in the delicious sight in front of him.

By the time the coffees were gone, Scott had also demolished half the biscuits. Gareth had only had a couple, but that was fine by him. He'd bought them when he had a craving, but that had passed by the time he got home, and he wasn't usually much of a snacker, so the chances were they'd have gone stale before he ever got around to eating them. He'd been thinking of taking them into the office anyway.

"I should get going," Scott said, breaking Gareth out of his thoughts. "Don't want to impose on too much of your Saturday, especially now we're busy tomorrow too."

"Oh, sure." Gareth nodded.

"Besides, the sooner I get home and write up our notes from today, the sooner I can start on this," he said as he waved *Ready Player One* in the air.

"Well, I just hope you enjoy it."

"I'm sure I will."

Scott laced up his shoes and grabbed his coat from the hallway as Gareth unlatched the door. They hovered for a moment in the doorway, the awkward shyness from earlier creeping back in. Before Gareth had any time to dwell on it, Scott leaned in, placed a hand on his upper arm, and brushed a kiss against his cheek.

"Thanks. For the coffee and the book." He smiled as he pulled back.

Gareth's cheeks flushed almost instantly, and his words

caught in his throat. He managed to nod and give a small smile as he watched Scott leave and trot down the stairs. Once he'd pulled himself together, he leaned over the railings and shouted down the stairs.

"I'll see you tomorrow!"

Scott looked up and grinned at him. "You will. Enjoy the rest of your afternoon."

Gareth grinned back and dove into his flat before the neighbours could come out and catch him leaning over the railings like a lovesick teenager. With a smile still plastered on his face, he gathered everything back onto his coffee tray and went to wash up. He felt his phone buzz in his back pocket and quickly checked the display. Faith. He opened the message.

How'd it go? xx

His grin grew, and he laughed loudly as he slid the phone across the kitchen counter and began running the water. He'd call her later once he'd decided precisely how much detail he would give her.

Chapter Fifteen

As soon as he arrived back home, Scott threw himself into writing up his notes. When nothing jumped out at him, he got out his laptop and started searching through Beth's social media, hoping he might spot something Gareth had missed. But no such luck. Even with the new information they had regarding Beth's secret love life, there seemed to be no connections Gareth could have missed.

Hitting a dead end, Scott turned his attention back to Beth's brother. Any information he could find ahead of their meeting the following morning could be useful, if only for giving them an idea of the type of person he was and how to deal with him.

A quick internet search didn't bring up too much. Paul O'Neil worked in finance for a large tech firm over in Manchester, according to his LinkedIn profile, but didn't seem to engage with much outside of finance and tech-related news. Comments he'd left on posts suggested he was clued in about his industry but spoke little to his character. His Instagram page was pretty bland too. A few holiday snaps of white, sandy beaches and shots of cocktails in high-end bars suggested the guy liked a life of luxury. Scott noted the distinct lack of people in Paul's photos. There were no photos of anyone, other than himself. No friends, no colleagues, and certainly no mention of his sister.

Frustrated, Scott pushed his laptop under his green velvet sofa. He was a firm believer in out of sight, out of mind. Shoving the case metaphorically somewhere he could no longer see it usually helped him take a step back and reduce his frustration. He padded into his kitchen and flicked on his coffee machine, momentarily tempted to call Gareth and see if he was free. He could play it as wanting to chat about the case. Thankfully, he managed to rein in the temptation and settled down with *Ready Player One* for a few hours. Eventually, the words began to swim in front of his eyes, and he decided to put the book down, shower, and head to bed.

His mind whirred with everything he wanted to tell Gareth about the book and how much he enjoyed it. And once the young man appeared in his thoughts, Scott's tired mind struggled to shake him out. He slid under the covers and closed his eyes, giving in to the visions of Gareth splayed out beside him.

As he drifted to sleep and regained control of his breath, Scott prayed he'd be able to control himself enough to keep Gareth comfortable the next day. Despite being given the go-ahead to pursue their attraction, he was still conscious of the young man's nerves and didn't want to spoil things before they started.

By ten a.m. the following morning, Gareth was waiting outside a city café. He peeked inside and spotted a man he assumed to be Beth's brother. They had the same sandy hair and thick curls. The same slanted nose and sharp chin. He quickly pulled back and stood around the corner while he waited for Scott to arrive. He didn't want the brother to see him loitering. Shifting from foot to foot, Gareth thought back to his conversation with

Scott the previous afternoon. Their words had been whirling around his head all night. He'd meant what he said. He didn't want anything that developed between them to affect work, but he didn't really know what that looked like or how to achieve it, especially when so much of their time together was due to their case.

A small, insistent voice in the back of his head kept telling him that he was being foolish for mixing his work and private life once again, that he was damaged goods, and that he should quit before Scott found out just how much of a mess he really was. But then he'd remind himself of Faith's words. What happened with Liam had nothing to do with how they had met. Nor had it been Gareth's fault. He deserved to move on and be happy. He deserved to be loved and cared for. And so did Scott.

As if summoned by the thought, Scott idled up the street, hands tucked deep into his pockets and a big smile on his face. One look at that smile and Gareth felt those nagging anxieties soften and fade into the background. He could deal with them later.

"Morning." Scott grinned.

"Hey, I think he's already here." Gareth nodded toward the café. "Guy at the back table with the grey jumper and blonde hair."

Scott leaned across and glanced inside. "Well spotted." He smiled and signalled for Gareth to follow him.

Paul O'Neil looked up from his phone as they entered. There was a disinterested look in his dull grey eyes as he watched them approach.

"Paul? Scott Parmer. Thanks for agreeing to meet with me." Scott extended his hand.

Paul scowled over Scott's shoulder towards Gareth. "I didn't realise this was a group meeting."

Gareth felt a shiver trail down his spine as Paul's cold gaze swept him over. The bile in his eyes triggered a host of unwelcome memories and Gareth fought hard to shut them out.

Scott kept a calm expression and sat down, gesturing for Gareth to do the same. "This is my partner, Gareth Hughes. I find it's often useful to have another perspective and a second pair of eyes and ears with these things."

Paul finally dragged his steely eyes away from Gareth, who finally felt safe enough to let out a heavy breath.

"Whatever," Paul said. His tone felt hard and clipped. Nothing like the broad warmth of so many local accents. "Let's just get this done so I can put the whole sorry affair to bed."

Gareth nodded. "Sorry, this must be hard for you to keep going over."

Paul scoffed. "It's a pain in the neck is what it is. She always did like to make things hard for other people. Even when she's dead she can't help bringing drama into everyone's lives."

Gareth's strangled expression of shock was thankfully drowned out by a waitress asking if they needed anything. Scott ordered a glass of orange juice to keep her from moaning about their free use of the café. Gareth shook his head, still reeling.

"You weren't close then?" Scott asked.

Paul snorted again. "I tried to stay out of her life as much as possible. She was all chaos, all the time. Even when we were kids. Always attaching herself to the local hooligans and bringing trouble with her. I always said it'd kill her in the end."

Gareth cocked an eyebrow and leaned into the table. "You think she was killed by someone close to her?"

Paul rolled his eyes and shot Gareth a look as if he'd just told him the sky was blue. "She was always sleeping around, getting involved with the wrong people. I wouldn't be surprised if one of them turned on her."

Gareth glanced at Scott, who kept his eyes firmly on the sour face of Beth's brother.

"Did your sister ever talk to you about a court case she had coming up?" Scott asked, careful not to reveal too much.

Paul shook his head. "No. Didn't know a thing about it until the police told me after she'd died. Wonder who it was at the top that dumped her to make her mad enough to squeal. She always did have one hell of a temper."

Gareth felt his blood boil. He hadn't known Beth. But the fact that she'd been willing to speak out against a very powerful and potentially dangerous company, and how she cared for Marie and her son, spoke to her character. The fact that her brother could sit here and talk about her murder so coldly snapped something inside of him.

"Had you spoken to your sister much in the last few weeks before she died?" Scott asked quickly as he placed a hand on Gareth's thigh before the Welshman could speak—it spoke as both a warning and something to settle him as his anxieties bubbled close to the surface.

Paul laughed harshly. "I think it's pretty obvious that we didn't really talk. If you've looked into us at all, you'll have seen that we live very different lives. I moved to Manchester for uni and haven't really come back much since, especially not since mum and dad died. Nothing worth coming back for."

"What brought you back this weekend?" Scott asked as he accepted his glass of orange juice from the passing waitress.

"Well, you see, being the only surviving relative of a murdered woman tends to keep you quite busy." Paul scowled. "I've been talking to the police and trying to work out when I'll be able to get into Beth's house, but they're dragging their heels. I doubt there's anything in there worth anything to me, but she might have managed to squirrel away some of mum's jewellery. That could be worth something I suppose."

"And you couldn't discuss that over the phone?" Gareth asked.

"Well, like you boys, I prefer sorting things face to face." Paul downed the dregs of his tea and planted his mug on the sticky tabletop. "Now, if you don't mind, I have a few things to do before I catch my train home." He raised his eyebrow, daring them to ask him any more questions.

Scott shook his head. "Well, thanks for your time, Paul. Let's hope this all sorts itself nice and quickly for you."

Paul scoffed a laugh again, grabbed his coat and headed for the door, mumbling about Beth managing to waste more of his time now she was dead than she did when she was alive. Gareth bristled and glared at his retreating back as he disappeared down the street.

"What a dick," Scott grumbled.

Gareth shook his head. "That's putting it mildly. I know my sister and I aren't exactly close, but I like to think we'd be a little more emotional than that if one of us were killed." He paused for a moment and took a moment to calm himself. "Do you think he could have done it? Got tired of the bad reputation she supposedly had and decided to cut ties once and for all?"

Scott screwed up his face. "I don't know. I don't see it. I mean, he's awful. But I think he'd be more likely to just pretend she didn't exist rather than kill her."

"You're probably right," Gareth mused. "Although, that

comment about the mother's jewellery was a bit off. Maybe she had something of worth that we don't know about?"

"It's a possibility. But I still don't think he did it. It seems too odd that he'd just happen to kill her when she was due to give evidence at a big trial he allegedly didn't know about."

"Maybe that's exactly why he did it. Maybe he did know, and he wanted to keep their family out of the spotlight."

Scott chewed his lip for a moment before shaking his head. "It doesn't feel right to me. Let's not rule it out though. We can do some more digging. Try and work out if he really didn't know anything." He glugged the rest of his orange juice and made a loud lip-smacking noise as he finished the glass. Gareth shook his head and rolled his eyes. Scott gave him a mischievous grin and picked up a sticky, laminated menu.

"Come on, we've got a couple of hours before we need to check out the hotel. Do you need breakfast?"

After Scott had demolished a large full English and Gareth had enjoyed a far smaller portion of toast and eggs, they began making their way to the hotel where Beth had worked. They took a longer route through the city centre to kill enough time to arrive in line with Beth's shift pattern. At some point, as they wandered casually through the streets, occasionally stopping to look in shop windows, Scott took Gareth's hand in his. Gareth initially jumped at the sudden but soft contact. But one look at Scott as he casually peered into the window of a high street clothing shop, holding Gareth's hand like it was the easiest and most natural thing in the world, and he relaxed. He curled his fingers around Scott's and stepped closer to look where he was pointing. They stayed that way, lightly holding hands until they reached the hotel, where Scott gently slipped his hand away to pull out his notes to double-check they had the right time and place.

The reception had a classic feel, with white marble floors and a glossy white reception desk. Bright light filled the room from crystal chandeliers. Black leather sofas and armchairs created a luxury waiting area on the far side of the room. It was fancy but somewhat cold for Gareth's taste.

A young, petite brunette stood behind the glossy desk, tapping away at a flat-screen computer. Gareth breathed a sigh of relief as he noted that the snooty manager he'd spoken to on the phone was nowhere to be seen. He gave Scott a quick nod to go ahead.

Side by side, they strode across the lobby, their shoes clicking against the cold marble floor. The woman behind the desk looked up and smiled as they approached. Her eyes were warm, and her smile lacked the forced politeness often found in overworked customer service workers. Gareth immediately felt his shoulders relax and his face soften. He wondered if this woman had had the same effect on Beth too. Whether the warm, inviting aura around her had let Beth open up and spill some of her secrets. Secrets that could potentially lead them to her killer.

The woman behind the desk — Charlotte, according to her name tag — greeted them brightly, her face slowly dropping as Scott explained why they were there. She looked around nervously. Her dark eyes lost some of their bright shine as sadness and fear crept into her features.

"We're not really supposed to talk about it," she whispered and bit her bottom lip. "Management are worried it makes the hotel look bad. One guy almost lost his job just for mentioning it in the breakroom."

Gareth nodded slowly and gave her a gentle look as Scott pressed her further.

"We'll do what we can to keep your name out of it and avoid management finding out you spoke to us. But if you can tell us anything about Beth's movements and activities in those last few weeks, it would really help."

Charlotte looked around nervously again. The hotel was silent save for the whirring of the heating unit above Charlotte's head. She bit her lip and wiped her hands down her thighs.

"I know she was seeing someone, but it was very hush-hush. She wouldn't tell me anything about him, which was odd because she loved a gossip about other people's love lives. I tried to get it out of her so many times, but she would grin at me and tell me she'd say more when she knew where it was going." She stopped and glanced around again before leaning a little closer. "We used to get the bus together sometimes. I live just a few stops along from her. A few weeks before she died, just when she said she'd started feeling unwell and things seemed to be going downhill with this guy she was seeing, I went to a bar not far from where we live. There was this guy there who looked kind of familiar to me. It was only a couple of days later, when I saw that case she was involved in reported in the papers, that it came to me. He was one of the guys I'd seen photographed as someone she was giving evidence against. Tony or Toby Littlefair. I thought that seemed a bit dodgy, right? Why was he hanging around near where she lived? Shouldn't that be illegal or something? I tried to raise it with her, but she just clammed up. She often did whenever the case got brought up, so I wasn't surprised. We weren't really supposed to know she was involved in it, but the rumour quickly got around the team when she started. But when I said she should call the police, she just brushed me off. Said she'd deal with it, but I never heard her mention it again and whenever I brought it up, she changed the subject. Then she stopped coming to work because she said she felt so ill, and then..." Charlotte trailed off, and her eyes watered. She tipped her head back and sniffed before quickly wiping her eyes.

Gareth reached out and patted her hand on top of the reception desk. He handed her a tissue from his pocket and gave her a soft smile, which she returned before cleaning herself up.

"She was always super nice to me. I knew she had a lot going on, but she was always on hand to support me when management were on my back about stuff. I'm not great with the booking system see, I'm better with people than I am with tech. But she really took the time to teach me and back me up when I needed it, even though I'd been here a little longer than she had. I just wish I could have returned the favour and had her back when she needed it."

"You're doing exactly that now," Scott told her.

She smiled at them both and gathered herself. "The Locus Bar. That's where I saw him. It's about a mile or so from Beth's house. I don't know if he's involved, but it's been nagging at me."

"Have you told the police?" Gareth asked.

Charlotte bit her lip again and shook her head. "I was too scared. Scared that management would find out. I really need this job see. And I guess...after what happened to Beth, I was scared to get involved in case..."

"In case the same happened to you," Gareth finished.

Charlotte nodded. Tears pricked her eyes again, and she dabbed at them furiously.

"We'll keep your name out of it as much as we can, okay?" Scott reassured her. He pulled a few business cards from his pocket—the same ones he'd given Marie. "If you need anything, or if you think of anything else, you give us a call. Okay?"

Charlotte nodded. Her head snapped up, and worry filled her face as footsteps sounded on the stairs in the corner. A pair of black heels tapped down the marble staircase, and eventually, Rachel stepped into reception.

Gareth followed Charlotte's gaze and quickly caught on.

He shook the hand he'd been holding and smiled at her. "Thank you so much for your help. We'll definitely be back to stay again. You've been wonderful."

Scott looked over his shoulder and spotted what, or rather who, the other two had been looking at. He quickly pocketed his notes and patted his hand against the small of Gareth's back.

"We best be getting a move on, babe. Don't want to miss our train."

He shot a quick wink at Charlotte, who smiled warmly at them again and mouthed a silent "thank you" as they waved goodbye and hastily made their way out of the building before Rachel could put two and two together.

Chapter Sixteen

Gareth spent the rest of his weekend mulling over what he knew about the case. He'd spent another several hours scouring social media to try and find any hint of who Beth's mystery boyfriend could be. When nothing seemed to check out, he'd begun to ponder Marie's theory that the man was married and had to keep up appearances. But even the few married men he'd found linked to Beth's Facebook page were accounted for in the days before Beth's death. That made him think about people she would have hidden all links with. He'd wondered momentarily if she was seeing someone on the defence's side but decided that didn't add up. If she'd thought she was pregnant and the father was potentially linked to the people she was standing against, she'd have withdrawn her statement. Unless, of course, the police had something on her too. He remembered Alex's words that the defence had accused her team of bribery and again felt frustration rumble at Scott's blind trust in Alex and Jake. There was undoubtedly more there than he was being told.

His mind continued to race as he pondered how to raise his thoughts with Scott without winding him up and ruining their growing relationship.

By the time his alarm went off on Monday morning, Gareth

was sure he'd gotten little more than a couple of hours of sleep. A few minutes under a cool shower and a freshly brewed coffee helped him wake up enough to look semi-respectable when he stood outside to wait for Scott.

As he watched Scott's car come around the corner, he was relieved the wind had picked up so he could blame his unruly hair on the weather and not the lack of sleep.

"I'm not late, am I?" Scott asked as Gareth slid into the passenger seat. "The traffic getting into the centre was heavier than I expected."

"No, I just thought waiting down here was easier than you having to ring up for me," Gareth replied as he fastened his seatbelt, both relieved and a little disappointed that Scott's attention was no longer on him.

"How was the rest of your weekend?" Scott asked, his eyes firmly fixed on the road.

"Yeah, good. Relaxed, you know? You?"

"Yeah, same really. I managed to read a fair bit," Scott grinned. "I'm really enjoying it so far."

Gareth smiled. Scott's easy-going nature went some way to relaxing his frayed nerves and the underlying annoyance that had kept him awake half the night. "That's great. I'll have to get thinking about what else I can recommend." He kept his eyes low and fiddled with the cuff of his jacket.

Scott must have picked up on Gareth's mood, if not the cause of it as he said, "You don't have to worry about this meeting. Hart's bark is definitely worse than his bite. It'll mostly be me he guns for anyway. He usually gets on at me for being...well for being a bit much."

"No," Gareth gasped. "You? Too much?"

Scott barked a laugh. "Don't you start. I was trying to be

reassuring."

"Thank you, but trust me, Dr. Hart doesn't worry me."

"Good to know." Scott nodded. He waited for Gareth to carry on, as if waiting for him to say what he was worried about. When he didn't, Scott turned the conversation to work.

"So, my plan is essentially to get as much information on the toxin found in Beth's body as possible. The more we know, the more doors it will likely open. Then we can go over our suspects lists and see how all the info we have fits together."

Gareth nodded and ran through his list in his head again. He knew full well who he wanted to speak to and hoped that Dr. Hart's information would bring his and Scott's opinions more in line.

By the time they reached the hospital, the strong winds had blown away most of the morning's clouds, and the weak sunlight was finally warming up. Scott led the way across the car park, letting the front desk know they'd arrived before striding back to Dr. Hart's office. He rapped on the door and waited. Gareth couldn't suppress a smile at Scott's shake of the head when Dr. Hart barked, "Come in, Parmer. Let's get this done."

Scott mouthed an apology before he led Gareth into the office. It was sparsely furnished with a wooden desk in the middle and almost bare bookshelves lining the walls.

"Sit down," Hart snapped from his chair on the far side of the desk. "What have you brought the help for?"

Scott bit the insides of his cheeks and lowered himself into one of the blue plastic chairs facing the doctor. "Gareth is my assistant. It's easier to bring him along than reiterate everything to him later."

The grumpy Northerner grumbled and slapped a brown paper

file on the desk. "So, you want me to explain my report on the O'Neil death for you? How slow do you need me to go?"

"Come on Oliver, you know me well enough by now to know I don't need stuff dumbing down. Stop being difficult. I read your report. I just need a few extra details," Scott growled.

Oliver Hart smiled from the corner of his mouth. A faint glimmer flickered in his dark eyes. "Go on, then."

"The toxin in Beth's blood. What can you tell us about it?"

"Well. It was undoubtedly the cause of death. There were no other fatal wounds on her body and levels of convallotoxin that high with no medical attention would eventually have put too much strain on her heart. Based on the toxins in her blood and the red rash I noticed on her neck and shoulders, I believe she ingested a large quantity of lily of the valley."

"The plant?" Gareth asked.

"No, the fair Welsh maiden," Dr. Hart deadpanned.

Gareth rolled his eyes. "Wouldn't she need to have ingested a hell of a lot for it to kill her?"

"Absolutely. Which is why I said a large quantity. But I couldn't say whether it'd been built up over time or ingested all at once."

"Marie said Beth had been complaining of dizziness and nausea for days," Gareth told him.

Oliver nodded. "That would make sense. The symptoms I'd expect to see would be nausea, diarrhoea, dizziness, and the rash I mentioned. She might also have felt something akin to fluttering or a sharp, stabbing pain in her chest."

"She thought she might be pregnant," Scott said. "But there was no mention of a pregnancy in your report."

"That's because there was no sign of one," Oliver said bluntly, crossing his arms over his chest. "Although I can understand why she'd think that based on the dizziness and nausea she said she felt."

"You keep saying she ingested the poison. Are you sure she wasn't forced or injected against her will?" Scott asked.

"No signs of any needle marks so it's unlikely she was injected. I'd say, based on everything else, that it was probably given to her by someone she trusted. She probably didn't even realise what it was," Oliver explained.

"But if it was making her ill, why would she keep exposing herself to it over such a long period of time," Scott mused aloud.

"Maybe she didn't realise her symptoms came from something she'd eaten," Gareth replied.

Dr. Hart nodded along; his eyebrows raised in surprise. "I agree. Based on what you're saying, it's likely she was being gradually slipped the poisonous substance without her knowledge and put her symptoms down to stress and the suspected pregnancy."

"But where would someone get that amount of toxin?" Scott asked.

"Well lily of the valley is a very popular flower in bouquets," Gareth chipped in. "Grows in a lot of places in the UK too. Between picking it in the wild or getting it from a florist, I'd think it would be quite easy." At Scott and Oliver's raised eyebrows, he explained, "I read an article about it once."

"Funny thing to remember," Oliver mumbled.

"Photographic memory," Gareth retorted.

Oliver smiled approvingly. "I think you've really lucked out finding this one, Scott."

"Don't I know it." Scott winked, as a smile tugged at his lips.

Oliver immediately sobered up. "Oh don't start that. I don't need to see you getting all flirty. And you don't need to go ruining another partnership by getting your dick involved."

Gareth's back stiffened, and he raised an eyebrow at Scott, who was shaking his head and chuckling again.

"What on earth are you on about?" He drawled.

"Well, you and Scullon haven't worked on anything together lately. I assume that all went pear-shaped," Oliver teased.

"You're such an old gossip," Scott laughed as he stood to leave. "We'll be in touch if we have any more questions."

Oliver nodded but didn't get up to see them out. "Try not to. I do have my own job to do."

Scott flipped the doctor off and closed the door on his laughter. The grin on his face soon died when he caught sight of Gareth's frown.

"Let's get back to the office," he said as he rubbed the back of his neck. "Then we can go over everything in more detail."

Gareth nodded in agreement and set off at pace towards the car. His back was ramrod straight, and his fists were balled in his pockets.

The drive back to the office was tense. Only the sounds of the car's aged engine and crackling radio filled the air. But Scott didn't pay any attention to the songs, the DJ's mindless chatter, or the stupid ad jingles – not that the quality was good enough to hold his attention if he'd wanted it to.

He glanced across at Gareth a few times. Each time, Gareth was staring out the passenger window and absently fiddling with his cuffs.

Scott clenched his hands around the steering wheel and racked his brains about what could have gotten Gareth's back up. He'd handled Dr. Hart's acidic nature well, so surely, he hadn't let the doc get under his skin. On several occasions, he opened his mouth to say something but wasn't sure what and immediately clamped it shut again. *The sooner we get back to the office, the better*, he thought.

Over in the passenger seat, Gareth was stewing in his frustration and self-doubt. Dr. Hart might have purely been trying to get a rise from Scott, but he'd inadvertently struck Gareth right where he was most vulnerable. He closed his eyes and bit back a sigh. He'd known. He'd fucking known Scott wasn't telling him everything. And now he knew why. Bringing Gareth along, calling him his partner. It was all a ploy to get at fucking Jake Scullon. He hadn't taken the case to help Alex. He was doing it to help Jake. Gareth cursed mentally. What an idiot he was. Of course, a man like Scott wasn't interested in or impressed by him. God, and he'd opened up about his past to him. Let himself dare to hope. He gritted his teeth so hard his jaw ached. He'd never even met the guy, and already he had a deep hatred for Jake Scullon burning in his gut.

Scott pulled up outside the office and shut off the engine. The silence pulled Gareth out of his thoughts. He jumped out, slamming the door behind him and fishing out his office keys. He didn't even stop in the doorway to wait for Scott to catch up. Instead, he made a beeline for the kitchenette and the coffee machine. The precision and process required to create the perfect cup often helped to calm him. He was so focused on his task that he missed the warning creak of the floorboards that signalled Scott's arrival. He jumped, clattering the mugs against the countertop when Scott suddenly spoke.

"Right, what's going on?"

Gareth steeled himself, drew up to his full height, and turned to stare Scott down. “You tell me.”

Scott raised his shoulders, a puzzled look on his face. Gareth wasn’t sure whether that soothed or irritated him.

“Okay, let’s start with how well you know Dr. Hart.”

“I told you,” Scott said, his brows still creased in confusion. “He worked with my ex, and he’s covered a few cases I’ve worked over the years. He’s a good bloke, despite his attitude.”

Gareth nodded. “So you know each other quite well?”

“Yeah, I...”

“Well enough that he knew more about your past with Jake Scullon than I do?”

Scott’s eyebrows shot up. So that was it? Gareth was jealous of his past with Jake. “Are you serious? You were the one who wanted to keep work separate from anything else and here you are letting petty jealousy impact a case,” Scott spluttered.

Gareth gawked at him, and Scott immediately realised he’d made a mistake.

“This isn’t about jealousy. You called me your partner multiple times but kept vital information from me. I don’t care that you and Scullon had a thing in the past. But you should have told me you had a history with a potential suspect.”

Scott shook his head and ran a hand over his face. “Jake isn’t a suspect. Trust me. He’s a little morally ambiguous in a personal sense. But professionally, he’s sound. Besides, Alex would have known if he—”

“You keep saying that but what if she didn’t? Think about it, Scott. They’ve already been accused of bribery and of meddling with the witness statements. Alex herself told us Scullon did most of the legwork checking in with Beth. The poison had to have been administered by someone she had regular contact with. Jake Scullon falls into that category.”

Scott took a deep breath and walked back through to the main office. He flopped into one of the leather chairs and steepled his fingers in front of his face.

Gareth followed quietly and lowered himself onto the opposite sofa. He stared at Scott intently. His blue eyes searched Scott's face for some sign that he was taking in what was being said.

Minutes passed, with the only sound being the movement of the people in the office above them. Gareth hoped that their raised voices couldn't be heard from up there. That wouldn't be good for business.

Eventually, Scott lowered his hands and looked Gareth in the eye.

"Okay," he started. "I'll give you Jake had the means to do this. But I can't see a motive. I know what you said but the investigation notes look watertight. Beth was a legitimate witness. Why would Jake kill the only person who could win them this case?"

"Because he's the secret boyfriend," Gareth said bluntly. "The sneaking around. Withdrawing from friends. The lack of social media links. It all fits. If she wanted to go public, it could destroy his career. She loved him, so she'd have trusted him completely, and he'd have easily been able to slip her the poison without her being suspicious. When you trust someone that much, it's easy to miss the obvious."

Scott closed his eyes and breathed deeply. "It's a decent theory, I'll give you that. But we still have plenty of angles to look at this from. Let's not put all our eggs in one basket just yet," Scott warned.

"I'm not," Gareth protested. "I'm just asking you to admit that Jake is a suspect. He has as much means and motive as anyone."

"We don't know he was sleeping with her."

"But you have to admit it seems likely," Gareth stated confidently.

Scott got up and moved slowly to sit beside him and gingerly reached out and put a hand on Gareth's thigh. There was a split second where Gareth felt his thigh muscle tighten involuntarily before he relaxed.

"Look, Gareth. You've been a huge help on this so far, and I really do think you have a knack for all of this. But..." He paused, and Gareth pulled away slightly, his stomach churning as his mind tried to race ahead with potential endings to Scott's sentence. Eventually, Scott gathered himself and pressed on. "But I wonder if you're projecting your past onto Beth and letting it impact your judgement."

Liquid steel slid down Gareth's spine and solidified, forcing his back straight. He slipped behind the cold hard mask he'd relied on when he first left Liam and shuffled away from Scott.

"How fucking dare you," he snarled. "I could say the same about you. You're letting your past fling – if it is in the past – skew your judgement of this case. Just because the two of you shagged doesn't mean you know the man inside out. Look at the evidence, Scott. For fuck's sake. You're meant to be the professional here. I opened up to you about everything with Liam and the first chance you get, you throw it back at me and use it as a weakness," Gareth panted through gritted teeth. His fists were balled at his sides, and his shoulders shook with tension. God, he'd never felt so mad. Even after everything with Liam had finally ended, he'd been more ashamed than angry, but now...

Rage bubbled in his veins as he glared at the man in front

of him — a man he'd hoped he could trust to handle his past. How wrong he'd been. His entire body shook, and he knew if he didn't get out soon, he'd explode, either by shouting or crying, and he wasn't sure which he least wanted Scott to see. He jumped up from his seat and grabbed his coat.

"I'm going out to grab some lunch. I need some air." With a rustle of his wool outer coat, Gareth swept out of the office and disappeared down the stairs.

Scott groaned and sank into the back of the sofa. He cursed himself for getting so defensive and being so insensitive. He spent his entire professional life dealing with hurt people, yet he was utterly useless when dealing with people he had a genuine personal connection with. With his head tipped back, he looked at the Styrofoam-tiled ceiling and sighed. His mind whirred through everything Gareth had said. They might not have solid proof that he was right, but there was nothing to say he wasn't either. Beth had been an objectively attractive woman; if Jake had one weakness, it was attention from beautiful people. If he stepped back and pulled himself out of his head, Scott could see that Gareth had a point. And even if he hadn't, that didn't excuse him bringing up Gareth's past so soon after the young man had let himself be vulnerable. Cursing, he dragged himself to the kitchen and poured a mug of coffee from the pot Gareth had made. As the perfect blend hit his tongue, he moaned loudly. For once, Scott acknowledged he was out of his depth. He whipped out his mobile and called Faith.

Chapter Seventeen

Gareth roamed the city streets with his hands thrust deep inside his pockets. He kicked a couple of loose pebbles into the road, watching as they skittered across the paving slabs and tarmac. God, he needed a coffee. He remembered the fresh pot he'd just made in the kitchenette and mentally punched himself. Bloody Scott would have helped himself to a cup, benefitting from his handiwork. Typical.

It was that time of year when the mornings were crisp and cool, but the midday sun now beating down was roasting. Gareth slipped off his coat and slung it over his arm as he approached the high street. He wandered in the direction of a favourite cafe of his almost absentmindedly, his focus still back in the office. He was sure Jake Scullon was more involved with Beth's death than it first seemed, but maybe he had been a little harsh on Scott. He certainly could have delivered his theory more sensitively. Then again, so could Scott. Neither of them had covered themselves in glory in the last half hour. He rubbed the back of his neck and tutted as he felt the hairs starting to curl slightly. He reached the cafe and ordered a sandwich for himself, and a sausage roll for Scott – as a peace offering. As much as he was pissed off at the American for bringing up his past, he hadn't been much better. They were both at fault to some extent and probably both right to a certain degree. Gareth had leapt into a theory based on speculation rather than facts. At the same time, Scott had let his closeness to the case scupper his judgement.

"A pair of fools cut from the same cloth," he muttered under his breath. He smiled shyly at the server and thanked her as she handed him his order. Food in hand, he left the cafe and returned to the Park Square. He found a nice quiet bench and settled down in what little shade there was. A small smile crept across his face as he tucked into his sandwich. Sure, he forgave Scott for his outburst. Neither of them were perfect, of course. But that didn't mean he couldn't let him stew for a while before returning to the office.

Gareth dropped the brown paper bag containing Scott's sausage roll on the wooden desktop. A sense of relief washed over him as the bag stayed intact and kept any stray pastry flakes from scattering across the brushed wood.

Scott immediately looked up, his pen hovering over the file in front of him. He smiled shyly, gingerly picked up the bag, and peeked inside.

"A peace offering." Gareth shrugged. "I went off the handle a bit."

Scott's smile lit up and covered more of his face. "I have a little peace offering of my own."

He got up and led the way to the kitchenette, where he pulled a paper bag from the top cupboard and handed it over.

"I popped across to Whittards while you were out," he offered.

Gareth looked inside the bag to find a small tub of marshmallows and a tin of mint hot chocolate powder. A large grin crept across his face as he placed the bag gently on the counter.

"You called Faith, didn't you?"

Scott chuckled. "You got me. I wanted to show you I was sorry and knew she'd know what would get me out of the doghouse quickest."

"Yeah, she's had plenty of experience when it comes to this situation." Gareth smiled.

"You know, some people would say you have something of a temper if you need placating so often." Scott smirked as he leaned forward slightly.

Gareth reciprocated and leaned closer, a smirk on his face. "I'm Welsh. Being cantankerous is part of our national identity."

He caught Scott's gaze for a moment and felt himself being pulled into those deep green eyes. His breath caught momentarily as his gaze dropped to Scott's slightly parted lips. An eternity seemed to stretch between them before Gareth could snap himself free. He glanced at his watch, surprised by how quickly the time had gone.

"What time do you think Locus opens? We could pop down and try to speak to Tony or ask around for information on him," he said. He tried to ignore the disappointment in Scott's eyes as he pulled back.

"Their website says they open from four p.m., we could head over there tonight?" Scott told him.

"Okay, sounds good. Did you find anything useful while you were going over the files?"

Scott cleared his throat and returned to his office. "Yeah, I read back through the initial crime scene report Alex took. She picked up on the fact that the house was freshly cleaned – impeccably so."

"As if the killer was trying to clean up after themselves? Scrub their presence from the scene."

"Exactly." Scott nodded. "The only real evidence they found was a single fingerprint on the inside handle of the front door—a fingerprint belonging to Jake Scullon."

Scott looked at him sheepishly and Gareth shook his head. "One fingerprint in the entire thing looks sketchy even to me. Like a classic frame job. Maybe it's time we spoke to Jake? I know Alex was against us speaking to many people but he's too close to this for us not to. Even if he wasn't involved in her death, he might have more information than Alex, right?"

Scott leaned back against his desk and crossed his arms over his chest. He stared at Gareth and smiled in that way that caused Gareth's pale skin to flush again.

"Yeah, that makes sense. You know, you've really got a knack for all this," he drawled.

"Must be all those books." Gareth blushed.

"No, it's more than that. You seem to know exactly what to ask or try next."

"Well, it's just logical, I suppose. I just walk through the problem step-by-step."

"Uh-huh," Scott mused, grinning at his assistant.

Gareth pushed his hands into his trouser pockets and avoided Scott's gaze. He cleared his throat and pulled himself up straight, looking slightly beyond the man in front of him. He couldn't guarantee he'd hold himself together if he looked straight at him. Deep down, he knew he should still be mad at Scott for what he'd said. But the other man's actions told him more than a spoken apology ever could.

"So, we're going try and speak to Tony or at least look into him tonight. Do you want me to try and arrange a meeting with

Alex and Jake for tomorrow to see if we can find any more about the crime scene?"

Scott nodded. "Probably a good idea. We'll need to update them on what Oliver and Marie told us as well. See if that sparks anything."

"And we can get a better read on what Jake knows if we can witness how he reacts to the information," Gareth pushed.

Scott frowned and made a non-committal noise.

Gareth rolled his eyes. It wasn't an acknowledgement that he might be right, but it wasn't the complete shutdown he'd had before. An improvement of sorts.

"I'll make a pot of coffee. Then I can do some digging into Tony and The Locus before we head out."

"I thought you'd never offer." Scott grinned. "Oh, and thanks again for lunch." He waved his wrapped sausage roll in the air.

"Don't mention it," Gareth said. "Just try not to get pastry everywhere, will you?"

"I can't promise that," Scott called after him as he left the room. Despite himself, Gareth chuckled. At least Scott was honest about the mess he would inevitably make. Gareth just hoped he'd keep the flakes away from his keyboard – that would be a nightmare to clean if not.

As he got to work on the coffee, Gareth began to ponder the morning's argument and his response. Although he knew he shouldn't, he began comparing it to Liam's arguments. Just as he could not stay mad at Scott, he'd never been able to stay mad at Liam. The key difference being that he never stayed mad at Liam because he always managed to convince Gareth that the argument had been his fault. This time, Scott had felt equally bad and gone out of his way to show Gareth he was sorry. Gareth tried hard, but he couldn't think of a single time in their relationship when Liam genuinely apologised. Any attempt at an apology was quickly followed by a 'but', and the but usually justified why Gareth had deserved the anger in the first place. He'd been too clingy. Too stubborn. Too insensitive. Too careless. The excuses always came thick and fast. It was hard to stay mad at someone else when you thought you deserved to be in the firing line. Scott might have needed a little help from Faith, but at least he'd known blame lay at both their feet. For once, Gareth didn't feel sole responsibility for the upset. He snuffed a laugh and smiled to himself as he set up a tray for three cups of coffee. It was crazy how clear these things seemed now that he had some space to think.

Chapter Eighteen

The Locus Bar was still gearing up for the night when Gareth and Scott arrived, meaning they were the only people there besides the staff. As they lingered in the doorway, a man in his thirties approached. He was dressed in a crisp white shirt and black jeans and carried himself with comfortable confidence.

"Evening, fellas. Help yourselves to a table. We'll have the bar open in a tick." He spoke with a soft Northern accent and a broad smile.

Scott returned the smile, cranking up the charm that Gareth was becoming so familiar with. "Actually, we're not here for a drink I'm afraid."

"He never takes me out unless it's work-related," Gareth teased.

Scott winked at him before pulling up a screenshot from an online article following the Elevate case. "We're investigating a case and wondered if you'd seen this man."

It was more up-to-date than the photo of Tony on Elevate's website, but it wasn't as full-faced. Still, it seemed to do the job as the young man nodded.

"Yeah, comes in most nights, him. Didn't click who he was at first, but the other customers soon started gossiping, you know? A few of 'em wanted him kicked out but to be honest, he looked so miserable I couldn't bring myself to kick him further. Besides, he doesn't cause any trouble. Just sits in the corner by himself and orders a steady flow of whisky."

"Is he local, do you know?" Gareth asked.

The waiter shrugged. "I'd guess so for the amount he's in here, but I couldn't say for certain."

"We could really do with talking to him," Scott explained again.

The young man shrugged again. "By all means. You can wait and see if he comes. He's usually one of the first people in. But good luck getting more than two words out of him."

"Thank you," Scott smiled.

"No problem. Just don't cause a scene, yeah?" The man turned on his heel and went back to organising his staff. As soon as he was out of the way, Scott winked at Gareth, grabbed his hand, and pulled him towards the Art Deco-style bar.

The lighting wasn't as dim as Gareth expected from a bar and gave off a warming glow. The deep teal walls gave the bar a luxurious feel and perfectly complemented the room's gold. It looked far more upscale than he'd imagined for a small, local bar.

"What do you fancy?" Scott asked, pulling Gareth from his observations.

"I thought we weren't having a drink?"

"Well, just one while we wait won't hurt." Scott grinned.

Gareth smiled back and shook his head. "Just a Coke for me is fine."

Scott chuckled. "You're a cheap date."

Gareth rolled his eyes. "If you think taking me out to question suspects counts as a date, we need a pretty serious discussion."

Scott laughed again. "Okay, okay. I get the hint." He quickly caught the attention of the woman behind the bar and ordered two pints of Coke before turning back to Gareth. "Just so I know we're on the same page –what would you class as a date?"

Gareth blushed and tried to hide it by taking a large swig of his drink. "Well. You know," he spluttered. "Anything, really, I suppose. As long as it's not related to work."

Scott nodded thoughtfully. "Got it. So, no stakeouts or witness questionings then?"

"Or suspect interviews, or investigation planning," Gareth added.

"You're quite picky, aren't you?" Scott teased as he gulped his drink.

"Just like to do things properly." Gareth smirked.

After reciprocating Gareth's smirk, Scott turned back to the bar, engaging the staff in conversation and sharing Beth's photograph. While a few of the bar staff were certain she'd been in once or twice, a lot of them didn't recognise her. Even the ones that did didn't have the surety of the manager when he'd recognised Tony.

Eventually, Gareth caught sight of their target and gave Scott a discreet nod to let him know they were on. Together, they kept a subtle eye on Tony as he took a glass of whisky and bundled himself into the farthest corner of the bar.

Even with the information they'd gotten from the staff, the appearance of Tony Littlefair was far from what Gareth had expected. His skin was pale and waxy, highlighting the dark purple bags under his brown eyes. The dark hair that had once been immaculately kept had now outgrown its style and become greasy and unruly. His high-end clothes hung from a frame that had lost a significant amount of weight and muscle mass. As he raised his glass to his lips, his hands shook.

Scott put down his empty glass and strode across the room, snapping Gareth back to the present, and he quickly followed suit.

As they approached the table where Tony sat, he raised his eyes and gave them a questioning look.

"Tony?" Scott clarified. "Can we ask you a few questions?"

Tony raised an eyebrow. "You reporters? I'm not speaking to reporters."

Scott shook his head. "Nope. Not reporters. We're looking into a murder case, and we think you might be able to help us out."

Tony looked at them, puzzled. "Murder?"

Scott nodded and slipped into a chair opposite Tony. Gareth quietly took up the chair next to Scott.

"Do you know a Beth O'Neil?" Scott asked.

Tony paused before answering, "We had a receptionist called Beth, but I don't know her last name. Is that her?"

"That's her," Scott confirmed.

Gareth watched Tony's face closely as Scott led the questioning. He took in the watery rims of Tony's brown eyes and the tremble of his lips. The pale tone of his skin and sunken cheeks almost made Gareth feel sorry for him. He was the shell of the confident young man the press had first splashed across their front pages. But, given everything he'd done in betraying the trust of his clients at Elevate – and what he was additionally suspected of – Gareth couldn't find any empathy for him.

"She was poisoned a few weeks ago and died as a result," Scott explained.

Tony dropped his head, and his shoulders sagged even further. "Elevate was cursed. I'm sure of it. No one got out of there intact."

"She was also the key witness in the case against you and the rest of the Elevate board," Scott finished.

A visible shiver travelled down Tony's spine as he raised his head and locked eyes with Scott. "You think I killed her?" His voice wobbled, and the tears rimming his eyes threatened to fall.

Gareth tried to picture this man leading meetings at a high-end finance company and ripping off millions of elderly customers. Tony could barely keep his voice steady, let alone have the mindset to poison someone so consistently. Beth's murder required a methodical mind, patience, and calm. They certainly didn't seem to be traits Tony had anymore.

"We're just considering all possibilities," Gareth reassured him, trying to calm their suspect before he got too flustered.

"You've been frequenting a bar just a short drive from her home, and her testimony could be the key to sending you to prison for a long time. We have to chase up a lead like that. You understand," Scott added softly. Like Gareth, he'd clearly picked up on Tony's fragile state and decided that the charm offensive would be more successful here than an aggressive approach.

Tony shook his head and let out a tearful laugh. "I live just up the road. It's a five-minute walk," he said. He held up his trembling hands in front of them. "My nerves are shot. I can barely hold a glass, let alone drive. Besides, even if I could, my car was vandalised as soon as the case broke in the press. Not that I didn't deserve it."

"Did you have any idea it was Beth that was testifying?" Gareth asked.

"No. I'd never given her a second thought, to be honest. She was just the receptionist. But if I did, I'd have been thanking her, not killing her. If she hadn't helped catch us, I don't think I'd have ever stopped. We needed to be caught, and I deserve everything coming to me. If I go down for this and serve my time, my family might be able to look me in the eye again." Tony chucked back the rest of his whisky and winced as the alcohol burned its way down his throat. "Is that it?"

Scott held his gaze for a few more seconds before nodding. "I think we're done for now. But if we need to talk to you again, we'll be in touch."

Tony grimaced. "I'll be here. Nowhere else for me to be. Now, if you don't mind. I'm going to get another drink." With that, he slid out of his chair and shuffled towards the bar, the weight of Gareth and Scott's stares pressing into his back as he went.

Chapter Nineteen

The shared entrance hall to Jake Scullon's flat stunk of disinfectant. A mop and bucket stood in the corner, dirty water just visible below the rim. The communal cleaners must be on their monthly visit. Alex stifled a cough. With any luck, she'd never smell bleach again – her sinuses were burning.

The flat door opened, and she grimaced. "Jesus, you look like crap. The stress of all this got you bad, huh?"

Scullon lowered his head, his dark brown eyes rooted to the floor as he stepped back to allow her inside the flat. His usually coiffed, sandy blond hair was flat and limp against his head. Lank tendrils of hair clung to his forehead. The usual golden glow of his skin seemed dull and his eyes were ringed with purple shadows.

"I think I have a bug," he mumbled.

Unlike her own, Jake's flat was a tip. Half-empty plates sat on the kitchen counter, and used takeaway packaging lay around the bin. There had to be twice as much rubbish as one person alone could make. She envied him. If she so much as left a stray pen lying around she never heard the end of it.

She took a seat on the far side of the living room. If it was a bug, she could do without catching it. Although, a vomit-splattered bathroom would create some fantastic entertainment. Marcus debating which to look after first, his sick wife or his ruined bathroom, holding her hair in one hand and gripping a cloth in the other.

"What can I do to help?" Jake's voice was weak, quieter than usual.

"I've asked Scott Parmer to look into stuff and try and help us out of this mess, but I could do with you coming with me to meet him. You were closer to Beth than I was, you'll have more information that he'll find useful."

She noticed his eyes widen briefly, and then they shrunk back to normal. A momentary reflex, a thought slipping into his mind and being pushed away. It was quick, but she noticed.

"Why on earth would you involve Parmer? He's not exactly my biggest fan these days." Jake twisted in his seat, pulling the woollen sleeve of his jumper over his hand.

"We need help, Jake. And despite whatever went down between the two of you – and I don't need the details – Scott is a professional. He's damned good at his job and you know it. So come on, get yourself cleaned up and let's go."

He shifted in his seat, resting his elbow on the arm of the brown leather armchair, his head balanced on his palm. His red eyes were wet as he stared ahead, chewing the skin around his fingernails.

He straightened his back and cleared his throat. "I'm not going to Parmer's."

"Oh for Christ's sake, Jake. Now isn't the time to let your vanity take over. I need you on this. Both our reputations are on the line here."

Jake groaned loudly. "It's not about vanity. I feel like shit. I'm not going anywhere other than my bed."

Alex's brown eyes narrowed as she fixed Jake with a cold hard stare. It was the look that had got him to heel on a number of their cases together. After just a few breaths, Jake sighed and shook his head.

"Look, I really don't feel well enough to traipse across town to see Parmer. How about, you tell me what you've already told him and I'll see if I can add anything."

Alex quickly ran through the information she'd passed on to Scott. The information about Beth's job and her brother. When she'd finished, Jake took a deep breath and raised his eyes to the ceiling.

"It sounds like you already have everything when you started digging into it. She didn't really do much with her spare time. So other than work and the contacts we already knew about, there isn't anything I can add. She was being cautious as far as I know."

"So, you think someone must have gotten to her at work? Or maybe someone we've already talked to who had access to her home?"

"I don't know, Al." His face was stoney and his voice steadied with the determination she usually heard him use in interviews.

"What about friends? People she spent time with?" She opened her notebook and held her pen poised and ready.

"I suppose, but she never mentioned anyone else to me. Scott will probably find someone doing his own digging. But there was no one else that I knew of."

"Come on Jake, you must be able to give me something."

He heaved a sigh. "Look, Al, I'm exhausted. You're right. The pressure of everything we're being accused of, coupled with this stupid bug, has really wiped me out. I could do without being interrogated by my own partner, okay? I'll call you if I think of anything else."

He stood and held his hands towards the door, making it clear her welcome had worn out.

"Well, thanks for all your help." She gathered her things, shoving her untouched notebook into her coat pocket. "Don't strain yourself seeing me out."

She stood, looking straight at him while he stared at the front door. She waited, expecting him to speak, to apologise for being so unhelpful. But he didn't. Whatever bug he'd caught had clearly affected his personality. Shaking her head, she marched from the flat, slamming the door behind her.

Once she'd settled in her car, she took a long breath. A rattling from inside her glove box caught her attention. She leaned over and fished out her vibrating mobile phone. She rolled her eyes the second she saw the caller ID. It was an involuntary reaction by now. She couldn't help it. Unable to put it off any longer, she took a deep breath and hit the green button.

"Hey, Marcus."

"I thought you were going to be home for lunch."

"Yeah, I thought so too, but I got held up." It would, of course, help if she didn't have to keep answering her mobile.

"It's nearly half one."

"I know that," she gritted her teeth, trying to keep her annoyance out of her voice. "You know to always give me an hour each way."

"Yeah, well, coq au vin waits for no one." His smirk was audible.

"Was that an attempt at a joke I just heard?" Sometimes she forgot he had a sense of humour. Warmed by his unusual calmness, she tried a joke of her own. "You're taking my lack of punctuality very well, are you feeling okay? You haven't got a bug too, have you?"

"No. Why?"

"Oh, I just popped round to catch up with Jake about this Elevate shitstorm before we meet with Scott. Reckons he's caught a bug of some kind."

"I see." The smirk was gone now. How did he do that? How did he go from light-hearted humour to petulant complaining in a single breath? "I thought you weren't on that case anymore. You said they were keeping you away from everything after that girl died."

"Marcus, my entire career is on the line here, you didn't seriously think I'd just sit back and not defend myself, did you?"

"Well surely by digging around where you're not supposed to you're only going to cause yourself more problems," Marcus sniped.

"I'm not digging. Scott is."

Marcus's eye roll was practically audible through the phone line. "Because you asked him to, Al. Surely you're just better off stepping away altogether."

"I'm not giving up on my career, Marcus. You know how hard I've worked."

"Don't I just," Marcus scoffed.

Alex tutted loudly and shook her head. "Listen, I've got to meet Scott now. You eat. But make sure you leave me some of that chicken, for later." She hoped not having to wait for her would salvage the situation. Maybe if he wasn't as hungry, he'd be less grouchy.

"Probably ruined by now anyway."

He hung up without a goodbye.

She revved the engine far more than she needed to. Its pained whirr satisfied her frustration. Pulling off at speed, she headed for the P.I. office, taking her frustration out on the engine.

Gareth had just finished making a fresh pot of coffee and placed his tray on the table when he heard the familiar squeak of the floorboards on the landing. Gareth swung himself around to poke his head through Scott's doorway.

"They're here."

Scott jumped up and brushed pastry flakes from the front of his shirt. Another lunch where he'd managed to get as much of it down his front as he had in his mouth. Gareth rolled his eyes and swerved back into the main office, his suit jacket flapping about his hips as he did.

Alex and Scott entered the room simultaneously from opposite ends, and Gareth gestured towards the sofas so they could all get comfortable. They greeted each other warmly and settled down for their meeting.

Gareth moved one cup closer to Alex and offered her the milk and sugar. She smiled politely and took the small milk jug. Gareth winced slightly at just how much milk she added and felt Scott stifle a chuckle next to him before quickly pulled himself together when Gareth sent him a glare and a raised eyebrow.

"Listen, first off, I'm sorry Jake isn't here. He says he's got a bit of bug, and to be fair he did look like hell when I went round. But he didn't really offer me anything new in terms of information. Maybe when he feels better, and his head is a bit clearer, he'll be more helpful."

Scott frowned, his brows bunching together in a way Gareth hadn't seen him do before. "Okay. Yeah, we'll check in again with him in a few days and see if he can give us anything else."

He cleared his throat and seemed to catch himself again, sitting straighter and relaxing his face. "On our side of things, we've managed to speak to Beth's friend, Marie. She seems to have been overlooked by the officers investigating the case, but she did offer us some useful information."

"Really?" Alex asked with a raised eyebrow. She blew on her coffee and took a sip. Both eyebrows flew up her forehead as the deliciously rich flavour hit her tongue. "Jake always said she didn't seem to be all that switched on," she finished.

"He spoke to her?" Scott asked, glancing at Gareth.

"Yeah, I think she was there a few times when he called to update Beth on the case. After her initial statement, Beth was always more comfortable around him than with me, so he handled most of the communication with her. He'd check in more, make sure she was safe and that she felt supported ahead of the trial. I think that's why this has hit him so hard. He feels like he let her down. We both do, really."

"Marie said much the same thing. She wasn't too impressed with how Beth's case has been handled," Gareth muttered.

Alex sighed heavily. "Yeah, even once we can prove the case was clean, I can't see the force coming out of it particularly well."

"Marie also told us that Beth had been seeing someone recently. Sounded like she was pretty serious about him, but he wanted to keep everything secret. Marie assumed he was married. We did some digging into her social media activity but couldn't find anything there. Is that something Jake might know if we visit him when he's better?" Scott asked.

Alex shook her head and drained the rest of her coffee. "I don't know. When I asked him about people you could get in touch with, he said there wasn't really anyone other than her brother and the staff at the hotel she worked at, both of whom I'd already told you about. He seemed pretty adamant that there was no one else that would be close enough to be worth speaking to. But by all means ask him again in a few days. I didn't want to push too much today. He looked rough as hell."

Gareth raised an eyebrow again and glanced at Scott, who nodded slightly.

"We spoke to Dr. Hart too. He said the poison would likely have been given to her gradually over several days, maybe even weeks. Which could fit with this secret boyfriend theory," Gareth explained.

"I also wanted to ask about the crime scene. You mentioned in your report that it had been cleaned to within an inch of its life leaving just Jake's fingerprint. But was there anything else you noticed?" Scott asked.

"I did note that things looked off. Empty spaces on the shoe rack and coat hooks. Like someone had stolen or moved her stuff."

"Or taken their stuff back to remove themselves from the scene," Gareth pondered and Scott nodded in agreement.

The more they chatted, the more uneasy Gareth felt about the case. It was like they were only being given half the information, and even that wasn't being given easily. They really needed to speak to Jake.

Scott reached out gave her hand a slight squeeze. "Listen, Alex. We've got this. I promise you. We'll talk to Jake. We'll find who really killed Beth, and we'll clear your name. Go home. Rest up. Lean on Marcus for once. You don't have to be the strong one all the time. I will talk to Jake and do some digging at the station."

Alex shook her head sadly. "I'm not sure Marcus is in the

right frame of mind to sympathise with me right now. I haven't exactly been open or attentive to his needs lately, have I?"

Scott lifted her chin to look her dead in the face. "He loves you. Anyone can see that man dotes on you. You have to remember to let him sometimes."

Gareth caught his gaze and gave him a soft smile. He knew Scott's words were ones they could all learn from.

After thanking Scott and Gareth several more times, Alex left, promising to let her husband take care of her for once. Gareth shifted uneasily on his feet as he watched her go. His mind was working at full pelt to digest everything Alex had told them. Or hadn't told them, as it turned out. He couldn't help but feel like the meeting hadn't gotten them anywhere.

Suddenly, Scott's voice broke him out of his thoughts, "I think you might be right."

He shoved his hands in his pockets and turned to face Gareth, his eyes still on the ground. He took a deep breath before looking Gareth in the eye. "Something doesn't feel right about this. Even if Jake felt too unwell to join us, why would he not give Alex all the information he had to pass on to us? I just don't believe that with all the check-ins he would have had to do that he couldn't think of any other contacts she might have. Besides, he's certainly not the type to just lie down and take shit from anyone. He would never just take such an accusation without a fight. Unless he was trying to lay low for some reason."

Gareth nodded but was humble enough to spare Scott an "I told you so".

Scott grabbed his coat from inside his office. "I'm going to try and speak to him. Maybe I can get something out of him. He must know something. He must." Scott paused, as if letting his thoughts catch up with themselves before slipping his arms into his coat. "While I'm gone, could you look into the poison some more? See if you can figure out where someone might get large enough quantities of it."

"You don't want me to come with you?" Gareth asked. He hated to say it, but a small part of him wondered whether Scott could keep his bias out of any chat with Jake. Another part of him was afraid that Jake would use their history to charm Scott into leaving him be.

"No, it's okay. I know him. I know which buttons to press to get him to open up. He's more likely to crack if it's just me alone. I'll try not to be too long."

Chapter Twenty

Scott pulled up outside Jake's block of flats and looked up at the familiar building. It was one of the newer blocks in the city centre, with glass balconies and landlords that hadn't given up on it. He could recall plenty of early mornings he'd spent on one of the balconies as he'd pondered the choices that had led him there and drank a disappointing cup of instant coffee. Their arrangement had never been serious enough for Jake to accommodate Scott's coffee needs.

He took a deep breath and forced himself out of the car. As he crossed the car park, he tried to push down the memories of the last time he'd been here. The sloppy, drunken kisses in the lift, the fumbling at Jake's door. All of which ended abruptly when Scott moved a pillow from the sofa and found a lacey pair of women's knickers. He'd never really believed that he and Jake would be more than friends with benefits. But that didn't mean it hadn't hurt to find out Jake was sleeping with other people.

As he stood facing Jake's front door, Scott pulled himself up straight, mentally and physically preparing for the confrontation. He shook his wrist to steady his hand before rapping on the smooth, grey uPVC door. From inside the flat came a series of scuffles and curses before the door swung open. Scott blinked in shock. Alex had been right. Jake looked like hell – but he wasn't ill. No. Scott had seen that look in Jake's eyes enough to know he was simply hungover. And, judging by the half bottle of vodka on Jake's coffee table, he'd decided to drink his way through it. His blond hair looked greasy, and where he usually styled it into a voluminous coiffe, it was now plastered to his scalp. His skin looked sallow and clammy, and the dark purple circles around his eyes almost masked their red rims.

"Jesus. You look a state." Scott grimaced as he looked over his ex-lover.

"I'm hearing that a lot lately. If I were a less confident man it'd really start to hurt my feelings," Jake slurred, his Northern accent thick with alcohol.

"Can I come in?" Scott asked, trying desperately to keep his disgust from his voice and expression. God only knew what he'd been thinking on the numerous occasions he'd stumbled into Jake's bed.

"You know, usually I'd love to. But you were pretty clear last time you were here that you never wanted to touch me again. Besides, I'm not really feeling it. Got some kind of bug I reckon." Jake belched, and Scott found it impossible not to recoil.

"Right," he scoffed. "Nothing to do with that bottle of vodka I can see."

Jake narrowed his eyes. His face hardened, and he brought a shaky hand up to rest on the doorframe. "Piss off, Parmer."

Scott lunged forward, slamming one hand into the door and the other on the frame just above Jake's hand. "For fuck's sake, Jake. Despite you being a monumental arsehole, I am trying to save your career," he spat.

"I never asked you to," Jake snarled.

Scott snarled back, "No, but Alex did. And despite you being a complete waste of space I know you care about her too much to drag her down with you. The least you can do is give me the info we need to work on this case properly and help her out."

For a moment, Jake looked like he was about to shove Scott away and slam the door in his face. But suddenly, something crumbled. He dropped his arms and stepped back to let Scott in as what little fight he had left evaporated from his body.

Scott followed a stumbling Jake through the flat. If it hadn't been for the smell of bleach bleeding from the hallway, Scott was sure the apartment would stink of vodka. As they moved, Scott took in the state of the place. Jake had never been especially tidy, but this was something else. There were dirty dishes and empty food cartons strewn across the flat. The bin in the kitchen was overflowing, and the floor was covered in crumbs and stray socks.

He watched Jake drop into his white leather sofa and pour a slug of vodka into a cloudy glass. A sadness washed over him as he stared at the man he'd once been so close to. It was a shock to the system to see him looking so distraught. He'd seen Jake drunk and hungover several times. But this was different. It looked more like another scene Scott had seen all too often. One he'd lived himself. Heartbreak. And Scott was pretty sure that Jake's heartbreak wasn't over him.

He sighed heavily and sat next to Jake on the sofa, slowly moving the bottle of vodka out of reach. "Jake, I need to know what's going on. I can't help you if you don't give me all the information."

"You can't help me anyway," Jake whispered and gulped down the glass of vodka. "It's all my fault."

Scott watched him closely, his brain ticking at a million miles an hour as he tried to put everything together.

Jake took a deep breath and looked up at the ceiling. "I was sleeping with her. You were right. I'm an ass, and I have no self-control. It started just as a once in a while thing, but after you and I..." He paused and waved his hands as he fished for his words. "Once we finished things, I went to her more often. She had feelings for me, which fed my ego after you and I fought. Because I knew you were right deep down. I am a mess. I certainly wasn't good enough for you. But she saw me as a hero. To her, I was a knight in shining armour. I was good."

"And then she found out she was a rebound, got angry, and threatened to out you and pull her statement," Scott stated.

"No. No. She was never going to pull her statement. She was never going to pull her statement. She wanted to bring Elevate down as much as anyone. No. She'd been feeling off and thought she was pregnant. I suggested she get rid of it. She didn't want to. We fought, and she kicked me out. After I didn't hear from her for a few days, I called round to check on her. I knew I was an ass, but I did come to care for her. I'm not completely heartless."

For the first time since he'd started telling his story, Jake turned and tried to catch Scott's eye, which Scott managed to avoid.

Listening to Jake's story had been far harder than Scott had imagined. Since he'd called off their affair, he'd known that he hadn't been the only person Jake was sleeping with. But somehow, realising he was now connected to Beth in some way made his insides squirm. What surprised him was that the unease far outweighed any hurt he'd previously felt at the hands of his ex. There was, of course, a lingering ache in his heart, but it was nothing like he'd felt at the time or had even expected to feel when he'd first arrived.

Once he realised he wasn't getting a rise from Scott, Jake relented and continued with his story. "I let myself in when she didn't answer, and that was when I found her. I panicked. I knew my DNA would be all over that house. I had some of my stuff there, for fuck's sake. So I scrubbed everything down, removed my stuff and left. Then I got home and doctored my reports to look like my last few check-ins with her had been over the phone to try and cover my ass and waited for someone else to find her."

Scott stiffened and glared at the man beside him. "You scrubbed the flat clean while the woman you were sleeping with was lying there dead."

"I panicked!" Jake cried. "You know how huge this case was for fuck's sake. My whole career was on the line. Alex's career."

"Don't make out like you did this for anyone other than yourself," Scott spat.

Jake shrunk back into himself and sniffled. His voice became thick with emotion, "You don't have to try and make me feel more like a shit than I already do, okay. I know I let myself get carried away and took my eye off the ball and an innocent woman died as a result. And then I let my selfishness get in the way again and completely disrespected her to try and save my ass. For once, I had someone genuinely care for me, and I let her down." He hung his head and whimpered.

Scott sighed heavily, closed his eyes and shook his head. Some part of him felt sorry for Jake, but all his speech had done was reinforce how blind and careless he was. He stood up slowly and looked down at the broken shell of his past lover.

"I'm going to do what I can, Jake. Not just because Alex

doesn't deserve to be dragged down by you, but also because I did care despite everything I said in the end. I can't guarantee you'll come out of it unscathed. I just hope you finally learn something from this." Before Jake could respond, Scott turned on his heel and marched from the flat.

Chapter Twenty-one

Gareth absent-mindedly drummed his fingers on the desk as he scrolled through the listing for florists in Beth's local area. He'd upped his search to cover a five-mile radius but wondered momentarily if he should be looking further afield. How far did one travel to obtain poisonous flowers to commit murder? Was five miles too far? Not far enough?

Frustrated with himself for getting stuck at such an early hurdle, Gareth locked his screen and headed back to the kitchenette to brew a fresh pot of coffee. While he waited for his brew, he ran a second quick search on his mobile. The results showed that lily of the valley didn't commonly grow anywhere locally, so the chances of the killer having a wild supply were slim. Hopefully, he'd have more luck talking to florists on the phone.

Scott's solo trip to see Jake had left Gareth even more desperate to prove his usefulness. He momentarily acknowledged the unhealthiness of that constant need before pushing it to one side. As if he was jealous of or felt inferior to a potential murder suspect. Gareth tutted to himself and rolled his eyes. He grabbed his freshly poured coffee and headed back to his desk to start calling through his list of florists.

Slowly but surely, he made his way through. His plan

worked nicely to collect as much information as he could as quickly as possible. He'd been able to rule out several options immediately by asking if they sold lily of the valley bouquets and finding out they didn't. Any that did, he managed to confirm their opening hours and promised to stop by in the following days. So far, he had a list of five to follow up with and just one more left to call.

He quickly dialled the 'Blooming Lovely' number, and a young woman answered after several rings.

"Oh, hi," Gareth said brightly. "I'm looking for somewhere to do a bouquet for my partner. She loves lily of the valley. Is that something you can do?"

The door to the office creaked open, and Gareth snapped his head around. Scott offered a small smile from the doorway as Gareth signalled he'd just be a minute.

"Oh, err, I think so," the young woman stuttered. "I'm sure we've used that before. The owner isn't here right now but I can make a note of your number and double-check for you tomorrow."

Gareth faltered slightly, he didn't particularly want to give out his phone number, but he didn't want to provide the office number and give their game away. He quickly composed himself, hoping he wasn't blushing in front of Scott again.

"Oh, no, that's fine. What time are you open tomorrow? I'll be in the area so I could just pop by."

"Of course, we're open from nine to five-thirty."

"Great, I'll stop by then. Thanks for your help." He hung up quickly and turned his chair. Scott was leaning against the office door with his arms folded over his chest. The soft smile Gareth was coming to associate with a fluttering in his stomach sat perfectly on Scott's face.

"Sounds like you've been busy," Scott drawled. He unfolded his arms and strode across the room to perch on the edge of Gareth's desk.

"Just doing what you asked me," Gareth shrugged as he quickly scribbled down Blooming Lovely's opening hours. "I can make a fresh pot of coffee and we can exchange notes?"

"Sounds good," Scott smiled and leaned over to peck Gareth's cheek. As he pulled back, the smile faded from his face at the sight of Gareth's confused expression. He shook his head quickly as he stood, putting some distance between them to make Gareth comfortable. "I'm sorry, I know you said to keep this and work separate. Did I overstep the mark?"

Gareth nibbled his bottom lip as his stomach churned violently, those deep-rooted self-doubts clawing at his insides once again. "Maybe, but that wasn't what I was thinking of...I don't want to be a second prize or a rebound after Jake..."

Scot barked a laugh. "Sorry, I'm not laughing at you, I just... Gareth, Jake and I had a very short-lived fling that ended well over six months ago. And honestly, I'm not sure you could pay me enough money to go back there." He started to step toward the young man in front of him but stopped as Gareth pulled back.

"But you still care enough to try and help him."

"Well, yeah, I don't want to see an innocent guy go down for something he didn't do. And I certainly don't want to see Alex get dragged down with him. But that's it."

Gareth nodded but managed to avoid looking directly at Scott. He slowly moved around the desk and grabbed his used mug. "I'll get us those coffees," he muttered.

As he swept past Scott, Gareth gently pressed his hand to Scott's hip. A small gesture, but one, he hoped, conveyed how he felt without overstepping.

Once Gareth was out of sight, Scott let out a breath he hardly realised he'd been holding and flopped down into the sofa in the waiting area. He closed his eyes and let his mind drift. For as long as he could remember, he'd been looking for someone to share a life with. Someone he could enjoy the basic stuff with. He'd never felt this content or comfortable in Jake's presence, and if he was really honest, he hadn't had it with David either – even though he'd followed him all the way from the States. As he listened to Gareth pottering around in the kitchen, he imagined that maybe he'd found exactly what he'd been missing.

"Scott?" Gareth's deep Welsh tones dragged him back to the present.

He opened his eyes and smiled as Gareth held out a mug of steaming black coffee.

"Thanks." He took the coffee and blew across the top of the mug as his eyes followed Gareth around the coffee table until he sat on the opposite edge of the small sofa. Once he finally caught Gareth's eye again, he began to fill him in, starting with an apology and letting him know he'd been right about Jake being the secret boyfriend. After explaining Jake's story, he waited for Gareth's response. His blue-grey eyes had been unwaveringly still the entire time.

"Well, it makes sense I suppose." Gareth nodded eventually. "Without Beth the Elevate case was in trouble and that could knock his career. But if it came out that he'd been sleeping with her, it would all come crashing down anyway. He was in a bit of a lose-lose situation, right?"

"Exactly. And Jake isn't a good loser. He's the kind to try and ride a situation out so he can manipulate a victory for himself rather than accept any kind of defeat."

"So, you think he's telling you the truth? That he found her and panicked?"

Scott took a large gulp of coffee, smacking his lips before answering, "We don't really have anything other than theory to suggest that he's not." He shrugged. "With any luck, your florist hunt will help give us some clarity on that. If any of them can identify him, I suppose that'll be the final nail in the coffin."

Gareth watched him closely for a moment, before reaching out to place a hand on Scott's knee, squeezing it gently. "Whatever happens, you know it's not on you, yeah?"

Scott smiled sadly and clapped his hand lightly on Gareth's. "I know. Still feels shitty though."

"Bound to," Gareth told him, "for you and Alex, I suppose. Do you think she knew about the affair?"

"I think she was starting to suspect. She'd have worked it out eventually."

They sat in silence for a few moments. Scott tried his best to focus his thoughts on the case but struggled to keep his attention off how comfortably their hands were resting together. Scott's thumb rubbed back and forth against the smooth skin on the back of Gareth's hand while Gareth's softly caressed Scott's knee through his slacks.

Eventually, conceding defeat and accepting that his mind had clocked off for the day, Scott glanced at his watch.

"Listen, it's half-five. We're not going to crack this tonight. Let's get ourselves home. Then, I want you to get yourself ready and I will stop by and pick you up at seven," Scott declared.

"What?" Gareth blinked his soft grey-blue eyes at him.

"I'll pick you up at seven and we can go out for dinner," Scott clarified.

"Like – a date?" Gareth asked as he nibbled his lip again.

"Only if you want," Scott blurted out. "I promise, no surveillance or witness questioning involved this time. Just you and me." His hands started to shake, and he began to pull away ever so slightly.

For once, Gareth didn't erupt into a deep blush. Instead, he leaned closer and brushed a kiss against Scott's lips. It was only the faintest touch. Barely a kiss at all, really. But it was enough for Scott to know that the lips he'd spent so much time admiring and fantasising about were as warm and soft as he'd hoped. He pressed against them again, a little firmer this time, and felt Gareth squeeze his hand in response.

All too quickly, Gareth pulled away, biting his lip gently and smiling. "I'll see you at seven," he whispered.

Scott nodded, a grin on his face as he watched Gareth grab his things and bound out of the office.

Chapter Twenty-two

Alex stared at the bright, white front door to her apartment. Her stomach felt like a lead balloon. She knew that in deliberately taking longer to get home than she would have normally, she would only have made the situation she was about to face that much worse. The front door was even brighter and more pristine than normal, suggesting Marcus's cleaning frenzy had extended beyond the confines of their flat. Things were even worse than she'd feared.

She took a deep breath and pushed into the flat, stopping in the doorway as she looked questioningly at the duffle bag that lay on the sofa. The lead in her stomach melted to a molten metal as her temper bubbled up inside her. She narrowed her eyes as Marcus stomped out of the bedroom with his toothbrush and spare toothpaste in hand.

"Running away again?" she snarled.

Marcus shoved his toiletries into his bag before glaring back at her. "If you took more of an interest in me and my career, you'd have remembered that I have a meeting with some suppliers in Liverpool tomorrow morning. I'm heading over tonight to save me a crazy early start. That's why I did us a nice lunch. Which is now dry and chilled in the fridge."

Alex felt the tension ease from her shoulders and lowered

her head. Now he'd said it, she did remember him mentioning something about having a nice lunch together before he went away for the night. She stepped forward and reached out to touch Marcus's arm, but he jerked away.

"I know my work might not be as flashy or exciting as yours, but it does matter to me. If you could at least take some interest, instead of zoning out on me or talking about yourself all the time we might actually stand a chance." He finished as he hauled his bag from the floor and pushed past his wife to get to the front door. "I tidied up those files you left on the dining table. They're in the paper tray you never use. Just so you don't have to call me and rant about where they've gone."

"I'm sorry," Alex whispered.

"You always are. Doesn't mean you'll change anything though, does it?" He sighed before leaning in to peck her on the cheek coldly. "I'll see you tomorrow evening if you're around. It would be nice if I got to spend some time with you this month."

Before Alex could respond, Marcus left the flat, closing the door behind him. She groaned and collapsed onto their stiff, cream sofa, closed her eyes, and leaned her head back.

A headache was starting to build at her temples, and she gently massaged the sides of her head. She tried to think through the pain and work out when their marriage had started to crumble so drastically.

At times she liked to shift all the blame onto Marcus, claiming he didn't understand her job and its demands. But the more often they had this argument, the more she couldn't help but wonder if she was just as guilty of doing the same thing. She sighed and shook her head before pushing off from the sofa and dragging herself to the kitchen. She flicked on the kettle and began preparing a cup of tea to help settle her mind, convincing herself that the stinging in her eyes was purely a reaction to the steam that now filled the air.

Chapter Twenty-three

"Okay, if you promise not to say, 'I told you so', I have some news for you," Gareth smiled into his phone.

"I promise to try," Faith smirked. "You know you want to tell me anyway."

"I could always phone someone else, you know?" Gareth teased as he neatly toed his shoes off and padded across the hallway to his bathroom.

"Yeah, right. Like who?"

"I'd have found someone," Gareth defended.

"Just tell me, twpsyn," Faith snorted.

Gareth took a deep breath that was half preparation and half in shock at the frigid cold of his bedroom. Unable to keep his news from his friend any longer, he blurted out, "Scott and I are going out to dinner – on a date."

"I..." Faith started before he heard her slap her hand over her mouth.

"You were going to say it weren't you?" He grinned.

"No. I was going to say, I'm happy for you. Both of you."

"Course, you were," he chuckled as he tucked his mobile between his ear and shoulder so he could open his wardrobe to consider his clothing situation.

Faith scoffed in mock hurt. "I can't believe you'd doubt me

like that."

They both laughed together until Faith sobered up, concern suddenly hitting her.

"I really am happy for you, Gareth. Just...I know you said before you weren't ready. I didn't pressure you too much did I? I know I've been teasing but I'd never want to push you into something you weren't ready for."

Gareth sat down on the thin mattress and felt it sag beneath him. He'd asked himself the same question and variations of it the entire walk home. He'd spent so long telling Faith and himself that he wasn't looking to move on. And he really didn't think he had been. He had a million and one concerns about becoming involved with anyone, especially in a situation that shared so many similarities to his past. But it was all the ways that Scott differed from Liam and the way he made Gareth feel that lit a spark of hope that maybe he could do this. He tried to explain his thoughts to his friend and breathed a sigh of relief when he heard her whisper, "I'm so proud of you, Gareth. You honestly amaze me."

He smiled wryly as he felt the heat rise in his cheeks. "Well, no offence, but I'm more concerned about amazing someone else right now."

He went back to his wardrobe and groaned. Frustrated at his lack of options, Gareth pushed his clothes from one side of the wardrobe to the other, wincing as the metal hangers squealed.

"You still got that red, scarf-print shirt?" Faith asked.

"Yeah, but I don't know. It feels a bit flashy for dinner," he replied as he frowned at his wardrobe.

"Okay, fair. You should definitely go for something red though. It always suited you."

Gareth gently fingered the cuffs of a deep scarlet silk shirt that hung on the left of his cupboard and smiled softly. "As long as my face doesn't end up matching it, I think I have just the shirt."

Faith giggled. "I always thought your blushing was adorable."

"Not really the vibe I'm going for," he muttered.

Faith's giggle bubbled up into a full belly laugh but was soon muffled by beeping on her side of the line. She went quiet for a moment before she continued. Her big toothy grin was evident in the tone of her voice. "I've got to go. Someone else is trying to call me."

Guessing her mystery caller's identity, Gareth quickly called down the line, "Don't let him wear anything to outdo me. And don't bloody grill him, okay?"

"I'll behave, don't worry. Get yourself ready and have fun, okay? Love you."

She hung up as Gareth shouted a response. His smile still fixed on his face, Gareth removed the shirt from his cupboard and gently laid it out on his bed, eventually laying a pair of slim-fitting jeans alongside it. He glanced at the time and decided he had enough time for a quick shower. Especially if Faith kept Scott on the phone for as long as he suspected she would.

For the second time that day, Scott stood in a car park staring at a familiar block of flats as his stomach flipped. At least this time, it was flipping with good nerves. His taxi revved back into life behind him and pulled off, dragging him out of his head and back into the present. He pulled at the sleeves of his trench coat and straightened the dark plum shirt Faith had helped him to pick. The evening was still and clear – typical for early autumn.

Before leaving home, he'd checked the forecast and hoped it had been right when it said it would stay dry and clear all night. The last thing he wanted to do was give Gareth pneumonia on their first date. Although, the vision that popped into his head of Gareth in tight wet clothes wasn't exactly unappealing. He cleared his throat and shook the image from his head, adding a boner to the list of things he didn't want to force on Gareth on their first date. If he was right, this was Gareth's first date since Liam, so he knew he needed to take things at the Gareth's pace – which was undoubtedly going to be slower than he would usually go. After a quick check of his reflection in the grimy glass of the building's front door, Scott took a deep breath and pushed the buzzer for Gareth's flat.

Three floors up, Gareth leapt from the sofa arm and grabbed at the intercom handset. He fought back a curse and rising blush as the receiver slipped from his grasp, swung on its cord and clattered against the wall before he could catch it. He bit his lip and closed his eyes as he raised the receiver to his ear again.

"Hello? Scott?"

"Yep – were you expecting anyone else?" The warm drawl crackled through the ancient device.

"Nope, just double-checking I hadn't accidentally double-booked myself with one of my other suitors," Gareth replied dryly. "Wait there, I'll be down in two ticks."

He hung up the receiver and raced back to the bathroom to check his reflection for the last time. Already wearing his shoes and leather jacket, he checked his pockets for his phone and wallet before he grabbed his keys and headed out of the flat.

The moment Gareth stepped out of the building, Scott's composure started to slip. The young man looked breathtaking. A deep red shirt that had been left slightly undone, exposing the faintest hint of a hair-smattered chest, was tucked loosely into the waistband of his slim black jeans. The black boots and leather jacket gave a nod to Gareth's love of biking and were the perfect pieces to complete his look. For the first time in years, Scott felt almost self-conscious and prayed his get-up of dark grey jeans, plum shirt, and long trench coat was having a similar effect on his date.

He smiled broadly at Gareth, projecting far more confidence than he felt, and stepped forward to brush a lingering kiss against Gareth's cheek.

"You look incredible," he whispered.

Gareth pulled back and smiled softly. "Is it okay for where we're headed? I wasn't sure if..."

"It's fantastic," Scott reassured him and gestured that they should start walking.

"You look good too, by the way," Gareth said as they walked side by side.

"Just good?" Scott pouted.

"Well, I'd sound like I was just copying you if I'd said incredible too."

Scott scowled and wrinkled his brow as he considered his date's response. "Okay. I'll allow it."

Gareth chuckled. "You don't have to fish for compliments you know." He playfully nudged Scott, whose nerves had left him off balance. He stumbled, and his foot slipped over the edge of the kerb as he wobbled toward the road. Both men cursed. Gareth shot out his arm and caught Scott's flailing wrist, pulling him towards him and catching him against his chest. Scott could feel their hearts pounding together, and

Gareth's muscles stiffened as he clung to him.

"I am so sorry," Gareth panted. "Are you okay?"

Scott caught his breath, chuckled awkwardly, and straightened himself up, his face inches from Gareth's.

"I'm fine. Apart from having to fight an overwhelming urge to make a hugely corny crack about falling for you already."

Gareth shook his head and rolled his eyes. "Maybe we should get to the restaurant quickly then. That way you can distract yourself with food and drink."

"I can think of better things to distract myself with," Scott leered.

Gareth cleared his throat and put a few extra inches between them as a blush spread across his cheeks. "This way, is it?"

Scott watched him for a few paces before he rushed to catch up.

"Sorry. When I get nervous, I tend to make stupid comments."

"Get nervous a lot then do you?" Gareth smirked, one eyebrow cocked.

"Around you, it certainly seems so," Scott laughed. "Come on. I need a drink."

Chapter Twenty-four

The Restaurant was humming with activity when they arrived. The main dining room was comfortably filled with people dressed to the nines. Gareth slipped out of his leather jacket and fiddled with the collar of his shirt.

Scott suddenly gripped his hand and led him through the room. The waitress smiled warmly as she seated them in a private booth, lined with green, leather banquet seats. A large gold, industrial style lamp hung above their heads and cast a warm glow over the marble-topped table. The waitress handed them their menus and disappeared. Gareth drank in the atmosphere. The elegant design and warm lighting was far fancier than anything he'd experienced on his meagre budget since moving to the city.

"This is beautiful, Scott. Thank you."

Scott smiled fondly. "Thank you for coming. Alex mentioned this place to me a while ago and I've wanted to come ever since but never really had anyone I wanted to bring. And it's not really the type of place you come alone."

Gareth nodded. "You're really close with her, aren't you?"

"Yeah, she's been like a little sister to me since I moved here. She kept me going and helped keep me focused when David left. I just hope I can return that favour now."

Gareth gingerly reached across the table and covered Scott's hand with his. "You will. And at least she has Marcus to support her at home in the meantime."

Scott wobbled his head from side to side. "I guess. I still worry about her though. I know they have their issues, but I hope they can put them to one side for a while so Marcus can support her properly."

"What does Marcus do, do you know?"

"I'm not sure. Alex never really says. I think he runs his own business though." Scott shrugged and waved the conversation away. "Enough about other people though. What're you fancying to eat?"

With smiles on their faces, they both began browsing the menu, making idle chit-chat about their options. Gareth teased Scott about being as much of a wine snob as he was a coffee snob. Scott returned the playful banter when Gareth complained about the amount of side salad that would inevitably come with their orders. After much to-ing and fro-ing and small bickers about the bill, they agreed to split the whole lobster and a bottle of sparkling wine between them. As long as Scott promised he'd let Gareth treat him to coffee and biscuits instead of paying out for dessert.

Once they'd ordered their meal and the bubbles started to flow freely, their light-hearted conversation became even easier. Gareth had never really been overly tactile with Liam – although, for once, that wasn't something he could pin on his ex's abuse. He was just more of an 'acts of service' kind of guy. But as the evening went on and the drink flowed, he found himself relaxing into fiddling with the fingers on Scott's left hand and not particularly caring whether anyone was watching them.

When their food arrived, they took turns feeding themselves and each other. Gareth licked his lips in delight. He'd never tasted anything so delicious. The sweet, soft flesh of the lobster melted in his mouth and the zingy garlic butter popped on his tongue. *At least they were both eating the same thing, so garlic breath wasn't going to be an issue*, he thought.

Scott swallowed hard and immediately signalled to the waiter for more wine as Gareth's tongue slid out of his mouth and licked garlic butter from his fingers and bottom lip. Wine and conversation flowed freely and Gareth could feel a pleasant buzz ringing through his veins. His pale skin was flushed, not the bright red of his usual blushes, but a soft pink hue from the wine and good food.

They quickly finished their second bottle of wine as they exchanged silly anecdotes from their childhoods and years at university. They shared a few stories Faith would be mortified to know they'd told. Wine drunk, stomachs full, and cheeks sore from laughing, the two men paid up and stumbled into the lift.

Gareth sighed and leaned into Scott's side, resting his head on his broad shoulder.

"Still up for a coffee back at mine?" he asked wistfully.

Scott dropped his gaze to look at the blue-grey eyes staring up at him and smiled. "If the offer's still open."

Gareth nodded and brushed his lips against Scott's bobbing Adam's apple in answer.

Giggling and fumbling for each other's hands, Gareth and Scott tumbled up the stairs and into Gareth's flat. For once, Gareth didn't hear his unseen, furry squatter scurrying around. He was far too preoccupied with the touch of Scott's hands on his hips, the weight of his head on his shoulder, and the warmth of his breath on his neck.

They pushed inside, Scott still seemingly glued to Gareth's back. As soon as the door closed, Gareth spun round to face his date. He slowly stroked his hands up Scott's arms and over his shoulders. His heart pounded in his ears, his legs trembled, and his throat felt dry. He dropped his gaze to Scott's slightly parted lips and felt his breath catch. Before his nerves could get the better of him, Gareth slid his hands up Scott's neck, cupped his face, and pulled him in for a long, lingering kiss. Tongues probed and explored as both men lost themselves in the kiss. The offer of coffee was momentarily forgotten.

Together, they stumbled through the dark onto Gareth's bed, chuckling as the mattress creaked beneath them. Hands roamed over bodies and shakily removed shirts and belts and unbuttoned jeans. When Gareth's jeans were halted by the boots he still wore, he burst into a fit of giggles. He pulled himself to the edge of the bed and removed his trousers before lying back beneath the covers and watching Scott do the same. His eyes roamed Scott's toned body as he wished he'd thought to flick a light on so he could get a better view.

Freed from his clothes and with a sloppy grin on his face, Scott crawled back up the bed and slipped under the covers beside Gareth, wrapping him in his arms.

Gareth smiled sleepily and pulled Scott back in for another messy kiss. Their kisses eased up, turning more into soft brushes of lips and cute smiles. The break to remove the last items of clothing and sliding beneath the cool covers had given the alcohol time to settle in their systems, and the initial heat of passion had slowed significantly.

"I'll make coffee soon," Gareth whispered as he stifled a yawn. His eyes remained closed, but from the soft breathing of his bed-mate, he could tell Scott was already well on his way to sleep. He sighed happily and buried into his pillow, his feet still entangled with his lover's.

Chapter Twenty-five

Gareth woke gradually and instinctively found himself burrowing deeper into the solid warmth behind him. Only when Scott huffed a warm breath in his sleep did Gareth remember what had happened the night before. His back stiffened as his mind surged into overdrive.

What had he done?

Had he embarrassed himself?

Had he said or done something that Scott would be mad at him for when he woke up?

His breath came in pants. His heart rate kicked up a notch as the panic began to boil over in his veins. But another soft snuffle from behind him, followed by the weight of Scott's arm suddenly draping over his waist, anchored him. The soothing warmth of Scott's breath tickled the back of Gareth's neck, sending the tiny hairs at his nape sticking up on end. Closing his eyes, Gareth took a few deep, grounding breaths, repeating his mantra. *You're safe. You're okay.*

After a few cycles, Gareth felt his heart rate slowing down, his breath returning to normal. He rolled his head, turning to look at the man lying against his back, and smiled.

Scott's face, with its striking cheekbones and sharp jawline, was much softer, transformed in a way that only a comfortable, contented sleep can manage. His lips were parted so slightly, breath slipping between them, in and out at a gentle rhythm. Gareth watched him, spellbound. Even as the wonder of their date returned to him, Gareth still found it impossible to see how the man next to him had taken such an interest in him. And he thanked whatever force it was that brought him this stroke of luck that he had.

As if sensing he was being watched, Scott sniffed and rolled onto his front, burying his face in his pillow. The duvet shifted as he moved, exposing the strong planes of his shoulder blades, and Gareth felt his body stir. His cheeks began to burn, and his heart rate picked up again – though it was far from unpleasant this time. A part of him wanted to plaster himself to Scott's back. To bring their bodies together in the most intimate and intense way he could think of. But the more cautious side of him signalled its warning. Was that what Scott wanted? They'd undoubtedly been heading that way last night before they fell asleep. But had that been Scott or the alcohol? Sure, Scott had stayed, but that didn't necessarily mean anything – did it?

Gareth groaned quietly and rolled onto his back. The cold of his room bit into his arms as he brought his hands up to rub his face. Before they went any further, all cards needed to be on the table. Gareth knew his history made things complicated. Their working relationship added another layer of complexity, too.

They needed to talk. And soon. And the bed was probably not the right place for that conversation. Closing his eyes, Gareth braced himself for the frigid temperature of his flat before slipping from the bed and setting about his morning routine. Hopefully, a bit of structure would help him get into the headspace he needed and calm the way his body was still reacting to Scott's closeness.

Scott woke up slowly and nuzzled further into his pillow. His teeth felt furry, and his head fuzzy. He rolled his head back and forth to try to clear his brain's alcohol-induced fog. As reality finally hit him, he pushed himself to sit up, the bed he was in creaking loudly as he did so.

The room was filled with the weak light and slight chill of an autumnal morning. The clanging of pipes told him someone, somewhere in the building, had put the heating on – and he hoped that someone was Gareth.

A rush of panic swept over him as he realised Gareth's pillow and side of the bed were biting cold. He must have been up for some time. Scott closed his eyes and prayed he hadn't done anything in the night to make the young man uncomfortable. He racked his brain for some clue. He remembered coming back to Gareth's flat. He remembered the kissing. God, did he remember the kissing. No amount of alcohol could remove that from his memory.

A clatter and curse from the kitchen broke him from his thoughts and immediately reassured him that he hadn't forced his date out of his own home. He smiled to himself and started looking around the room for his clothes. His eyes fell on a neatly folded pile by the foot of the bed, and he felt his smile grow, knowing he hadn't been the one to fold anything. Next to his clothes lay a soft flannel dressing gown and a note in loopy handwriting – *Didn't want you to get cold.*

He laughed softly and slipped the cosy material over his shoulders. He usually wasn't averse to naked mornings, but Gareth's flat was especially chilly. Besides, he wasn't sure how comfortable Gareth would be with his penchant for nudity just yet. He quickly tied the belt around his waist and slipped his socks from the previous day onto his feet. It probably wasn't the most fetching look, but then he supposed Gareth didn't like his lovers frozen either. Quietly, he padded through the flat, following the sounds of Gareth pottering around in the small kitchen. He leaned casually on the doorframe. His hands rested in his dressing gown pockets as he watched Gareth lay out two coffee cups and a small plate of pastries. At some point, Gareth had slipped into a pair of tartan patterned pyjama bottoms and a soft grey hoodie. His hair was ruffled at the front, and his skin still had a sleep glow. He looked deliciously cosy.

"Morning." Scott smiled, finally announcing himself.

Gareth jumped and spun round, a freshly capped milk bottle in his hands as his eyes settled on Scott.

"Morning." He smiled back as he composed himself. "You been up long?"

"Nope, slept solidly all night. Thanks for letting me stay by the way."

"No, problem. I'm not really one to kick sleeping guys onto the street," Gareth teased, though his confidence was slightly belied by the blush spreading across his cheeks.

Scott's confidence stalled. Had he fallen asleep while they were...No. He couldn't have. Wouldn't have. He'd thought they'd fallen asleep together, but now...

He took a deep breath. Time to take a leap of faith. "Hey, listen, I just wanted to apologise for falling asleep when I did. I was so caught up in my nerves and not wanting to push you that I think I went too far the other way. I honestly didn't mean to fall asleep on you."

Gareth huffed a laugh and shook his head before looking back at him. A wave a relief spread through Scott at the sight of the small smile that tugged at Gareth's mouth. "Well, it was a pretty eventful night. I think we were both a little exhausted." Gareth stepped forward, his hands still buried in the pockets of his soft joggers. "I do think we need to talk though."

Scott swallowed heavily, his mind throwing up every possible issue Gareth might have. But he simply nodded and waited for Gareth to continue.

"I think we need to be better at communicating. With balancing this," he gestured between them with a small smirk, "and work, we need to be especially clear of what we want and how this is going to work."

Scott nodded vehemently, his brain racing so fast that he almost wasn't aware of the words that came spilling from his mouth. "Absolutely. I know what I want. I want you. I want you as my partner at work and I also want to see where this goes. But I also don't want to push you too fast. I know everything with Liam must still be raw for you and..."

Gareth shook his head, stepped forward, and pressed his lips to Scott's, silencing his babbling.

Scott cupped Gareth's face in his hands, his thumbs stroking the Welshman's cheeks as the kiss deepened. His body rapidly responded to Gareth's kisses and he automatically rutted his hips. The flannel gown and Gareth's light pyjamas did nothing to separate their bodies. A soft whimper escaped Gareth's lips as their sensitive erections brushed against one another.

When the need to breathe became overwhelming, Gareth pulled back. He rested his forehead against Scott's, a sheepish grin on his face. He pressed several small kisses to Scott's jaw before whispering, "I'm not broken, Scott. And I don't want you to treat me like I'm fragile. I appreciate the concern. I do. But please. Trust me. Trust that I know what I want."

Scott smiled softly and nodded, before he leaned in for another toe-curling kiss. Slowly, he began moving backwards, doing his best not to tumble down Gareth's hallway as they frantically stripped each other. By the time they crawled underneath the covers, they were both completely naked – and this time, there would be no dozing off. Hands were desperately groping and running across whatever expanse of skin they could reach. Gareth squeezed Scott's arse firmly and pulled their bodies flush together as he did so. Scott's hands ran up Gareth's chest, his fingers dancing in the soft smattering of hair he'd only caught glimpses of previously before they continued upwards and curled in the thicker hair on the back of Gareth's head.

Gareth whined as Scott pulled back from their kiss, but his protests were quickly silenced when Scott pressed soft, kiss-swollen lips against his throat, then his collar bone, then the tip of his shoulder and back again.

Soon, they were both groaning loudly, and Scott quickly learned that Gareth had no problems communicating in the bedroom. Here, the quiet, reserved gentleman he'd grown to know unleashed hidden layers of passion that took him by surprise and drove him mad. Gareth's accent thickened as he explained, in detail, all the things he wanted to do. It was so hot Scott began to tremble. He'd always loved being talked dirty to, but he'd never expected it to come from such a seemingly mild-mannered man.

When he feared he couldn't take anymore, Scott felt Gareth roll away. Feeling bereft at the sudden loss of contact, he opened his eyes to see his lover with his arm dangled over the edge of the bed as he rummaged around for what he needed. When he rolled over, he slid a foil wrapper under his pillow and showed Scott the bottle he'd retrieved from under the bed. Scott's heart pounded, and he nodded his head before diving in to plunder his lover's mouth again. He could hear nothing except the racing of his own pulse. He didn't hear Gareth clicking the bottle open or closed and gasped when he suddenly felt two slick fingers stroking over him.

Scott gasped and swore but wasted no time rolling them so he straddled Gareth's lap. He thrust his hips back, driving himself further on Gareth's fingers which were still buried inside him. He leaned his upper body forward and slid his hands up the mattress alongside Gareth's head. He grinned lecherously at his partner before dropping down for another kiss. His tongue explored Gareth's mouth as his hands searched under the pillow for the packet Gareth had stashed there. Once he'd reached his prize, he pushed himself back up to a sitting position. He ripped open the packet and slowly rolled the condom down Gareth's penis, revelling in the moans the movement elicited from his lover.

The moment Gareth removed his fingers, Scott lowered himself and bit back a cry as the familiar burning and stretching sensation spread through him.

Gareth ran his hands up Scott's toned stomach and chest, both now lined with a soft sheen of sweat. He brushed his fingers lightly over Scott's skin as his lover adjusted. Once he was ready, Scott grabbed Gareth's hand and kissed his knuckles before slipping his fingers into his mouth and sucking them one by one as he started to bounce slowly. Gareth groaned loudly, tipping his head back as he lifted his hips to meet Scott's bouncing. They quickly found a rhythm with one another. Gareth's cock hit Scott's prostate over and over, and they both let go, getting louder as they got closer to the edge.

Scott gasped, his breath coming faster and faster until he suddenly reached his peak. He came with a cry, his release shooting across Gareth's chest as the Welshman simultaneously shouted and swore through his own release.

Spent and breathless, Scott collapsed against Gareth's chest and let Gareth wrap him in his arms. He nuzzled closer, breathing in their combined scent, and closed his eyes.

"Don't go falling asleep on me again, old man," Gareth teased.

"I'll have you know, thirty-four is not old," Scott gasped as he poked Gareth in the side, causing him to squirm and laugh.

"A whole eight years on me, sir."

"Jesus. I feel like a cradle robber now," Scott mumbled as he buried his face further into Gareth's chest.

Gareth laughed loudly and held Scott tighter. He pressed a kiss to the top of Scott's head and smiled. "All jokes aside, I haven't felt this happy or comfortable in a really long time. And a lot of that seems to be down to you. So, thank you."

Scott raised his head and smiled. "Same here. You really are something, Mr. Hughes. There's a lot more to you than smart suits and a refined exterior. You continue to surprise me."

"And you're not as brash and overconfident as you first seem. Looks like we're both full of surprises."

"Don't go telling anyone though, yeah? Can't lose my reputation," Scott winked.

Gareth chuckled, kissed Scott's forehead, and held him closer.

"So." Scott patted Gareth's chest. "Next time it's my turn, yeah? I believe that was one of the things on your list."

He wiggled his eyebrows, and Gareth laughed. "See. We're definitely not as bad at communicating as we thought."

Chapter Twenty-six

Alex woke with her neck bent against the sofa arm and files spread out on the coffee table in front of her. She'd tried to go through her case notes again when she'd struggled to sleep in the night, but she'd found nothing she hadn't already known. She checked her watch and saw that somehow, she'd managed to sleep through till midday.

Clattering and swearing from the front door suddenly caught her attention. She smiled to herself. For all the effort he put into cleaning the flat and the focus he put on looking as though he had everything together, her husband was still one of the clumsiest people she knew. He'd probably been busy fumbling with his keys, phone, and bag and dropped one, if not several, of his belongings on the floor. She propped herself against the sofa's backrest and watched as the living room door creaked open and Marcus peered around it.

His eyes skimmed over her crumpled pyjamas and messed hair and whispered, "Did I wake you?"

"No, I must have sensed you were due back. I woke up just before I heard you come in."

He nodded as he padded across the room towards their bedroom, his head hung low. His timid movements reminded her of the early, awkward days when they had first started dating. How little he had changed. He still had thick blonde hair, which was currently dripping stray drops of water over his forehead. His eyes still twinkled with a friendly and welcoming shine, and his jaw was still sharp and clean-shaven. He was really quite attractive when he wasn't being moody or obsessive. And he could be funny too, though she seemed to laugh less at him these days.

"What've you been dreaming about?" Marcus leaned against the doorframe to the bedroom and broke her train of thought.

"What?"

"You were sat there with a big grin on your face." He bent down to grab his bag from the floor again and moved back into the bedroom. "You must have been somewhere nice."

She smiled at him. Sometimes amongst all the rows, she forgot how jovial and attentive he could be. She got up and followed him. She dropped down on the bed and watched as he began methodically unpacking his bag. "I was just thinking about how little you've changed."

"In a good way?" He raised his eyebrows and smiled.

"Sometimes." She smiled back. "I'm sorry I was rude yesterday."

"Don't worry about it." Marcus moved to sit next to her on the bed.

"No, Marcus. I'm really sorry, you went to so much effort, and I just shot you down."

"It wasn't that much effort really." A grin spread across his face. "I got it out of a packet."

Alex gasped and gave him a slight push. "You total twat. You had me feeling so guilty!"

He laughed and gave her a slight shove, so she fell against the mattress. With the laughter still on their lips, he gently lowered himself and kissed her. Alex relaxed in a way she hadn't in months. When was the last time she'd let him show her affection without shoving him off or sarcastically rebuffing him? She quickly slipped his shirt over his head and ran her hands down his back, feeling his skin in a way she hadn't for too long. A small moan escaped her throat as she felt his hand brush against her thigh. Her heart raced as she felt his breath hot on her face. She kissed him more, her lips trailing over his jaw and neck.

A loud clattering from her bedside table caught her attention. She instinctively pulled away and looked towards the noise. Her phone was buzzing away with an incoming call from the superintendent.

"Leave it, Al. Please." Marcus breathed heavily against her neck. She could feel his heart pounding in the same way hers was.

"It might be about the case." She pushed herself back into a sitting position.

"Of course, it's about the case. Al, please just silence it for a moment."

"I should just check."

The phone continued to rattle against the bedside table. She pushed Marcus to one side and answered, "Sir."

"Al, we need you to come into the station. We've arrested Jake for Beth's murder."

"What?" Alex gasped and sat bolt upright.

"We found evidence that he'd been sleeping with her in the lead up to her death and we identified his DNA on clothing samples from her laundry basket. You're going to need to come in and answer a few questions yourself, just to help us fill in some of the gaps."

"Of course," she stammered.

"One hour." As usual, Pickering didn't leave her a chance to reply.

She looked over to Marcus, who was already sliding off the bed.

"I'm sorry. I have to go."

"Of course you do." He was already pulling a fresh T-shirt over his head.

"It's my job Marcus."

"And I'm your husband!" He rarely raised his voice, even when he was mad at her. It wasn't like him to let rage overcome him. That wasn't his style. "You're always so quick to jump and do whatever the force needs you to do. But what about me?" His voice wobbled again. "Do you ever stop to wonder what I need from you?"

"I can't stand here arguing with you Marcus; I have important things to do."

"And I'm not important, is that what you're saying?"

"You know damn well that's not what I'm saying. Stop twisting everything!" She yelled at him, but unlike him, she held her voice steady. She raked a hand through her hair, trying desperately to think of a response that would calm him down without her having to waste more time before she got to the station. She came up blank, grabbed her dressing gown from the hook on the door and locked herself in the bathroom. She turned the shower on full blast, drowning out any response Marcus could muster. Stepping under the water, she took a deep breath and scrubbed her face, hoping she could wash away the argument. She'd pushed him too far. She knew that. She wouldn't have gotten so angry with him if he wasn't so childish and needy. That's what she kept telling herself over and over again. Maybe, the more she told herself that, the less she'd beat herself up about the fact that really, deep down, she knew he was right. She did put him second to her job. She did belittle his work compared to her own. How else did she expect him to act when she treated him so poorly?

Marcus had gone when she got out of the shower and crept out of the bathroom. Just as well, really. She only had twenty minutes left to get herself sorted and didn't need any more distractions.

It was almost three-thirty p.m. when Alex arrived back home. Marcus was sitting at their small kitchen table with his laptop open in front of him. He barely looked up as she entered.

"Get all your important work done?"

"I've been officially suspended pending investigation." She could barely get the words out. They seemed so unreal to her. Everything she'd worked so hard for was crumbling away before her eyes. Everyone who knew her knew how much her integrity and role in protecting people meant to her. Now, all of that was being questioned, both by her colleagues and by herself.

"What?" Marcus pushed his laptop to one side and stared at her.

"They've arrested Jake for Beth's murder. They were sleeping together apparently. And now they've suspended me while they complete their investigations and work out how much I knew and whether I was covering for him."

"Jesus. I knew Jake was a sleaze, but I didn't think..."

"He didn't do this, Marcus," Alex snapped. "Something isn't right. I have to call Scott."

"Parmer? What's he got to do with anything?"

"I asked him to look into things when they shut me out of the case. I knew something wasn't right. I knew it."

She started fumbling in her bag, searching for her phone. Once she'd grasped it in her hand, she felt her husband's hand encircle her wrist. She looked up at him, and for the first time in years, she opened up to him. Or rather, she cracked in front of him. He wrapped her in his arms and pressed a kiss to her head as she folded into his body and sobbed.

Marcus ran a soothing hand down her back and whispered softly to her, "I know it may not seem like it now, but maybe this is a bit of a blessing in disguise."

Alex felt her body stiffen, and she pulled away from the hug. Where there had been a vulnerability a few seconds ago, there was now a hardness. "What the hell does that mean?"

Marcus reached for her again and tried to pull her towards him. "Don't push me away again, Al. I just mean, maybe having some time away from it will help you refocus on us. Give us the time we've lost out on."

Alex pulled away sharply, her temper flaring as her emotions raged through her veins. "Don't you dare pin all our problems on me. What the hell have you done to help our relationship? Other than whine when you don't get what you want."

"Al, you have no idea what I've done for this relationship," Marcus snarled as his lip curled up on one side.

"So, enlighten me. What lessons can you teach me as the relationship expert you apparently are?" she cried, her voice thick as she blinked back tears that she refused to let fall.

Marcus threw his hands in the air and paced back to his laptop. "I put my entire business on hold so you could build your career and all I asked for in return was a little of your time to help me keep this relationship running. And now, I finally have an opportunity and idea to grow my business, to go into something that's really exciting for me, and you can't even pretend to be interested."

His voice cracked under the weight of his emotions. He pulled out a chair and collapsed into it. The cold white wood creaked beneath him as he buried his head in his hands. "Sometimes I think you forget I'm even here, or wish I weren't. And honestly, I don't know which hurts more."

Alex's shoulders sagged as all her pent-up rage left her body. The sight of the man she loved looking so broken, and knowing that her behaviour had caused it, was too much. She moved to his side, dropped to her knees, and pulled one of his hands into hers.

"You're right," she whispered as she pressed a kiss to Marcus's knee through his jeans. "I've been so focused on my work, and the importance of it, that I forgot there were other things that needed my attention too. I got so wrapped up in trying to be the best investigator I could that I dropped the ball on being the best partner. I'm sorry."

Marcus patted her hand gently and wiped his face with the arm of his jumper as he waited for her to continue.

"I know what you do is important to you, and how much you love that shop of yours. And I love you. And I'm sorry I made you doubt that."

They stood, wrapped their arms around each other, and clung on as if letting go would emphasise the distance they'd both previously put between them. Alex pressed her lips to Marcus's neck, whispering more apologies between kisses as she nuzzled her tear-streaked cheeks against her husband's warm skin.

"No more talk about cases or Jake or Scott," Alex promised. "Not tonight. Tonight, I want you to tell me all about that meeting you had today and what you've been planning."

Marcus held her tightly and sighed, "It's okay, you don't have to listen. I know it's not interesting for you. It's just nice to know you're not tired of me and my little shop."

When Alex pulled back again, she saw Marcus smiling sadly, accepting what little he clearly felt he deserved. She shook her head and cupped his face in her hands. "I want to know. It's important to you, so it's important to me."

Marcus let out a breathy laugh and sniffled, and tears pricked the corners of his eyes again. He grabbed her hands and pressed delicate kisses to her palms as he whispered his thanks. "I'll make us some tea and then I'll talk you through my plans."

Chapter Twenty-seven

After Scott had taken his 'turn', the couple hopped in the shower. Still spent from their activities in the bedroom, they managed to keep the distractions to a minimum – Gareth decided he could save his shower fantasy for another day. Once they were clean, Scott slipped into his clothes from the previous night, and they finally sat down to drink their coffees.

Scott sank into the old sofa in the living room, and Gareth curled up next to him, cradling his coffee cup in both hands.

"We should eat up and get into the office," Gareth said as he took a sip. "We're already late opening up."

"I'll have a word with the boss, I'm sure he won't mind." Scott winked. "There's no rush."

Gareth rolled his eyes. "Have you always been this irresponsible?"

"Only when I get distracted by something pretty," Scott smirked.

Gareth pushed Scott gently with his foot, sending the American's coffee slopping up the sides of his mug.

"Idiot," he tutted. His smile gave away his true feelings, though, and he tried to cover it by taking another swig of his coffee.

Scott grinned and picked up the plate of pastries they'd

placed on the floor. He tore a croissant in half, popped one part in his mouth and offered the other the Gareth.

"We have all afternoon to scope out those florists you researched yesterday, right? No other client meetings or anything?"

"Nope. The diary is clear until tomorrow morning," Gareth replied once he'd swallowed his half of the croissant. "All the same though, I'd like to get in and just check messages et cetera."

"If you want me to leave you can just say, you know," Scott teased as he polished off another pastry and washed it down with the last of his coffee.

"Of course not. But I meant what I said about trying to keep 'us' and work separate – and that means taking them both as seriously as each other," Gareth insisted.

Scott reached out and grabbed Gareth's hand. "I know. I was only teasing. I appreciate that about you. I need someone to keep me on track."

"I'm starting to see that," Gareth smiled before quickly turning back to his coffee and breakfast. He grabbed another pastry and meticulously began pulling it apart as he deliberately ignored the fact that he'd so easily referred to himself and Scott as an 'us'. In part because it felt so normal that it barely registered as something to comment on. But also partly because it terrified him to think such a thing had happened so quickly and easily. He'd already opened up to Scott so much that it was hard to believe they'd only known each other a week.

The speed at which his feelings were developing was concerning for Gareth. The last time he'd gotten caught up in a whirlwind romance hadn't exactly panned out well for him. But then, he supposed Scott's experience with David hadn't turned out much better. They'd both loved and lost enough to be wary. But something in his gut told Gareth that this was different. Keeping it as separate from their work as possible meant he felt more secure in his work too. It was a win-win scenario. Especially if the work and the sex continued to be as much fun.

Pastries and coffee finished, Scott helped tidy things away before leaving Gareth with a soft lingering kiss. They agreed to meet at the office in an hour. That would give Scott time to get home so he could change and give Gareth time to check the phones and organise his list of florists before they headed out.

As he sat in the back of his taxi and headed for home, Scott's mind whirred louder than the engine. Since David had left, he'd been reluctant to let anyone in on a romantic level. He'd by no means been a saint. His fling with Jake was proof of that. But that was all it had been. A fling. No-strings-attached sex. But, based on his reaction to finding out Jake had been seeing other people at the same time, Scott had to admit he maybe hadn't been as careful with his feelings as he thought. While he didn't think Gareth would betray him that way, he knew the young man's situation was complicated. It was perfectly possible that he was just enjoying the attention, and some (pretty fantastic) rebound sex. And if that was all it ever amounted to, Scott was fine with that. He really was.

Chapter Twenty-eight

By ten a.m., Gareth had unlocked the office and was busy checking their diary. Despite Scott's reassurance, he'd felt uncomfortable about being late. But thankfully, they'd had no calls that morning, which helped ease his guilt.

Inbox and phone checked, he stood up, smoothed his suit trousers, and made his way to the kitchenette. As his morning progressed, Gareth's nerves slowly resurfaced. His initial doubts over getting involved with his new boss whirled around his head, and his stomach churned. He methodically started brewing a fresh pot of coffee, hoping the process would ground and settle him before Scott arrived and undoubtedly sent him into a tailspin again. He laid out a tray and placed two mugs on top. Once everything was prepared, he leaned against the counter. He closed his eyes, focussing on the sounds of the coffee machine working its magic. The grinding of the beans and the boiling water soothed him, and by the time the rich aroma of a fresh brew reached his nose, he felt much calmer.

Of course, he had nothing to worry about. He'd been open with Scott and vice versa. They knew where they both stood. Neither one had done anything they hadn't wanted to. Besides, if anything did go wrong between them, Faith was sure to knock their heads together.

He chuckled to himself and lifted the fresh pot onto his tray. As he stepped into the main office, he heard the familiar squeak of the landing floorboards and seconds later, Scott stepped inside. As soon as he locked eyes on Gareth, a bright grin lit his face.

"Is that for me, or the coffee?" Gareth teased.

"A little of both maybe," Scott smirked as he slipped out of his coat and hung it by the door. "You want to sit in here or at my desk?"

Gareth paused for a moment. He'd intended to take Scott's coffee to the small sofa area, but now he was doubting himself again. He thought back to their cosy breakfast on his sofa. He panicked that they'd be too close to crossing that boundary between working life and their new relationship if they sat too comfortably.

"Let's head through to your office, that way if anyone turns up all my notes are out of the way."

Scott smiled softly and nodded, indicating that Gareth should lead the way. Once Gareth placed their coffee tray on the desk, he turned around and pointed behind Scott, gesturing that he needed to get past Scott.

"My notes are just by my computer," he started.

Scott gingerly reached out, squeezed the top of Gareth's arm, and offered a reassuring smile. "You okay?"

"Fine. Just...Not entirely sure how we do this now. Everything feels different suddenly."

"You wish we hadn't...?" Scott waved his hand, as if afraid of speaking the words aloud.

"No," Gareth's immediate response eased the knot that had started forming in his gut. The instinctiveness of it reassured him of his initial, deep feelings.

"Things don't have to be any different at work, you know? We just do our jobs as before and I'll try to keep my hands to myself at all times," Scott reassured him, a sly grin creeping onto his face. "You wanted to keep things separate and I respect that, especially knowing what you've been through previously. But, I want to reiterate, I'm not Liam. If I do something wrong, you can tell me. Those communication skills come in handy outside the bedroom too, you know?"

Gareth huffed a laugh and nodded as he nibbled his lip. "I'll just grab those notes then, sir."

Scott took a sharp breath and moved out of the way to get to his own desk. "You're really going to have to stop with the whole 'sir' thing now though. It sounds way too kinky. And if you want me to behave myself..."

Gareth laughed loudly. "Duly noted...Scott."

Scott put his hands together in front of his chest and dipped his head in thanks.

By the time Gareth returned, notebook in hand, Scott was busy pouring each of them a cup.

"Okay, tell me what you got," Scott said, leaning back in his chair with his coffee clasped just below his chin.

Gareth settled himself in the opposite chair and dropped his pad on the desk so they could both see his looping scrawl. He picked up his coffee with one hand and, with the other, pointed his way through his notes as he explained his plan.

"I split the florists I called last night into different areas we should be able to cover on foot before moving onto the next lot. I suggest we start with these ones because they're closer to Beth's house and the furthest from us, so we can gradually work our way back to the office. Not all of them could give me a clear answer on whether they supplied lily of the valley or not.

Most of them were just kids doing the afternoon shifts. I've asterisked those ones so we can make a point to try and speak to someone more experienced."

When he looked up, Scott smiled broadly over his coffee cup and watched him intently. Immediately he felt his cheeks flush. "What?" he asked before taking a sip of his coffee, hoping it would cover up some of his blushing.

"Just thinking how well you did with all this. Are you sure you weren't a detective in a past life?"

Gareth shrugged and let a small smile break out on his face. "Just like to be organised, I guess. One of us has to be. Come on, drink up. It'll take us about thirty-five minutes to drive out to this first set."

"Yes, Sir." Scott grinned and gave a mock salute.

Gareth rolled his eyes and tutted again. "Idiot. Don't you start."

Chapter Twenty-nine

The chill bit into Gareth's sharp cheekbones as he and Scott stepped onto the street. It seemed as though it was growing more autumnal by the hour now, and Gareth regretted not bringing a scarf with him – though he was sure it would have gotten lost in the mess of Scott's car if he had.

As he followed Scott back to the car, Gareth crossed the latest florist off his list. His brows were knitted together, and he was chewing the inside of his cheek. They'd managed to get a few dates and quantities for lily of the valley purchases, but nothing to link any of those purchases to Beth. The good news for Jake was that none of the owners so far had recognised him as a customer. So, while he was looking less and less like the culprit, it left Gareth feeling further and further from the truth. He shoved his notepad and pen into his pocket with a huff.

Scott reached out and caught his forearm. "Don't worry, we've still got plenty of places to look and people to speak to. There'll be something we can use, somewhere."

Gareth sighed. "Yeah. But we haven't even started looking into the possibility of online florists, which just extends our search parameter. If anything, I feel further from a result than closer to one."

Scott wobbled his head and raised one shoulder – a movement Gareth was starting to recognise as a tick of his. "Maybe," Scott drawled. "Of course, buying online offers a sort of facelessness. But it would be linked to their bank cards, home address etc. At a florist, or several florists, they could pay in cash, keep their name and address out of it. That seems far more likely to me."

"Maybe," Gareth conceded. "Next shop's up this way."

They started walking again, Scott still lightly holding Gareth's forearm. A part of Gareth initially cried out to pull away, but instead, he felt himself leaning slightly closer as they walked. For now, they weren't around any potential witnesses or suspects, so he reasoned it didn't count as a working environment. As a result, he felt the tension seep from his shoulders as his arms relaxed.

They wound their way through the streets, huddling together against the occasional bursts of an autumn wind that sent leaves and litter skittering up the road. The air was pretty warm when the wind died down, the sun was low in the sky behind them, and there were very few clouds. Gareth would have said it was a perfect day if their investigations had been more successful.

When they reached their next stop, Gareth held back and gestured for Scott to go ahead of him. A small bell tinkled above the doorway of Blooming Lovely as they pushed into the balmy shop interior. The walls were lined with green potted plants, and buckets containing pre-made bouquets and fresh cuttings were placed in neat displays at various focal points in the room. At the back stood a small workbench that doubled up as a counter.

An elderly woman emerged from behind a bright pink curtain that covered the entrance to the back of the shop. Her face had that squishy softness that often came with old age. Her white hair curled on top of her head in a stereotypical blue-rinse perm, starkly contrasting the bright colours and modern cut of her clothing. She wore emerald green cigarette trousers and a silk fuchsia blouse. Around her neck hung a delicate chain that held a pair of pink-rimmed glasses.

"How can I help you boys?" She smiled.

Gareth let Scott handle the initial spiel as always. His natural charm and charisma often put people at ease, even once they knew he was an investigator.

Scott introduced the idea that they were investigating the poisoning of a local woman, and the florist shook her head.

"I heard about that—such a terrible thing to happen. I don't think I'll be much help, though. I'm just minding the shop for the new owner. I help out now and then. The place used to be mine, you see, so I know the clientele and the business better than the part-time girls that work here. Although, I'm fairly sure the new owner would have already spoken to the police about everything."

"We're sure they will have, we just want to check a few things out ourselves," Gareth reassured her. "Do you know if the owner stocks lily of the valley?"

The elderly woman answered immediately, "Oh, no. We did back when I owned the place, but Mr. Cooper doesn't. He's trying to expand the business to include a herbalism range and he doesn't want to risk having potentially toxic plants mixing with that."

Gareth caught Scott's eye momentarily, trying to determine if any of what they'd learned was helpful.

"What sorts of things does the herbalism range include, do you know?" Scott pressed.

"Err, aromatherapies, teas, herbal remedies, that sort of thing, I think. I'm not totally clear on it all. But he says it's good for all kinds of things. Stress relief for one. But I think he's trying to ensure the range has something for everyone."

"Well, we could all do with a bit of stress relief now and again, couldn't we?" Scott smiled in his charming, Hollywood magazine kind of way.

The elderly woman returned the smile, completely enamoured – not that Gareth could blame her. "He has a sign-up sheet for people who want to know more."

She rustled around beneath the counter. When she stood up, she had a deep frown etched onto her face. "I can't find the bloody thing, but here's the business card he had made. I'm sure if you give him a call tomorrow, he'd add you to his list. I know he's really keen to grow this."

Scott smiled his thanks and took the pale yellow card from her outstretched hand, looked at it briefly, and handed it to Gareth. On the back was a phone number for the shop and a website address. On the front was a pale green logo of some entwining herbs and flowers. Thanks to the soft colour palette and sweeping design, it had a calming, serene look. He slipped the card inside his notebook and smiled at the elderly woman, who seemed to be watching him eagerly.

Scott slipped his hand into his jacket pocket and pulled out a business card of his own. "Can I leave this with you? Just in case you think of anything else. Pass it over to the owner if not."

"Of course, anything I can do to help." She smiled.

They said polite goodbyes and left Blooming Lovely. The sun was starting to dip in the sky as they headed back towards Scott's car, and the wind started picking up.

Gareth pulled his coat tighter and buried his hands in his pockets, once again lamenting his lack of a scarf. "I can't tell if that was useful or not," he mumbled.

"Everything is useful," Scott reminded him. "We know where the killer won't have got the flowers from. That cuts our search down a little further."

"I suppose. But we don't have any solid leads on where they could have gotten the flowers."

"Not yet. We will." Scott smiled as he gently nudged Gareth's shoulder with his own.

When they returned to the car, the sky was ablaze with burnt oranges, and the ground was full of stretching shadows. They slipped inside the vehicle, and Gareth subconsciously brushed the seat before sitting down. "We probably have time to get a few more shops in before five p.m.," he said as he stared at his list.

Scott nodded as he buckled in and reached for his GPS. "Okay, give me the next address and let's get going."

The next shop was as unsuccessful as the others. The owner was a curmudgeonly man who was utterly immune to Scott's charms and annoyed at being questioned after already speaking to the police.

They'd quickly moved on and reached their final stop for the day at around four-thirty p.m. It had a much more pared-back look than many of the shops they'd visited. The walls inside were bare brick, and the flowers and plants on display all consisted of soft white or cream petals, rich green foliage, and natural hessian ribbons.

"We like to keep things simple and natural," the young woman in charge explained. "Some shops like to go all out to catch attention or feel they have to do more than just flowers, but here, we believe less is more."

Scott nodded as if agreeing. Gareth smiled and said, "It certainly feels very soothing in here. Less chaotic than most places."

"Exactly." The young woman smiled as she looked him up and down with her dark eyes.

Gareth risked a glance over at Scott and noted the way Scott's back had straightened in a manner that looked almost painful. His shoulders had raised slightly, and Gareth could practically see the tension building in his muscles. Gareth swallowed the anxiety he could feel building. Memories of Liam's anger whenever Gareth had received attention and the not-so-subtle backhanded compliments and put-downs that followed. He took a deep breath through his nose and mentally ran through his growing list of all the reasons Scott was different to Liam.

As if sensing Gareth's discomfort and rising anxiety, Scott cleared his throat and drew the woman's attention back to him. "We're specifically interested in sales of lily of the valley, do you keep records of who you might have sold those to?"

The young woman dragged her eyes back to Scott, a frown threatening to break onto her face. "We don't take names or anything unless it's for an event or something. I can find those for you if you like?"

"That'd be great," Scott smiled, but Gareth could sense the forced nature of it. Something hard and heavy settled in his stomach at that realisation. "And if we could get copies of your receipts or stocktakes for the last two months, that would help us link any potential sales."

The young woman flicked her hair over her shoulder and disappeared into the back room. As soon as she was out of earshot, Gareth glanced over at Scott and mumbled, "I'm really sorry."

Scott blinked and shook his head. "What for?"

Gareth rolled his eyes and awkwardly shifted from foot to foot. "That. All that flirting. I didn't want to disrespect you or anger you or..."

"Woah, woah, woah," Scott whispered fiercely as he held his hands out in from of him. "Gareth, I'm not angry with you."

"You're not?" Gareth breathed, cautious but hopeful.

"Of course not. I can't deny I felt a bit jealous and annoyed, but not with you. You can't help being so gorgeous people want to flirt with you." Scott winked.

Gareth chuckled and Scott reached out and caught his hand. "Just breathe. I never want you to feel the way you would with him because of me. Okay?"

Gareth nodded. Tears prickled his eyes. Scott's gentleness was almost overwhelming in how different it was from what he was used to. He squeezed Scott's hand and managed a small smile.

A soft click from behind the counter made them jump. They whipped their heads around to see the young florist move through the door towards them. They dropped each other's hands, and Gareth shoved his back into his pocket as his blush rapidly rose up his face. A small pang of guilt hit him as he caught the flicker of disappointment on the girl's face as she slipped a small note out of the file she held in her hand before handing the Manilla folder across the counter.

"Everything should be in there. They're all copies, so there's no need to bring them back. Just make sure you destroy anything you don't end up needing for the case," she said softly.

"Of course." Scott nodded. "Thank you."

They nodded their goodbyes and Scott motioned for Gareth to lead the way out of the shop.

Chapter Thirty

Scott shook his hands, sending water droplets splashing up against the large wall mirror. Having flung most of the water away, he wiped his now-damp hands on his trousers. Once he was satisfied his hands were dry, he picked at the front of his hair, ensuring it sat just so.

Watching Gareth organising the information they'd gathered from the florists while they'd driven home had filled him with both a sense of fondness and an acute arousal – apparently awakening a competency kink he never knew he had. Gareth had noticeably relaxed after their quick check-in at the last florist's store, but he'd still held his shoulders high and tight and Scott couldn't shake the desire to bury his thumbs into the tense muscles, easing the tension from them with focused touches and soft kisses. There was an element of lust to his motives of course, but beyond that was an overwhelming desire to simply be with Gareth for as long as possible, to take care of him, and show him he was cared for in a way that he'd clearly lacked in his relationship with Liam.

Scott had planned the entire evening in his head the moment they'd returned to the office. They could head back to his place, look through their files, have dinner, and then he could show Gareth just how thankful he was for all his help.

Finally happy with how his hair was styled, he turned on his heel and headed back down the corridor to the office. When he entered, Gareth was in the inner office, bent over Scott's desk with his back to the door. A sly smile crept across Scott's face as he took a moment to admire the view. He almost lost his composure when Gareth shifted his weight to reach across the desk pulling his suit trousers tight against his arse.

Gareth turned his head and rolled his eyes. "Are you planning on standing by the door much longer or are you going to come and sort this work out?"

Scott tried to look insulted as he brought a hand to his chest. "How do you know I've not just got here?"

"The floorboards on the other side of that door creak," Gareth called before he turned back to look at the sheets of paper in front of him. "You know, for a P.I. you're not exactly very stealthy."

"Maybe I wanted you to know I was there," Scot retorted, his eyes dropping back to Gareth's arse as he moved through the office. He just caught sight of another trademark eye roll and headshake as he came level with Gareth. He slipped an arm around Gareth's hips. "Come on then, talk to me through what you've been doing."

Gareth cleared his throat and shifted away to point out the various piles of files he'd made. "So, this is all the bulk order information we got. Weddings, events, that sort of thing. These are the receipts we got from single transactions. That last one is stocktake information. With both of those, I've highlighted which bouquets include lily of the valley, so we don't miss any. I figured one of us could check events. One could take a look at the stock lists. Then we can go through the single transactions together and see if any sales line up with

Beth's timeline etc."

"You're amazing. You know that?" Scott smiled broadly and reached out to grab Gareth's hips again. He pressed Gareth back against the desk and brushed his lips against his neck, just above his shirt collar and nuzzled against him. "Why don't we take these back to my place? We can get something to eat, go over everything, and then I can show you just how much I appreciate everything you've done today," he whispered.

"Actually, I was sort of looking forward to a night to myself," Gareth spluttered.

Scott frowned and squeezed Gareth in his arms as the urge to cling on and never let go threatened to overwhelm him. Surely, Gareth couldn't be pulling away from him already? They'd only just begun. Even he couldn't have cocked things up that badly yet. Could he?

"I was just really hoping you'd spent the night at mine this time." He tested his voice. When it didn't break instantly, he pushed further, hugging Gareth closer to him as he did. "I'd really miss you tonight otherwise. Besides, we've worked hard today, I figured we deserved a little fun, you know?"

Gareth immediately froze, and Scott knew instantly that he'd made a mistake. Before he could backtrack and make things right, Gareth pushed him away and grabbed one of the folders from the desk. He hugged his chosen file against his chest as though it was some kind of shield.

"I think I'm just going to go through these at my desk if I'm honest," he said, his voice barely staying steady as he spoke. His hands shook around the edges of the folder, either from emotion or from the tension held in his muscles, Scott wasn't sure.

Scott shook his head and took a breath, trying to keep his

voice calm and reassuring, "Gareth, it's nearly six o'clock; you need to eat."

"I'm quite capable of deciding what I need thanks." This time there was a clip to Gareth's voice. His shoulders rose again as his back straightened.

Scott tried again, pressing on. "Look, why don't you come back to mine and we can work through them together?" Scott reached out again, only for his heart to thump in his chest as Gareth withdrew further.

"I don't think that's a good idea, do you? You clearly have one thing on your mind right now." Gareth glared, his hands still shaking.

"And? It's nothing we haven't already done. We're..." Scott waved his hand as his brain searched for the most appropriate word for their relationship.

"We're colleagues," Gareth said, his voice sounding stronger than his shaking body looked.

"Right," Scott clipped as he folded his arms. "And that's it, is it? Because that's not the impression you gave this morning. Or all the times you held on to me earlier."

"Stop being petulant," Gareth spat. "You know what I meant. I've told you over and over again that I want to keep that separate from work and you're just blatantly ignoring me."

"I'm sorry! I can't just switch off my feelings for you because we've got work to do. What you're asking for is impossible. You're being ridiculous!" Scott yelled, exasperated. But, as soon as the words left his mouth, he wished he could take them back.

Gareth's face dropped, and his eyes darkened, though his shoulders stayed stiff and his back straight. "Ridiculous, am I? Okay, well I'm glad we cleared that one up early on," he growled.

He grabbed his coat from the rack and put a hand out to stop Scott from advancing closer. "Clearly, as you say, this isn't possible. So, sir, I'm going to go home and look at these files. In the morning, we can debrief before your meeting with Mr. Collins. Goodnight," Gareth snarled before storming out, leaving Scott standing speechless in the middle of the office.

Scott closed the Manilla folder in front of him and added it to the pile to his left. He grabbed a yellow sticky note and slapped it onto the file to remind himself which pile was which in the morning. He blew out a huge sigh and checked his watch – eight-thirty p.m. Not quite the evening he'd had planned. He groaned as he rubbed his hands over his face, dragging them down his cheeks so that the skin stretched unattractively.

When would he learn, he wondered. He knew he tended to push too hard, too fast, and not doing so had been even more important with Gareth. And yet he'd blustered around in his usual way and had done the one thing he'd promised he wouldn't – made Gareth uncomfortable. Then, to top things off, he'd let his embarrassment and frustration at his behaviour boil over and sent it lashing out at the one person who deserved it least. He lowered his head and hit his forehead against the cold wood of his desk twice. God, why was he such a jerk?

His phone vibrated across the desk, the clattering ripping through the silence in the office. He flung out a hand to catch it before it jumped over the edge. His heart, which had momentarily dared to hope, dropped at the sight of the caller ID. He bit the inside of his cheek and braced himself before answering.

"Hey, Faith, what's up?"

"You tell me," she huffed. "I didn't realise introducing the two of you meant I'd become your bloody go-between every time you fall out."

Scott chewed nervously on the skin around his thumb nail. "You've spoken to Gareth then I take it."

"Not really. I text him to check in and see how last night went seeing as neither of you bothered to update me. All I got back was that he didn't want to talk about it right now. So, come on. What did you do?"

"Why do you assume it was me who did something?" Scott pouted.

"Oh, don't worry. I'll be asking him the same question when I finally speak to him. I know you're both as bad as each other."

Scott gave a wry chuckle. "And yet you still thought it a good idea to set us up."

"I did not set you up. I merely introduced Gareth to you as a friend and colleague. It's not my fault the two of you had romance on the brain and started making googly eyes at each other," she defended. "Anyway, stop trying to change the subject. What did you do or say?"

With a heavy sigh, Scott explained the brief but fiery argument.

"Do you think I should call him?" he asked when he was finished.

Faith tutted. "No way. Just give him some space for tonight. He needs time to realise that while your delivery wasn't great, you weren't wrong. It isn't fair for him to expect you to keep the two aspects of your lives totally separate, especially not with the nature of your job. And he will realise. It's not like you can stick to nine-to-five hours where you're completely in work mode, and then have your evenings totally free for couple stuff. Then tomorrow you can both grovel and set some proper boundaries, okay? Sensible ones."

"Thanks, Faith. I don't know what I'd do without you." Scott smiled for the first time that evening.

"I dread to think," Faith mumbled. There was a moment's silence and Scott could hear the cogs in her mind talking as she worked through her next point. "And, maybe, a night apart every once in a while will be good. For both of you. With Liam, he was barely given room to breathe. For a while he'll need his own space to avoid feeling like he's slipping back under someone else's control."

Scott rubbed a hand over his eyes. "I'd not even thought about it like that. Jesus. What an idiot."

"Don't worry about it," Faith reassured him. "He'll be okay. Just apologise in the morning. Liam never would, so even something small will remind him how different this situation is."

"Yeah. Yeah, you're right. Just need to keep myself under control," Scott chuckled. "You couldn't have suggested a less brilliant friend to take over your maternity leave?"

"And leave you without a firm hand to keep you in line? No way," she laughed. "You sure you're okay now?"

"Fine," he reassured her. "I'm gonna close up the office, grab something to eat, and plan my grovelling technique. Go and get some rest."

Faith barked a laugh. "Fat chance of that at the minute. Every five minutes, Robin Jr. either kicks me in the ribs or bounces on my bladder."

From the background, Scott could hear Robin make a sarcastic retort, although the exact words were muffled. Chuckling, the two friends said their goodbyes and hung up. Feeling slightly less uneasy, Scott pushed away from his desk and headed out of the office.

Gareth threw his mobile onto the bed and turned his attention back to the papers spread out around him. He loved Faith fiercely, but right now, he really couldn't face her enthusiasm or her trying to counsel him. Whichever approach she took would have only riled him up further.

The bare bulb above his head was burning bright, and his eyes felt dry and sore. He stared a little longer at the lists of events he'd made based on those that ordered lily of the valley. He'd noted the venues, contacts, and quantities for each and had made a note to speak to Dr. Hart to clarify just how much would be needed to kill someone.

Satisfied that he'd done everything he could for the night, he gathered his papers and placed them back in their files, with his list lying on top. He slipped off the bed, which groaned loudly no matter how smoothly he tried to move. He shuffled down the hallway and left his work on the small wooden bench by the front door.

Huffing a sigh, he made his way to the kitchen, set up his coffee machine, and leaned against the kitchen counter with his eyes closed. Now that he had no work to focus on, his mind was racing over his argument with Scott. His cheeks started to flush, and his heart raced. He'd known that everything with Scott had been too good to be true, and he'd been foolish to give so much so early. A growl bubbled past his lips as the coffee machine finished its cycle. He clattered a mug against the counter, poured his coffee, and closed his eyes as he inhaled the rich scent. His eyes sprung open again as something clicked in his mind.

I can't just switch off my feelings, that's what Scott had said. Gareth had been in such a heightened state of anxiety at the time that he hadn't taken the words on board. But Scott had admitted to having feelings, which motivated his actions. He wasn't acting on pure lust or a need to keep Gareth close so he could watch him and control him. He wasn't Liam.

"Maybe I am being ridiculous," he mumbled to himself.

He sighed heavily and trudged to the living room, where he flopped down onto the sofa. A spring clanged loudly somewhere beneath him as he did so.

Deep down, he understood what Scott was saying because he couldn't turn off his feelings either. Despite being cross, Gareth wanted to tell Scott what he'd found in his notes, to share a pot of coffee with him, and enjoy an evening together going over their findings before having dinner together and then...

He closed his eyes and shook his head. "Boy, have I got some making up to do in the morning," he groaned.

Chapter Thirty-one

As was often the case when he felt anxious, Gareth woke early the following morning. His stomach churned almost constantly, and he couldn't decide whether it was more or less intense than his first day on the job. Determined to smooth things over with Scott, he showered, shaved, and brushed his teeth at double speed. He even skipped his morning coffee in favour of getting out the door early. He placed his files in his bag and left the flat, ignoring how his hands shook as he tried to lock up.

The streets were barely beginning to fill with the early morning buzz of city life. A few delivery vans whizzed past to get to their first drop-offs of the day, and buses carrying early-morning commuters rattled along the roads. The air had that chilly dampness that only comes with an autumnal morning. Wet leaves squelched beneath Gareth's feet as he stepped carefully through the rain-slicked streets.

Despite the grisly weather, Gareth deliberately took a longer route to work so that he could pass one of his favourite bakeries. He ducked inside and took a deep breath, inhaling the sweet smell of sugar and pastry. A small smile grew on his face as he thought of the way Scott's face would glow on receiving such a delicious peace offering. It was almost worth the mess he'd create with the flakes of pastry and the cleanup that would inevitably follow for Gareth.

He ordered a collection of pastries for Scott to sample and a sugary glazed doughnut to perk him up in the afternoon – if it lasted that long. When he left the bakery, the morning air had started to dry out. The low sun was starting to peek through the clouds and fog. The stone pavements were beginning to dry, too, meaning Gareth could pick up his speed a little. By the time he reached the office, the sun had burst through the morning clouds and threatened to turn anyone daring to rush in its presence into a sticky, clammy mess. The front door to the building in Park Square was already unlocked, and Gareth slipped inside. He smiled politely at the security guard at the front desk, once again promising himself that he'd learn the man's name soon.

He hopped up the narrow, creaking staircase and fumbled with his office keys. To his surprise, the P.I. office door was already unlocked. Confused, he slowly pushed open the door and poked his head inside. The rich aroma of coffee wafted towards him as Scott stepped out of the kitchenette carrying a tray with two mugs and a fresh pot.

Scott smiled warmly as Gareth stepped through the door. "Excellent timing as ever."

Gareth returned the smile and dropped his bag of pastries on his desk before cupping Scott's face with one hand. He leaned in, carefully avoiding the tray in his lover's hands, and pressed a soft kiss to his lips. Tears pricked his eyes, and his heart swelled in his chest. From what Faith had told him and what he'd seen so far, he knew that Scott was rarely, if ever, in before nine a.m. It may only have been a small gesture, but to Gareth, who was so used to being the one to go out of his way for others with nothing in return, it was everything.

"Thank you," he whispered.

"I figured I owed you after yesterday," Scott replied. "Some of the things I said..."

"You weren't wrong," Gareth told him, stroking his thumb over his lover's smooth cheek.

"Maybe not. But I could have said it in a better way."

"I think we both lost our heads a little. You were right, what I was asking of you wasn't fair. I panicked because I didn't want to feel trapped or controlled like I was before."

Scott put down his tray and grasped Gareth's hands in his. "Gareth, I would never try to trap you. I just wanted to spend time with you, but I know with your past I need to let you take more of a lead at times and not let myself get carried away." He paused to look at Gareth closely, as if trying to read his thoughts through his eyes. He took a deep breath before continuing, "At the same time, you have to trust me. I'm a tactile guy and I like you – a lot. So I'm probably going to get caught up in that at times and we need to find a way of you telling me when it's too much without just flat-out rejecting me."

Gareth smiled softly and squeezed Scott's hand. "I don't have a problem with you touching me. It was more that I freaked out about spending so much time together so soon. I just need my own space a little more often right now. I don't want to repeat the mistakes I made with Liam, that's all. You touching me was never really the issue. Although, maybe don't do it in front of clients or potential witnesses."

They both chuckled, and Scott took a relieved breath, "I think I can manage that."

"And no funny business when we're supposed to be concentrating," Gareth smirked before taking on a more serious expression. “I don’t want anyone to be able to use our relationship against us in a professional matter – even each other. I want this and I want you, but if it doesn’t work, I need to know that the job won’t be affected.”

Scott’s brow creased into a frown, and his eyes grew serious. “Gareth, I promise you, whatever happens between us, you’re welcome to work here for as long as you’re comfortable doing so. You have to trust me on that.”

Gareth bit his lip and nodded sharply, though his eyes turned to the floor.

“Besides,” Scott laughed, “do you really think Faith would let me get away with treating you any less than fairly? If you can’t fully trust me yet, trust her.”

Gareth’s lips quirked into a small smile as he nodded again. “Have faith in Faith.”

This time it was Scott’s turn to roll his eyes. “Something like that, yeah.”

Gareth laughed and pulled Scott towards him, wrapping his arms around Scott’s broad shoulders and burying his face in Scott’s neck. He breathed in his aftershave’s rich, earthy tones and smiled as he felt Scott’s arms tighten around him. He quickly kissed Scott’s jaw before grabbing the bag of pastries from his desk.

“Come on. Let’s eat breakfast and catch each other up on what we found last night.”

Scott smiled and snuck in another quick kiss before Gareth moved into the kitchenette to grab some plates.

Once their breakfast was laid out, Gareth hung up his coat and retrieved his list from his backpack. He settled down on the small leather sofa and, for once, easily ignored the tiny voice in his head that told him to keep a respectful distance between himself and Scott. They sat comfortably close but with enough room that they could each reach everything they needed.

"My list is quite small so I can go first if you like?" Gareth asked as he took his first sip of coffee. He wasn't sure if it was because he hadn't had a caffeine fix since last night or because of the sentiment behind it, but the taste hit his tongue like a symphony. He swallowed his mouthful and pulled up his list. Scott leaned closer to see his notes. He had a flaky croissant in one hand and a small plate in the other but seemed to need to learn how the two items should work together. Gareth scoffed a small laugh, knowing his earlier prediction had come true almost immediately.

"Okay, so there were only a few events we had info on that included lily of the valley. But I did take notes of a few that seemed to request a lot of arrangements or bouquets that used it and fit within our timeline. I want to speak to Dr. Hart again and get a better idea of how much toxin someone would need to ingest and how many flowers would be needed for that."

"Good plan. I've also highlighted the shops where the stock patterns line up with our timeframe, but I doubt any of them add up to enough to do harm on their own. But I made a list of shops that could potentially fit together to make enough sales to poison Beth." Scott pulled out his own notes and looked over them before passing them over to Gareth. "Could you see if any of those add up with what Oliver tells you?"

Gareth took the list and nodded. "Absolutely. I'll give him a ring while you're in with Mr. Collins."

Scott smiled and popped another mouthful of pastry into his mouth. He checked his watch and took another swig of coffee.

"How long have I got before this meeting?"

"About half an hour. Do you have everything you need?"

Gareth asked as he bit into a pastry of his own.

"Yep, we're all good. It's only a first appointment so it's more just a case of getting as much information from him as I can so I know what to do next."

"Another divorce case?"

Scott nodded as he brought his coffee cup to his lips. "Yep. Back to more familiar ground. You never know. It might give us an excuse to test your dancing skills again."

Gareth raised an eyebrow. There was a mischievous glint in his eye as he leaned in, pressed a quick kiss below Scott's ear, and whispered, "We don't necessarily need a case for that. You just have to ask nicely."

Scott almost choked on the coffee in his mouth. Before he could recover from his shock enough to respond, Gareth gathered the empty plates and food bags onto their tray and hurried into the kitchen.

Chapter Thirty-two

Scott gave a small nod and soft smile as he closed his office door on his meeting with Mr. Collins. Gareth gave him a returning smile and soft mock salute before picking up the phone and dialling Dr. Hart's office. He balanced the handset between his ear and shoulder and pulled his notes closer, twiddling his pen between his fingers.

The call connected, and Dr. Oliver Hart answered in the short, sharp way Gareth had expected.

"Yes?"

"Dr. Hart, it's Gareth Hughes from P.I. I just wanted to run a few questions by you."

"Parmer got you doing the grunt work again, has he?" Hart scoffed. "What does he need now?"

Gareth bit his tongue and scrunched his eyes, determined not to let the snarky doctor get under his skin. "We have a few possible sources for the poison that killed Beth, but we wanted to confirm with you just how much she'd need to ingest to kill her."

The doctor took a long breath. "Well, every part of the plant is poisonous. That thing is loaded with toxins. As little as five berries from lily of the valley can be enough to kill a small child if they don't get help soon enough. But Beth was almost six foot tall and fit and healthy. So, it could have been as little as a single bouquet crushed down and given to her over time. But realistically, until we know how she ingested it, it's going to be tough to say. If she was feeling unwell in the prior week, it suggests that she was gradually being exposed to more and more, so it would have to come from a consistent supply. Without medical attention, her symptoms would have worsened over time until she eventually succumbed to them."

"But you can't say specifically how much?"

"That's what I said. Did the line break up or did you need me to talk slower?"

Gareth gritted his teeth and took a deep breath. "No, all fine. I just wanted to double-check. Feels like we did all that work for nothing."

Oliver sighed. "Listen, with time and proper tests, I could find out exactly what quantity of the plant would produce the level of toxin I found in her blood, but this isn't my job." He groaned again. "I'm not an arse, I want this guy caught as much as the next person. I'll see what I can do. In the meantime, I'd say the key will be to find out how she was exposed to enough so gradually that she didn't feel the need to see a doctor. Once you know that, you might have a better shot at finding where and who it came from."

Gareth rubbed his eyes and ran a hand through his hair. "Okay. Thanks."

"Yeah. Just catch this bastard will you."

"Yup. Trying to," Gareth mumbled before hanging up. He shoved the notes he and Scott had made away from him, collapsed against his backrest, and threw his head back to stare at the white Artex ceiling. Through the closed door, he could hear the muffled bass of Scott's voice, and he closed his eyes, letting the comforting sound wash over him.

As his frustration began to ease, Gareth pulled his notepad closer and tapped his pen against his lips. How would they go about working out how Beth had been given the poison? They knew it had taken time and repeated exposure, meaning it was someone she saw regularly. Gareth flicked back to his original suspects list.

There were obviously people linked to Elevate. But there was no reason for Beth to let them get close enough for such a prolonged period of time. Even Tony Littlefair seemed to be uninvolved. He'd seemed pretty shocked when they'd spoken to him, and his unfamiliarity with Beth had seemed genuine. Aside from that, Gareth couldn't imagine Beth falling for someone who was as much of a mess as Tony had become since the fall of Elevate.

Gareth's eyes continued down the list and his eyes fell to Paul's name and he screwed up his face. Paul had clearly disliked his sister, but was that enough to kill her? And would he have been willing to spend the length of time with her it would have taken for the poison to take effect?

They'd ruled out Jake after none of the florists could identify him, but Gareth supposed he could have bought the flowers online – though he agreed with Scott that it seemed unlikely.

Thinking of Beth's affair brought Gareth's mind back to Marie – who'd first fed them the story. She and Beth often met up, so she could have poisoned Beth gradually and made up the affair as a way to redirect the attention of the investigation. But what would be the motive? Beth appeared to be one of Marie's only friends and means of support. He just couldn't see it being her. His frustration bubbled again. He tore through his notebook to find a blank page, but he wasn't sure what to write.

The muffled sounds of Scott's voice slowly grew louder. Gareth looked up from staring blankly at his pad just as Scott opened the door and let Mr. Collins out of the small office.

They approached Gareth's desk, and Scott requested a meeting for two weeks' time. Once everything was sorted, Scott shook hands with the middle-aged man and saw him out. As the door closed, Scott turned around with a frown on his face.

"Everything okay?" Gareth asked.

"Fine. Just feel like that might be a non-starter. Guy reckons his wife is cheating but couldn't give me anything to go on or any reason why he thought that."

"Sounds like insecurity to me. And maybe a slight control issue," Gareth replied, squashing the image of Liam that popped into his mind as he spoke.

Scott nodded. "Yeah, that's what I'm thinking."

He moved round to Gareth's side of the desk and perched on the edge. The old, cheap flatpack creaked and rocked slightly before Scott planted his feet on the floor and palms on the desk's surface. He grinned in triumph as the desk stopped moving. Gareth rolled his eyes but couldn't keep a soft smile from his face.

"How'd your call with Oliver go?"

The smile dropped from Gareth's face.

"That bad huh? Don't take it too personally. He's an arse."

Gareth started fiddling with his pen again and shook his head slowly. "It's not that. I've got tougher skin than that – I'm Welsh."

Scott laughed loudly, and Gareth smiled sadly. "No, he basically said that as little as five berries from the flower could cause a reaction, so really, we've been chasing our tails the whole fucking time we've been looking for the source. It could be any sale. Any."

"Shit," Scott groaned. "So we're back at square one."

"Yep," Gareth popped his 'p' and went back to staring at the ceiling. He racked his brain and tried to come up with some kind of next step. "We could try looking round Beth's house. See if we can work out how she took the poison. Speak to neighbours, see if they can tell us who visited her before she died."

"The police will already have been there," Scott grumbled.

"They might have missed something, though. If they weren't sure what they were looking for."

Scott nodded slowly. "It's possible. I'll try and speak to the super. See if I can pull some strings."

As he stood up to fish his mobile from his back pocket, the device started ringing.

"It's Alex," he muttered before accepting the call. "Hey, Al. Anything for us?"

"Scott, hey, it's Marcus," a soft male voice came through the speaker.

Gareth raised his eyebrow and leaned in closer to listen.

"Alex is in bed, I think the stress of all this is getting to her. They officially suspended her and arrested Jake yesterday."

"They what?!" Scott gasped. "On what evidence?"

"Apparently, they found out he'd been sleeping with that girl that was killed. But I don't know any more than that."

"Right. Well, could you tell her to call us when she's feeling up to it?"

"Well, that's why I'm calling. She's really unwell. I think the stress of all this is tougher on her than she'll let on – you know what she's like. She likes to be the strong one, in control, keeping everyone else safe. Anyway, I was really calling to ask that you don't get her involved anymore. For her sanity and career, I think it's best she stays as far away from this as possible."

"Right. Are you sure she'll be okay with that?"

Marcus chuckled dryly. "Probably not. But it's what's best for her. Don't worry, I'll look after her. You know I always take care of her." With that, Marcus hung up.

Scott looked between his phone and Gareth. "They've arrested Jake."

"Yeah, I heard. And now we can't speak to Alex to find out more."

Scott ran a hand over his face and groaned. "Well hopefully a few days' rest are all she needs."

Gareth nodded and continued to fiddle with his pen. His mind was whirring, and something gnawed at his gut. As much as he'd suspected Jake, they had found little to tie him to the case.

"What's in the diary for the rest of the day?" Scott asked.

"Nothing until Mrs. Jackson at three-thirty." Gareth sighed without even looking at his computer, his head tipped to the ceiling again, eyes roving the patterns in the Artex.

Scott grinned. "Come on, let's go to the police station, see what we can do." He hopped off the desk a little too vigorously. Gareth gripped the edge to stop it from wobbling. He rolled his eyes again, shook his head, and grabbed his coat before following Scott out of the office.

Chapter Thirty-three

Scott pulled his car into a parking space and glanced at his companion. Gareth had been fidgeting for the entire car journey. He was now fiddling with the cuff of his jacket for the umpteenth time and staring straight out of the windscreen.

"You okay?" Scott asked.

Gareth nodded but continued to fiddle. Scott watched him closely, the cogs in his head turning as he tried to get a grip on what was playing on Gareth's mind. The pieces clicked into place, and he reached across the car and placed a calming hand on Gareth's to hold them still.

"It brings back memories, right?"

Gareth bit his lip and nodded again. "Sorry," he whispered.

"Hey, hey. Nothing to be sorry for. I can speak to Derek myself, you don't need to come in."

Gareth twisted his wrist to squeeze Scott's hand. "No, I'm fine. Just needed a minute." He looked up, gave Scott a small, watery-eyed smile, took a deep breath, and nodded more confidently. "Let's go."

They hopped out of the car, and Scott slipped around to give Gareth's hand a final squeeze before leading the way across the car park. Gareth followed close behind, his hands thrust deep into his pockets and his eyes focused on the ground, watching each step he made with precision focus. He let the gentle slap of his shoes on the damp tarmac ground him and provide a distraction from the memories that were threatening to overwhelm his mind. With any luck, this visit would be more successful than the last time he'd been in a police station.

Scott glanced over his shoulder and gave a slight nod to Gareth as he reached the entrance. When Gareth returned the nod, Scott pushed inside and approached the front desk with his usual brash confidence.

"Scott Parmer, here to see Superintendent Price."

"Is he expecting you?" The desk sergeant asked.

"Not exactly, but he'll see me." Scott grinned as Gareth rolled his eyes behind him and the desk sergeant stifled a giggle before straightening her face and picking up the phone.

Scott rocked on his feet and shot Gareth a quick wink.

"He'll be down in a tick," the desk sergeant told them, gesturing toward the seating area.

Scott flashed her his best Hollywood smile and settled into a plastic chair at the side of the room.

Gareth took the chair next to him and leaned in to mutter in Scott's ear, "He must really owe you one to just come down like that."

Scott chuckled and muttered, "Sort of, but he also knows I'll kick up a fuss if he doesn't see me."

Gareth mock gasped. "You? Make a fuss?"

Scott laughed loudly, and the officers behind the desk shot them a stern look. He ignored them and nudged Gareth playfully. "Feeling better?"

Gareth nodded, but continued to fidget in his seat. Scott gave him a reassuring smile before leaning back in his chair in the hope that if he relaxed, Gareth would too. He began humming absentmindedly and smiled internally when he caught Gareth smirking.

Gareth watched Scott from the corner of his eye, trying to work out what he was humming but eventually giving up. He was just about to ask when the door behind the reception opened, and a portly man with thinning sandy hair and a thick moustache stepped in.

Scott stood up immediately and offered an outstretched hand and megawatt grin. "Derek! Good to see you again. Looks like you've lost some weight, you been working out?"

Gareth wasn't sure how, but he avoided rolling his eyes.

Derek Price chuckled and shook his round head, whisps of blond air waving as he did. "Nice try, Parmer, but I'm not going to be flattered into releasing your fuck buddy for you."

Gareth's eyebrows shot up his forehead, not just at the superintendent's choice of words but also at the fact that Scott was blushing for the first time since they'd met. And here, he'd thought Scott was unflappable. The desk sergeant giggled and snorted, which made Derek smile even more. The smile dropped suddenly as he, too, caught sight of Scott's discomfort.

"Oh Jesus. That is why you're here isn't it. Surely not? Really?"

Scott shook himself and straightened his back. "Not exactly. We had a few things we wanted to ask you. Is there somewhere private we can talk?"

"We?" Derek moved his attention to Gareth for the first time. Scott stood to the side to let the young man step closer.

"This is my new assistant, Mr. Gareth Hughes. We've been looking into the murder of Beth O'Neil."

"Pleased to meet you, Sir," Gareth smiled politely.

Derek ignored him and smirked at Scott. "Of course you have. Alright, let's hear what you have to say. In here."

He led Scott and Gareth into a small side room with low, bobbly, blue cushioned chairs that reminded Gareth of a college common room, and a low coffee table.

Derek dropped into one chair and motioned for Scott and Gareth to do the same. He leaned back, folded his arms and lifted an eyebrow as he waited for Scott to speak.

"Right, I'll get straight to it. We want a look inside Beth's house," Scott said.

"We already checked the house. It was clean. Too clean. Seems our killer was quite keen to remove all traces of themselves from the house. There's nothing for you to find. Besides, we've already made an arrest – as you know."

"An arrest based on purely circumstantial evidence that won't hold up. Come on, Derek. Humour me." Scott smiled. "I've helped you out enough times, it's about time I cashed in a favour. You never know, two fresh sets of eyes might just help."

Derek shook his head and sighed. "Scott, look, you know we value you as an investigator; we do. You've helped us plenty of times, and we acknowledge that. But I can't help but feel you're letting your somewhat personal connection to our primary suspect cloud your judgement. I know the two of you fell out, and maybe this is your way of getting back in his good books. But we have good reason to believe Jake did this."

Scott laughed. "Derek, believe me, I'm not doing any of this to win Jake back. That ship sailed a long time ago."

Derek caught sight of Gareth's blossoming blush and clucked his tongue.

Frustrated by the superintendent's stubbornness, Gareth

leaned forward. "With respect, sir. Jake was on my prime suspect list for a while too. But nothing we've found definitely ties him to Beth's murder. Surely we have to take another look at the house with an open mind."

Derek rolled his eyes and leaned forward. "We have several neighbours who've identified Jake as having frequently visited and stayed the night at Miss O'Neil's home. And his DNA matched a sample we found in her laundry basket."

"All that proves is that he slept with her, not that he killed her," Gareth reaffirmed. "We couldn't link him to any potential source of the poison that killed Beth."

"Maybe you just haven't found it yet," Derek defended as he narrowed his eyes.

"Neither have you," Gareth huffed.

Scott held up his hands. "Regardless, if we look around the house and speak to the neighbours, we could hit something you missed in that initial investigation when you didn't know what you were looking for."

He took a deep breath and scooted to the edge of his seat, reaching out to rest a hand on the coffee table. "You and I both know that if Jake goes down for this, Alex is going down with him. Whether she's implicated or not, her reputation will be destroyed. She'll be guilty by association. Do you really want to risk one of the best tech investigators you have on – at best – circumstantial evidence?"

Gareth smirked as he watched Scott argue their case and the superintendent deflate at his words. There was a long pause. Gareth held his breath, and Scott locked an intense stare on Derek. The phone on reception rang through the stud wall, and life in the station continued to tick by, even while it felt to Gareth as if time stood still in their little side room.

Eventually, after what felt like an eternity, Derek collapsed against his chair and pressed the heel of his hands into his eyes with a loud groan. "Okay, fine. I'll make some calls, let the team know you're heading down there. But you'll have one of my guys with you at all times. All eyes are on us with this one, Scott. I can't risk things being cocked up by you and your assistant."

Derek used his fingers to signal air quotations as he said the word 'assistant' and gave Gareth a sideways look.

Gareth sat on his hands, and his fingers gripped at the bobbly upholstery to prevent them from making an obscene gesture in Derek's direction.

Scott nodded firmly and stood. "We'll head straight over."

Derek closed his eyes, frowned, and waved them out. They were just about to open the door when he called, "Parmer, listen. I don't want to see one of my best officers dragged through the mud on this one. But if we find out DI Scullon did do this, we can't let him get away with it. No matter what that means for Alex."

Scott nodded; a frown now etched into his face too. He clapped Gareth on the shoulder, signalling him to open the door, and they left quickly. All three men suddenly felt heavier than they had just half an hour before. The pressure was on.

Chapter Thirty-four

It still managed to surprise Scott how strong the draw of death was. Like flies to shit, spectators were still buzzing around the now-empty house on Garden Crescent. The usual suspects were there: the greasy-haired teenagers dressed in black, ripped clothing, eager to get a whiff of death; the 'shocked' suburban neighbours who couldn't believe something like this could happen in such a lovely area; the mothers who feared for the safety of their young ones, and yet most of them brought their kids with them. They all lingered, desperate for gossip despite the time that had passed.

To avoid walking through the hordes of spectators and press mobs, Scott circled to the second entrance to the crescent street and parked his car far enough away that they wouldn't draw attention to themselves.

Thankfully, Gareth had felt much calmer on this trip than he had on their ride to the station. Instead of fidgeting, he'd spent this trip furiously scribbling in his notebook. He tapped his chin with the end of his pen a few times before he realised Scott was watching him. He closed his notebook and smiled sheepishly.

"What've you been scribbling down?" Scott asked.

"Just a couple of notes to myself. Things to keep an eye out for, questions to ask the neighbours, stuff we can try and ask whoever Price has asked to babysit us." Gareth shrugged.

Scott nodded. "Sounds good. You ready?"

Gareth looked down the street and took in the front of the house. The exterior had been updated compared to the others on the road. An attempt had been made to paint the flaking wooden panels below the first-floor window, and where other houses had ageing wooden doors, Beth's home had a bright white uPVC structure. Personally, Gareth preferred the older doors. They gave the houses a sort of rustic charm. The plastic looked cheap and tacky, but he could understand the appeal. He, too, had recently opted for sturdiness over rustic charm. Not that it had helped Beth in the end.

He dragged his gaze further up the street and began taking in the groups of spectators and reporters hiding out in their vans. He hesitated at the sight of the television cameras, and a shiver ran down his spine. Thoughts of his location being given away on national television flashed in his mind and panic rose in his throat like bile.

Scott reached over and squeezed his knee. "They probably won't bother with us. They're not likely to know who we are so we should be able to slip inside before they're able to try and ask us anything."

"And when we come back out?"

Scott shrugged. "I'll block you from the cameras. No one will see you."

Gareth took a deep breath and nodded. They burst from the car and strode towards the house.

A row of officers stood at the blue and white tape surrounding the house. The one closest to them recognised Scott and lifted the tape to allow them in. Where, as Scott predicted, they were able to slip inside just as the reporters began to swarm.

Inside the entry hall, the two men found a squarely built, middle-aged man with a bald, sweaty head and a grimace that seemed to be permanently etched into his face.

"Here to bail out your boyfriend, eh Parmer?" the detective grunted.

"No Andy, just here to work out if we can aid the investigation any and spot anything you boys might have missed when you were busy trying to find facts to support a theory, rather than taking everything in as it was," Scott sneered.

The detective – Andy – scoffed and lifted his chin in Gareth's direction. "Who's the suit?"

"My assistant. Price must have told you there were two of us coming," Scott grumbled.

Andy didn't answer. Instead, he stepped further down the hall and pointed to a small wooden shoe rack. "Shoe covers and gloves are on there. Grab yourself a set each, and we'll walk around."

Scott grabbed the items and handed Gareth a set. He mouthed an apology and Gareth waved him away. He was pulling on his second glove when Scott pointed at the shoe rack. "Did you guys move any shoes from here?"

"Obviously not," Andy snapped. "There were loads of empty gaps around the house when we searched it. Reckon Scullon quickly grabbed anything he'd left on view and took it with him when he left to try and keep us from figuring out what he'd been up to."

Scott pursed his lips but nodded in agreement. They knew that much was true from what Jake had told Scott when he'd been round to question him. Still didn't make him the killer, though, Gareth reminded himself.

"The place still stinks of bleach," Gareth noted. "I like a good clean, but this place must have been soaked in it for it to still smell this much."

"Like I said," Andy snapped again, "Scullon really didn't want us to know he'd been here. Even doctored his reports to say he'd been checking in over the phone rather than in person, but neighbours said they'd seen him here plenty of times. Last time was the night we reckon she died."

Gareth and Scott nodded. What Andy said added to what Jake had told them, and while it looked suspicious, it didn't technically prove anything. Still, it wasn't looking good for Jake.

"She was found in the upstairs bathroom, right?" Scott clarified.

"Yeah, we assumed it was an overdose at first, you know. Guessed the pressure of testifying and fear she'd be found by someone from Elevate got the better of her. That was until we got the autopsy report anyway."

"You sent anything for testing to see where she could have encountered the poison?" Gareth asked.

Andy folded his arms and scowled. "Obviously. A mug we found unwashed by her bed, bottles of juice, and some salads from the fridge. Results aren't back yet."

Gareth nodded thoughtfully, and they followed the detective through a doorway on the left. Immediately, his nose started burning as the thick smell of cleaning products got stronger. The walls in Beth's open-plan kitchen-living area were the same crisp beige as the hallway, and everything was spotless – not a speck of grime in sight. In the centre of the room was a light wood dining table that separated the bright white kitchen from the soft, cosy living room. Gareth looked around in shock.

A part of him had expected the house to feel cold, as though death was still clinging to every surface. Instead, it merely felt as though the owner had gone on holiday. If it wasn't for the stench of bleach and the presence of a grumpy detective, you'd be hard-pressed to believe anything untoward had happened here.

His eyes scanned the room, and he was aware of Scott doing the same thing. Nothing seemed out of place, which gave Gareth an awkward feeling. How had the police not disturbed everything when they initially searched the property? Then he remembered Andy's comments in the hall. They'd thought it was an overdose; they weren't considering it a murder until they got the autopsy report several days later. By then, rumours would have already been circulating about the circumstances of Beth's witness statement and Jake Scullon's relationship with her. The whole thing had become a pretty open-and-shut case in the eyes of many. The property looked untouched because it probably was. He caught Scott's eyes and knew they were thinking the same thing.

"Did you guys want to look at anything in particular or were you just hoping something would jump out at you?" Andy sneered from the doorway.

"Just trying to take in the bigger picture," Scott replied before turning a small, sideways smile in the detective's direction. "You just stand there and take notes, Andy. You never know, you might learn a thing or two."

Gareth chuckled and received a glare from the detective, which only served to feed his humour.

Scott turned to him and smiled broadly. "You want to take the living room or the kitchen?"

"Decisions, decisions," Gareth mused. "I'll go root through

the kitchen cupboards."

He moved away and left Scott to rifle through the living room. He looked back and watched for a moment as Scott bent over the beige, two-seater sofa and began running his hands between all the cushions. A blush blazed on his cheeks as he caught the detective watching him watching Scott a little too closely. He turned sheepishly towards the cupboards and pulled open the one nearest to him. He scanned the contents – several small cereal bowls, side plates, and serving dishes were crammed in haphazardly, and Gareth smiled. Despite keeping a neat home, it seemed Beth followed the mindset of out of sight, out of mind. It didn't need the same care and attention if it was hidden away. Sometimes he wished he was more like that.

Over the next half hour, he made his way strategically through the cupboards that lined the back wall of Beth's kitchen. The further along he got, the less hopeful he began to feel. So far, he'd found nothing unusual, and Scott had been equally quiet on his side of the room, suggesting he'd found nothing. With a heavy sigh, Gareth pulled open the small cupboard above the sink. His breath immediately caught in his throat.

He froze as he stared at the small, lemon-yellow box on the bottom shelf. On the front was a pale green logo depicting entwining herbs and flowers. He knew that logo. His heart hammered in his chest, and a lump formed in his throat, preventing him from calling Scott. His hand trembled as he reached into his back pocket and pulled out his small pad. With shaking fingers, he flicked through the pages and pulled out the small yellow business card he'd tucked in there just the other day. He laid the card on the counter and pulled down the box to sit them side by side. They were definitely a match.

The top of the box was labelled 'Chamomile and Lavender – Calming Tea'.

Gareth slowly lifted the cardboard lid and stared at the teabags inside. They looked just like any other herbal teabag he'd ever seen. But the smell that reached him through the stench of bleach wasn't the familiar soothing scent of lavender or chamomile. It was a spicy yet creamy smell that he couldn't place but one that he could guess. He looked back at the shelf and spotted a stray piece of lemon paper lying where the box had been. He pulled it down and read the hand-written message on the page:

Beth,

Thanks for your support and eagerness to help taste-test our newest products. Hopefully, this calming blend is as much of a help to you as you have been to me.

M

Gareth finally shook himself, found his voice, and called out to Scott.

"I think I've got something."

In seconds, both Scott and Andy were around him. He grabbed his copy of the business card and used it to point to the box of tea bags.

"These are from that shop we went to yesterday. The one where the woman said they were branching out, remember?"

Scott nodded. "But she made it sound like it was early days still. She didn't seem to think they were selling products yet."

"I don't think they are," Gareth panted, lifting the note for the others to see. "It sounds like she signed up for updates and offered to taste-test the products before they became available."

"We need to get back over to Blooming Lovely," Scott said firmly as he squeezed Gareth's arm. "You did good. Andy, you need to take a sample of these back and get them tested ASAP."

Andy's eyes were bulging from his head, and his mouth opened and closed like a fish as he tried to take in what was happening. He nodded and held out a hand for Gareth to pass the tea box to him. Wordlessly, he followed Gareth and Scott out of the house, stopping only to alert the uniformed officers watching the building as to what was happening.

Gareth and Scott raced down the front yard and towards their car at such a speed that the press had no chance of catching up to them. Tyres screeched, and the ancient gearbox of Scott's battered car screamed into life as he raced towards Blooming Lovely. They were on their way before Gareth had even had a chance to buckle himself in.

"I'll tell Mrs. Jackson we need to rearrange her three-thirty appointment," Gareth panted.

Chapter Thirty-five

Alex rolled onto her side and curled into a foetal position as her stomach clenched and twisted again. She scrunched her eyes and buried her head in her sweat-soaked pillow. She'd first felt off the night before and assumed her body had finally caved to the stress she'd put it under by working and worrying so much. Marcus had, surprisingly, been exceptionally attentive and hadn't once gloated. He'd lain down and stroked her inky dark hair when she needed soothing. When she'd been too shaky to get to the bathroom, he'd fetched her a bowl and held her hair back as she vomited. The circumstances were crap, but she couldn't remember a time when they'd been this close and connected since their university days. Before they got married even. Once she'd achieved her dream of getting into the police force, she'd become obsessed with keeping hold of that dream. It was only now, as she lay spasming on her side, that she realised just how close she had come to losing everything else by being so tunnel-visioned.

The bedroom door hissed against the cream carpet as Marcus entered. Alex rolled her head to look at him and tried to offer a smile before her stomach turned again. He placed a glass of water on her bedside table and knelt by the side of the bed.

"Still feeling rough?" he asked as he smoothed her clammy

hair.

Unable to talk without risking another vomit purge, Alex nodded.

Marcus pouted at her before pressing a kiss to her forehead. "Wait here," he whispered. "I'll go grab a book to read to distract you and when you start to feel a bit less sick, I'll make you a herbal tea for your nerves."

He disappeared back into the living room. The seconds dragged past in a steady string of sweats, stomach cramps, and heart palpitations. Alex tried to groan in pain but felt too weak to vocalise her discomfort. If she wasn't so dehydrated, she could cry. She'd never been so ill – at least not that she could remember. If she didn't start to improve in the next twenty-four hours, she'd see a doctor. Another heart palpitation rattled her chest, caught her breath, and sent her stomach rolling. She tossed and turned, but that made her feel worse.

Marcus returned with a dog-eared copy of *Northern Lights* – a long-standing comfort read for both of them. They'd been to see the movie adaptation on a date back in the day and had been bitterly disappointed. He settled next to her on the bed, and she rolled to nestle as close as was comfortable.

Marcus smiled and stroked her head. "You know, as shit as all this is, at least it's finally given us the time to be together. And we're not bickering. You know that's all I ever wanted, right? Us, together. And for you to realise that you need me just as much as I need you."

Alex lay still, cuddled into his side. Her head felt so fuzzy that his words didn't register. All she heard was the soft, low tone he used. She closed her eyes and let his voice wash over her as another wave of stomach cramps and heart palpitations hit.

Chapter Thirty-six

Gareth gripped the overhead handle, and his shoulder slammed into the side of the car. Again.

Scott gripped the steering wheel so hard that his knuckles had turned white. The engine screamed as Scott pushed it to its limit. The chassis rattled around them, and Gareth wasn't sure they'd make it to Blooming Lovely in one piece. His mind conjured up images of them pulling up in just a frame on wheels. Thankfully, the shop wasn't too far from Beth's home, so Scott's rusty old car didn't have to endure the torture for too long. It was certainly close enough that Beth would have known about its existence. Possibly even frequented the shop on trips to the town's high street. They screeched to a stop outside Blooming Lovely. Scott cranked his handbrake on and ripped his keys from the ignition. Together they leapt from the car and raced into the shop. The well-dressed older woman they'd met the other day gasped as they thundered through the door. A hand flew to her chest as she jumped.

"Goodness, you boys almost scared me to death. What on earth's going on?"

"We need to check a few extra things with you," Scott panted. "Did you find that list of people who'd registered an interest in the herbalism business?"

The woman smoothed the front of her plumb jacket and straightened her glasses. "I did. I stumbled on it earlier."

"Can we see it?" Scott pushed.

The former owner of Blooming Lovely hesitated. Her eyes darted between the two men in front of her, sizing them up and considering her position.

"I don't know. I'm not sure I should be giving out contact information. There are so many rules around that sort of thing now," she responded, unsteady and unsure.

Gareth stepped forward and placed a hand on the counter in what he hoped was a reassuring gesture. "We understand. But there's a chance the product batch for customer testing was contaminated. One woman is already dead. We need to make sure we can warn others that they may be in danger."

"That's not possible. The products aren't ready yet," the woman insisted.

"We don't think that's the case," Gareth said firmly. "We found a box of tea with Blooming Lovely's branding in the kitchen of a woman poisoned by lily of the valley."

The woman opened and closed her mouth and blinked several times before speaking, "But he doesn't stock lily of the valley."

"You're absolutely sure about that?" Scott pushed.

The woman gaped again and looked between the two men. She sighed heavily, and her shoulders drooped. "I did find a recent order for it in the system when I was trying to sort the daily takings. But I didn't call you because I couldn't find any in the stock room and there were no sales receipts for it, so I assumed Marcus cancelled the order and forgot to update the system. He's had a lot going on, you know? Trying to grow the business and fix his marriage, though," she huffed, "I don't know why he bothers. That wife of his doesn't deserve him.

Always puts herself and her work before anything. Even poor Marcus."

Gareth felt a chill run down his spine as something exploded in his mind. Marcus. It wasn't an uncommon name, he supposed. But a Marcus who ran his own business. A Marcus who liked to be in control. A Marcus experiencing problems with a career-driven wife. Surely that was too many coincidences to go unnoticed. Gareth swallowed and glanced at his partner. Scott's eyes were wide as he connected the dots and panic for his friend hit.

"Is Marcus coming in today? Can we speak to him?" Gareth asked, silently wishing he could reach out and place a reassuring hand on his lover's arm. Pain and worry were etched on Scott's face as his mouth moved silently.

The former owner of Blooming Lovely shook her head, and the tiny droplet earrings she wore swung against her jaw. "No, he's at home. That's why I'm here again. His wife's really sick at the moment. Stress, I'd imagine, from the amount she works. Honestly, Marcus is beyond devoted to that woman and I can't say she deserves it. Always prioritising work over everything and everyone."

Scott's face went bright red, and Gareth finally broke free of his self-restraint. He reached out and gripped Scott's arm giving his lover a reassuring squeeze, while the stern look on his face warned Scott to keep it together.

"Go outside, call an ambulance, and get them to go to Alex's. Then call Andy. Tell him we've found the source and that we need officers to search the shop," Gareth said in a low, calming voice.

The elderly woman tutted. "I already told you. The plant isn't here. And even if it was, it couldn't have gotten into the teas. They're not made on premises. Marcus didn't want to risk it."

Gareth rolled his eyes. If he wasn't careful, it wouldn't be Scott that exploded. He gritted his teeth and seethed. "Where was he having the tea made?"

"I don't know. I just help out at the shop," the elderly woman spluttered. She looked to the sky and took a shaky breath. "He mentioned a facility in Liverpool he was looking at renting. A tiny place so he could still keep an overview. He was very concerned about cross-contamination."

"I bet he was," Scott growled.

"Can we get the police to search for rentals in Marcus's name?" Gareth asked.

"I don't even know his surname," Scott groaned, wishing he'd been a better friend and asked more questions instead of letting Alex solve all his problems and support him without asking anything in return. "Alex didn't take his or vice versa. It was simpler."

"Cooper," the woman offered. "Look, if something has gone wrong, Marcus wouldn't have meant any harm. All he wants to do is care for people."

Scott pulled out his phone and began dialling. "Gareth we need to get to Alex." Without looking back, Scott fled the shop.

Gareth gave a curt nod and quickly thanked the former owner for her help – even if she hadn't been as forthcoming as they would have liked.

"Wait," she called. "Don't forget this."

With a shaky hand, she held out a piece of headed paper. Gareth skimmed the list of names in front of him, and there she was. Right at the top. Beth O'Neil. He quickly dove out of the shop and followed Scott to the car, bracing himself for another bruising drive. He could only hope they were barking up the wrong tree. For Alex's sake and Scott's.

Chapter Thirty-seven

The green SUV in front hadn't noticed the traffic light change, and Scott growled and smashed his horn in frustration.

"If I'd gone into the fucking force instead of being a stubborn ass and going private, then I could at least use the blues and twos to get there faster."

He swerved to overtake before immediately swerving back to avoid oncoming traffic. Cursing again, he glanced across at his partner. A double take revealed that Gareth was utterly oblivious to what was happening around him. Once again, Gareth was blankly staring out of the windscreen and fiddling with the edges of his clothing.

As if he realised he was being watched, Gareth sighed, blinked, and turned his head to look at Scott.

"I should have picked up on something sooner."

Scott blinked and shook his head. "We might not be right. And even if we are, there's no way you – or I for that matter – could have worked this out sooner..."

"I should have seen there was something off in their relationship," Gareth interrupted. "What good is going through everything I went through with Liam if I can't use it to stop the same thing happening to others?"

Scott tightened his grip on the steering wheel and shifted in his seat. "I think you're too hard on yourself. You hardly know them."

"I knew about the incessant calling. The unhappiness. That last call from Marcus. It screamed of control. And I was blind to it. Again."

"What about me? I saw all that plus several years more. Besides," Scott sighed as he pulled off from another traffic light and began to accelerate. "I made that comment about you projecting your past onto this case. I probably subconsciously put it in your head to not think of things in that way."

Gareth frowned momentarily before leaning across the car's middle console, pressed a light peck to Scott's cheek and left his hand resting on Scott's upper thigh.

"We might have completely the wrong end of the stick, Scott."

"Hmmm," Scott bit his lip and nodded. "And if we haven't, at least the emergency services are on their way. With any luck they beat us there."

Gareth gave Scott's thigh a tight squeeze and sat silently watching his partner speed through the streets – his face a picture of despair and desperation. Gareth's heart broke. However guilty he felt over not spotting the red flags surrounding Alex and Marcus, he knew Scott was feeling it tenfold. He kept his hand planted on Scott's thigh and hoped that at least some comfort passed to Scott through the small action. As he became aware he was staring, he turned to watch the streets fly past them but kept his hand resting firmly in place. The rest of the journey took no more than five minutes, but for Gareth and Scott, the roads seemed to stretch out for hours.

Alex's flat was on the outskirts of the city centre, worlds

away from Gareth's inner-city block. The underground car park was full of mid- to high-end hatchbacks and family cars, and Gareth had seen a young mother leading her smiling, well-dressed toddler through the front door as they pulled up.

"Doesn't look like the emergency services are here," he panicked as they abandoned the car and raced for the front door.

"We can't risk waiting for them," Scott groaned as he dragged a hand through his hair. He glanced down the street in both directions but there was no sign or sound of the emergency services. Gareth watched as Scott's last shred of patience visibly evaporated from his body. He jabbed at the intercom for Alex's flat and waited.

Chapter Thirty-eight

Alex opened her eyes and rolled over, relieved when for the first time in almost twenty-four hours, her stomach didn't churn. The slapping sound of water hitting the floor and trickling down the screen in the en-suite told her Marcus had hopped in the shower. He'd probably been itching to wash away the germs she'd passed on.

She pushed herself to sit up for the first time in almost a day. She smiled when the movement didn't send her lurching for the nearest receptacle to hurl up the contents of her already empty stomach. Slowly, she swung her legs over the side of the bed and wiggled her toes in the carpet's fibres. Desperate for information, she managed to stand, a hand planted on the bedside table for support. She'd left her phone on the coffee table last night. If she could make it to the sofa, she could drop Scott a message and then snuggle up and watch films until she felt better. Her legs shook as she took unsteady steps to the bedroom door. She leaned against the doorframe to gather her strength as she tried to estimate how many steps it was to the sofa. Ten? Fifteen? She'd have to make most of it with no support too. She took a deep breath and pushed away from the door frame, the momentum carrying her some of the distance. She swayed before stumbling the last few steps towards the sofa and collapsing against the arm. The corner of their modern, square sofa dug into her hips, and she found herself once again lamenting Marcus's preference for style and appearance over comfort. Another groan escaped her lips as her eyes fell on the coffee table. Her phone wasn't there. She lowered her head and gritted her teeth as her heart fluttered again. Damnit. She needed her phone. She needed to message Scott and call her doctor. As her heart rate stabilised, she raised her head and scanned the room, finally spotting her mobile lying by Marcus's laptop on their small white dining table. She took a deep breath, straightened her body, and shuffled around the sofa. When she reached the opposite end of the sofa, she counted how many unsupported steps she'd need to get to the dining area. Another ten, maybe? She could do another ten.

"What are you doing?" Marcus's voice broke through her thoughts, and she jolted in shock. She turned to face the bedroom door. Marcus stood in his jogging bottoms and university hoodie. His hair was still damp from the shower but not so wet that it dripped. He'd never risk dripping anything on the pristine carpet – not even water.

"Jesus, M. You scared me. I didn't hear you get out of the shower," Alex breathed.

"Why are you out of bed?" Marcus asked as he stepped towards her.

"I was feeling better, so I decided to grab my phone and see if I could get an update on the case from anyone."

Marcus sighed, and his shoulders dropped. "I called Scott earlier and told him not to bother you for a few days. Just until you felt better."

"Well, I am feeling better," Alex said firmly as she folded her arms and tried to stand still and straight.

"Al, you can barely stand. Just sit on the sofa. I'll make you a nice tea."

"I just want to check in with Scott," Alex pleaded. "I need to..."

"What you need is to listen to me for once in your life," Marcus snapped. "Now, sit down and..."

"And what?" Alex cried. "Be a good little wife? Do as I'm told? Give you my undivided attention?" She gasped for breath and collapsed further into the back of the sofa. Every muscle in her body screamed, and her bones felt like jelly. But she refused to sit down. She gathered herself and pushed off the sofa, the momentum carrying her to the dining table.

In an instant, Marcus was by her side. He snatched up the phone and grabbed her upper arms. His fingers dug into the tender flesh beneath her soft cotton pyjamas, and she cried out in shock.

"You're so skittish, Al. Just sit down. I'll make you a tea to calm your nerves." He steered her back to the sofa and dropped her into the seat. Her head spun again, and she pulled her feet underneath her. She couldn't fight anymore. Tears pricked her eyes. God, she hated being so weak. So helpless.

Minutes later, Marcus returned and handed her a small porcelain cup of warm, flowery-smelling tea. She thanked him quietly and took several greedy slurps. She hadn't realised how thirsty she was. Before she knew it, she'd drunk the entire cup. She placed it gently on the coffee table and glanced over to find Marcus staring at her.

"What?" she asked.

Marcus shook his head and sighed. He leaned back into the corner of the sofa and locked his eyes on her.

"Everything I've done for you. It's never enough, is it?

There's always someone or something that means more to you than I do."

Alex shook her head and went to question what he meant, but her stomach rolled, and she heaved. She closed her eyes as her stomach clenched and she felt rather than saw Marcus leave the sofa. As she retched again, he returned and placed the washing-up bowl in front of her.

"Even now. Here I am, taking care of you in your hour of need and you still can't bear to give me the time of day," Marcus sighed. "I really did try everything, Al. I read all the advice columns and self-help books. I thought, if I could just be the best version of myself, you'd be happy. But it wasn't enough. I tried talking to you about taking a step back from work and you flipped. Every time."

He slid closer and smoothed her hair as she heaved into the bowl again.

"And then, just when I thought we were out of options, who walks into my shop and enquires about the herbalism business, but Ms. O'Neil. I recognised her from the files and photos you brought home. You know you really should leave those at the station – no telling who might catch a glimpse of them otherwise. I knew this case, the biggest case of your career, you'd said, would fall apart without her. And then, to top it all off, Scullon went and slept with her and put himself in the frame. That I didn't see coming, but it sure helped. I thought then, surely now, she'll take a step back. Your career-making case in tatters. Betrayed by the partner you adored. Isolated by your colleagues. But no. You still couldn't walk away. You went to another man to help the partner you thought had betrayed you." He sighed again and pressed a kiss to her sweaty head. She felt her body stiffen as he spoke. But her stomach rolled too much for her to pull away.

"I never wanted it to go this far, Al," he whispered into her hair as he tightened his grip on her. "All I ever wanted was for us to be together. And now we are. I'll take care of you, I promise."

The intercom buzzed suddenly, making both of them jump and popping the bubble around them. Marcus stroked her back as she shook and vomited again, but his eyes were now firmly fixed on the front door.

"They'll go away soon," he whispered. "Then it'll just be the two of us again. Just how it's meant to be."

The intercom buzzed again. And again. Marcus began to tremble. He staggered over to the receiver on unsteady legs, leaving Alex slumped, barely conscious, on the sofa. He watched the front door camera in panic as he saw the large frame of Scott Parmer and a lithe young man push through the door as it was left open by a departing resident.

He leapt into action – sprinted across the room, and shoved his hands under Alex's armpits.

"Come on, love," he muttered in her ear. "Let's get you to bed."

He began to haul her into the bedroom, trying to keep ahead of the thundering footsteps on the stairwell. He pulled her through the doorway just as Scott pounded on the front door and yelled to be let in.

Alex tried to call back, but her voice wouldn't obey. Her entire body felt as though it was shutting down. She couldn't make anything work the way she wanted.

"It's alright, baby. I'll get rid of them," Marcus grunted as he dragged her the final few steps and dropped her onto the bed. He'd just pulled the bedroom door closed as the front door burst open.

Chapter Thirty-nine

Now fraught with panic and out of patience, Gareth bounded up the stairs after Scott, who wasted no time barging through the door to Alex's flat. The door splintered beneath his shoulder, and he tumbled into the open-plan flat. Gareth stood behind him and watched with admiration and just a little too much lust at the display of strength. An image of those strong shoulders lifting him as he was pressed against the nearest flat surface flashed in his mind. Definitely not the time or the place. He shook himself and followed Scott into the room, quickly sweeping with his eyes to take in their surroundings. Like Beth's home, the flat was freakishly neat and tidy. Every surface was a slightly different shade of cream or white, with a few soft grey accents strewn about. He liked things clean, but this was something else, more like a show home than a lived-in space. Sterile was how Gareth would describe it in his notes later. Cold and sterile.

"What the hell are you doing?" Marcus snapped at the two men standing at the edge of his living room.

"Where's Alex?" Scott growled as he prowled into the living room.

"She's in bed," Marcus hissed. "I told you, she's not well. She's been vomiting all morning. She needs rest."

"And you're taking great care of her, I'm sure," Scott snarled at the weedy blond man in front of him. The air around his body seemed to ripple with a mix of fear and anger. His body shook, as if he was struggling to hold himself together.

Physically, Marcus wasn't much to look at. With his plain features and slight build, he didn't seem like he could pose a threat to anyone. But now he was backed into a corner, Gareth could see the feral need for control that blazed in Marcus's pale grey eyes. A look he was all too familiar with.

"The game's up, Marcus," he said. He gently laid a hand on Scott's arm, giving a soft squeeze. Scott's shaking calmed ever so slightly. "We've already linked your shop to Beth's murder, and we've got cops searching for your brewery and more on the way here. Whatever you've done, I know you don't want Alex hurt, so just let us get in there and check her out."

Marcus's eyes skipped from Scott's face to the young man who stood by the smashed front door. He took one last glance at the bedroom door behind him and sighed. His shoulders sagged, and he dropped his chin to his chest. Wordlessly, he stepped to the side and moved toward the kitchen, where he leaned against the glossy white island units.

Scott nodded firmly and glanced back at Gareth, who urged him along and gave a small smile to let him know he had the situation under control. He moved closer to the kitchen space, limiting Marcus's movements and keeping the wiry blond in sight at all times.

Relieved at the assured presence Gareth offered, Scott opened the door to the bedroom and slipped inside.

Alex lay on her side, facing away from the door. She stirred and groaned as she heard someone enter the room, but her eyes refused to open, and she couldn't work her muscles to roll over. Scott whimpered slightly at the state she was in and once again felt the guilt churn in his stomach that he hadn't picked up on Marcus's dangerous behaviour sooner.

He perched on the edge of the bed and pulled her closer. He rested her head against his chest and put the untouched glass of water on her bedside table to her lips, hoping it would help neutralise some of the poison already tearing through her body.

Alex scrunched her face and whimpered slightly as the cool glass touched her lips.

"It's okay," Scott whispered. "Gareth and I are here, and the police are on their way. You're going to be fine. We just need to get some water in you, okay? Flush out your system and keep you hydrated."

Slowly, Alex parted her lips and took a few sips of water. Scott praised her gently and rocked her from side to side once she'd curled up with another stomach cramp. He heard Gareth's deep Welsh accent through the partially closed door, and his ears pricked up. He glanced at the door and tried to listen to what was being said. He hadn't heard anyone else enter the flat, so he doubted reinforcements were here. He waited a few seconds, just in case it was the emergency services, but no paramedics came through to the bedroom, and he heard soft footsteps as the muttering got further away.

He squashed the panic that rose in his throat. Slowly, he slid off the bed and rested Alex against the pillows.

"I'll be right back, okay? I just have to check a few things. The paramedics will be here soon," he whispered.

Chapter Forty

Scott pulled the bedroom door closed behind him, and Gareth immediately snapped his full attention back to Marcus. For the first time, he could put an image with the name and voice he was already familiar with. Average height, slim – some would say, skinny – build. Sandy blond hair, pale eyebrows, and cold grey eyes. If they'd passed in the street, Gareth wouldn't have looked twice at him. He supposed that was what most people like Marcus used to their advantage. Men like Liam and Marcus always seemed to have the uncanny ability to blend in – to fit everywhere without really being part of anything. They weren't especially loved, but they were always well-liked. They were the type of people who, when asked about, you'd always say, "Yeah I know them. Quiet, but nice." That's how they get away with it for so long, he thought. No one suspects them because they just go about their business, smiling and saying polite things when necessary, without ever making a fuss. That was what made them monsters.

"You trying to size me up?" Marcus asked quietly, that soft voice Gareth had heard on the phone earlier breaking through his thoughts.

"Don't need to," Gareth told him bluntly. "I know enough about people like you already."

"Really?" Marcus asked, a grimace on his face. "Tell me, what do you know about 'people like me'."

Gareth shook his head and glanced down at the counter between them. There was no point in answering. He wasn't going to get sucked into a conversation with this lunatic. All he needed to do was keep him in sight until the police arrived.

"You don't know a thing," Marcus sneered. "Look at you. Boyish good looks and pleasant manners. Bet you have people like Parmer fawning over you all the time. You've always been able to get the attention you need and deserve. Whereas people like me, the average Joes of society, we have to adapt. Find new ways of standing out, of making sure we keep hold of the few treasures we find in life because people like you and Parmer are always lurking around the corner, ready to steal them away from us."

"There's nothing average about people like you," Gareth spat. "Average people don't knowingly try to control or poison the people they care about."

He regretted speaking as soon as the words left his mouth. He could feel Marcus's presence prickling under his skin and hoped the police would arrive quickly.

In the blink of an eye, Marcus pulled open the drawer he'd been leaning on and pulled out a long-bladed kitchen knife. *Right*, thought Gareth, *I should have seen that one coming*. He instinctively took a step back from the counter as Marcus rounded it, knife held in front of him. The blade glinted in the bright whiteness of the flat, reflecting light in all directions. Gareth's heart pounded in his ears, and he swallowed hard as he attempted to push down the fear rising in his throat like bile.

"I don't want to hurt you," Marcus whispered. "Just move

out the way and I'll leave quietly."

"What, so you can start again somewhere else? Find yourself someone else to control and poison? I don't think so," Gareth managed to keep his voice steady and low.

Marcus lunged forward, swiping with the knife. He wasn't close enough to make contact, but close enough that the threat felt very real. Gareth's nerves were heavy in the pit of his stomach, and he took several steps back, moving closer to the open front door. The floor creaked on the opposite side of the flat, drawing their attention towards the bedroom door as Scott stepped through. Gareth immediately held out an arm, telling Scott to stay where he was, that he had everything under control. The last thing he needed was for Scott to come blasting in and get hurt.

Marcus recovered from the distraction and raced forward. Scott cried out, and Gareth fell to the floor, sticking his legs out. There was a clatter as Marcus dropped the knife and tripped over Gareth's outstretched legs.

From his position on the opposite side of the room, Scott could see nothing but a tangle of limbs. He raced across the room and let out a shaky breath as he spotted the knife a foot away from the two men grappling on the floor. He grabbed the knife and moved it to the coffee table, safely out of the way. He was even more relieved to see up close that the blade was still clean. When he looked back around, Gareth had pinned Marcus to the floor with his hands behind his back.

A grin spread across Scott's face as he saw Gareth's flushed face. He dug his hand into the pocket of his coat and snapped a pair of handcuffs over Marcus's wrists.

"You carry those around all the time?" Gareth panted,

raising an eyebrow.

"Professional habit." Scott shrugged.

"Good to know." Gareth smirked.

Scott chuckled, adrenaline still coursing through his body. "Well, you just never know when they might come in handy..."

"Mmhmm, I can imagine." Gareth smiled.

"Oh, come on guys. Time and a place," Andy's voice sounded from the hallway as several other officers and two paramedics flooded the room.

Gareth blushed, his cheeks burning with embarrassment. The adrenaline must have gone to his head. A few weeks ago, he couldn't have imagined flirting with anyone, let alone flirting with his boss over a handcuffed suspect. He stood up, pulling a grumbling Marcus with him, and handed the suspect over to the detective.

"I'll need those cuffs back, Andy." Scott grinned and winked.

Gareth felt his blush darken a shade further. Andy shook his head, a faint blush now colouring his own cheeks. Gareth gave the detective what he hoped was a sympathetic look as he uncuffed Marcus and replaced Scott's pair with his own.

"We'll get him down to the station and get all this sorted," Andy said, clearing his throat. "Alex okay?" He asked nervously.

"She's fine," Marcus snapped.

"Wasn't asking you," Andy snapped back, giving the wiry blond man a shake.

"She was pretty out of it, but I managed to get her to drink some water," Scott informed him. "We'll follow them to the hospital and give you an update later if you want?"

Andy nodded. "Please. And let her know I'm sorry. We all

are."

With that, he instructed his officers to search the flat and collect any potential evidence – including Marcus's laptop. He started down the stairwell before stopping and calling, "Oh, Scott. Do you want me to get Scullon to give you a call when he's out?"

Scott laughed loudly. "No. Just tell him Alex is being taken care of. I'm sure he'll want to see her when he can."

Andy nodded with a cheeky smile as he pulled Marcus out of the flat. Once he was out of sight, Scott grabbed Gareth's hand and dragged him into a fierce hug.

"You okay?" He muttered into Gareth's dark hair.

"Yeah fine," Gareth breathed. Relief was flooding through his veins hot on the heels of the adrenaline rush.

"Where on earth did you learn to pin someone down like that?"

Gareth chuckled. "Saw it in a film once and did my best to imitate it."

"Course you did." Scott laughed back.

Gareth felt him tighten his grip and breathe deeply, grounding him once more. His heart rate settled and he wound his arms around Scott's waist, giving him a slight squeeze.

They finally pulled away as the paramedics came from the bedroom with Alex bundled onto a stretcher. Scott looked at them expectantly.

"We'll get her sorted, sir," said the older of the two paramedics. "She'll probably be out of it for several hours, but we can call you once she comes round."

Scott looked round at Gareth, who shook his head, knowing without speaking what each other was thinking.

"No, that's okay. We'll follow you to the hospital if that's okay. So she has someone with her when she wakes up."

The paramedics nodded and led the way out of the building. After a final glance around the sterile flat to ensure the officers had everything under control, Scott grabbed Gareth's hand and they left the building together.

Chapter Forty-one

Gareth thanked his driver and hopped out of the car, checking his watch for the millionth time. He didn't want to be late, but he absolutely did not want to be too early either. In fact, he wasn't actually sure which option was worse. Thankfully, he'd made it with five minutes to go to their agreed time, which didn't seem too early. He strode up the front path to Scott's terraced house and rang the doorbell.

In the weeks following Marcus's arrest, Scott had spent several nights at the hospital, trying to keep Alex company and reassure her that she was not at fault for what had happened. Gareth had stayed with him every time, and he and Alex bonded quickly over their experiences of control – although Gareth had been forced to concede that at least his ex hadn't snapped and turned to murder.

After several days in each other's non-stop company, Gareth and Scott had finally started referring to themselves as 'together'. As Scott had feared, the speed of their relationship did cause Gareth to have a slight wobble, as he feared his life was becoming too entwined with and indebted to Scott. In a rash attempt to alleviate some of Gareth's concerns, Scott worked on updating the Welshman's working contract to reflect the more investigative role he often undertook, hoping this would give him more security and reassure the young man that whatever happened, Scott recognised his potential as part of the team.

At first, Gareth had resisted that, too, questioning whether the changes were being done on merit or because he was shagging the boss. But after a few stern words from an exceptionally exhausted Faith reassuring him that he did far more than she ever had and seemed to have more of a talent for investigating than her, he eventually caved.

Now, they finally had a night to themselves. No ongoing surveillance to conduct and no struggling friends to keep company. Somehow, in all the chaos, Scott had finally finished reading *Ready Player One*, and they'd agreed that tonight they'd sit down and have the movie night they'd discussed over a month ago.

He rocked on his heels as he waited, more out of habit than nerves now. He remembered the first time he'd been to Scott's and chuckled. He'd been so nervous he'd paced up and down the front path several times, not realising Scott had been watching him from the upstairs window the whole time. He glanced up at the window in question and smirked as memories of that night flooded his mind. He'd made sure Scott gave that window a wide berth when he'd found out.

Scott opened the door and grinned as he greeted him with a quick kiss.

"Come on through," he said. "I'm just dishing everything out."

"You haven't gone to too much trouble, have you?" Gareth warned.

"Just the essentials for a movie night," Scott called as he moved down the hallway, tight jeans framing his arse perfectly as he did so. "Pizza, popcorn, soda."

Gareth smirked. He wasn't sure he'd ever get used to Scott's Americanisms.

"Sounds perfect," he smiled as he pressed a kiss to the back of Scott's neck. "I brought a bottle of wine, in case we feel a little more refined later."

"Always prepared," Scott smiled as he turned to face his partner and boyfriend. In moments like this, when they were by themselves and so in sync with one another, Scott had to remind himself to keep calm and take things slow. Every instinct in his body constantly screamed at him to take things further, to tell Gareth exactly how he felt. But then he'd remember how that had worked out for him in the past and reminded himself of Gareth's experiences too. That was usually enough to keep him from blurting out something he shouldn't. It didn't always stop him from trapping the young man in a tight embrace or stealing a quick kiss.

Gareth grinned, slipped the wine from his ever-present backpack, and placed it inside the fridge before helping Scott carry their snacks and drinks to the living room. They settled together on the squishy green sofa that Gareth had become incredibly fond and jealous of over the times he'd visited Scott's home.

By the film's halfway point, they'd swapped their soft drinks for the wine Gareth had brought. Scott sat with his wine glass resting on the arm of the sofa and his other arm wrapped over Gareth's shoulders. Gareth had nestled himself into Scott's side, with his wine glass balanced on his knee. They watched in companionable silence, exchanging brief comments about the effects or a particularly stunning shot.

When the film finished, they both agreed – reluctantly in

Gareth's case – that they'd enjoyed it more than reading the book. Although they both decided that was more likely to be because of the visual effects than any failure of the original writing.

They chatted for hours, as they often did, losing track of time and revelling in each other's company. Eventually, at eleven p.m., Gareth checked his watch and emptied his wine glass before placing it gently on the coffee table.

He turned to face Scott and pressed a soft kiss to his lips. "I should make a move," he whispered.

Scott moved his wine glass out of harm's way before cupping Gareth's face and pulling him in for another kiss. The crisp, zesty flavour of the wine still lingered on their lips.

"Stay," he whispered.

"Don't think I brought any pyjamas with me," Gareth smirked as he brushed his lips against the late-night stubble forming on Scott's jaw.

Scott let out a low growl and pulled the Welshman into his lap.

Gareth grinned and rolled his hips as Scott nuzzled his neck, moaning softly. He grabbed Scott's face and pulled him into a searing kiss, nibbling his lover's lips before diving in to explore his mouth with his tongue.

Scott ran his hands over Gareth's back, reciprocating the kiss and losing himself in it. He moved his hands down Gareth's body and cupped his arse, pressing to put more pressure on the spot where their bodies met. Gareth rewarded him with a soft whimper and a jerk of his hips as he, too, tried to increase the friction between them. The kiss finally broke, both of them panting.

Scott blindly groped beneath the sofa cushions and let out a frustrated groan. "I forgot to bring stuff downstairs."

Gareth chuckled against his lips. "Race you upstairs then. First one there gets to be in charge."

Scott grinned, wrapped his arms around the Welshman's waist and threw him onto the opposite end of the sofa before darting up the stairs.

Gareth smiled as he grabbed his backpack with everything he'd need for the following morning. He uttered a silent thank you to Faith, and followed the trail of discarded clothes his lover had left up the stairs and along the hallway.

Acknowledgements

The People We Trust has been a passion project that has taken me far too long to be happy enough with to publish.

What started as a project during my university course, eventually got abandoned on the depths of my laptop before I eventually felt confident enough to start writing again several years later.

Throughout that time, I was lucky to have the continuing support of my husband, Carl, my mum, my sisters and the rest of the family, who always believed I could get this finished. Thank you for keeping me motivated.

Huge thanks also go to everyone who eventually read and reviewed early drafts on Critique Match – Scott H and C Miller in particular. You guys were invaluable in ironing out those last few plot holes and sections of waffle.

Thanks also to Lucy Littlejohns – the most wonderful proofreader I could have asked for. Thank you for fixing all my inconsistencies and getting The People We Trust into a publishable state.

And finally, thank you to you for buying and reading this book. I can't begin to put into words how much joy it brings me to think of people buying (and hopefully enjoying) my work.

About the Author

S.J Gathercole lives in Leeds with her husband and dog. She works full time writing marketing content and fills her free time with writing and reading fiction.

9781836907725
WS - #0099 - 200525 - C0 - 203/127/15 - PB - 9781836907725 - Matt Lamination